John,

Because of your
concern for the
environment —
you'll enjoy.

Maeven

Extinction Village

a novel

Michael Beres

ISBN: 9798670632805
Imprint: Independently published

ALSO BY MICHAEL BERES

Sunstrike
Grand Traverse
The President's Nemesis
Final Stroke
Chernobyl Murders
Traffyck
The Girl With 39 Graves

"The Grim Reaper's favorite disguise is disease."

—From *Warnings* by Richard A. Clark and Randolph P. Eddy (2017, HarperCollins Publishers, New York)

"You say you love your children above all else and yet you are stealing their future in front of their very eyes."

—Greta Thunberg, December 2018

"What concerns epidemiologists more than ancient diseases are existing scourges relocated, rewired, or even re-evolved by warming."

—From *The Uninhabitable Earth—Life After Warming* by David Wallace-Wells (2019, Tom Duggan Books, an imprint of Crown Publishing Group, a division of Penguin Random House LLC, New York)

"Once it becomes possible to disregard the welfare of future generations, or those now vulnerable to flooding or drought or wildfire—once it becomes possible to abandon the constraints of human empathy—any monstrosity committed in the name of self-interest is permissible."

—From *Losing Earth, A Recent History* by Nathaniel Rich (2019, MCD, Farrar, Straus and Giroux, New York)

Thank you to Colleen for our shared experiences of climate, geography, humans, and the other species struggling in our changing world.

Extinction Village

a novel

Michael Beres

Chapter 1—Bats

Bats were everywhere, especially predawn in the long-term parking lot at the Gerald R. Ford International Airport in Grand Rapids, Michigan. Mixed in with predawn bats might be a drone or two. These days, following viruses and social and political unrest of the previous decades, it was anyone's guess.

The lot's charging station section roofed over with solar panels was dark until a small SUV entered, triggering motion detector lighting. The lighting, and several bats, followed the SUV to its parking spot, the lights above the space staying lit as a man and woman exited. Both pulled facemasks up over their mouths and noses. The woman had curly gray hair and her facemask was beige, lighter than her skin but matching her jacket. She opened a rear door and pulled a wheeled carryon to the asphalt. The man was bald and his facemask was brown like his jacket and almost as dark as his skin. He pulled his carryon from the back before slamming the rear door on his side and walking to the front of the SUV to plug in the vehicle charging cable. The bats that had followed them into the lot darted in and out of light beams above the man and woman. The man waved one hand over his head, swatting at the bats after he parked his carryon and held his phone up to the charging station port with his other hand.

The woman wheeled her carryon to the charging kiosk. "Why are you waving? They won't get tangled in your hair because you don't have any."

"Doesn't mean I have to love them," said the man. "My grandfather in Mexico was bitten by a Brazilian bat and nearly died when he was a kid. I'm lucky I'm here."

"Your grandfather survived and you're here. These little guys are after bugs."

"What if one of them takes a shit?"

"Come on. Once we're in the shuttle to the terminal you'll be safe. Here it comes."

In the distance the self-driving shuttle, having been triggered by the signal from the charging port, was on its way. The motion detector lighting followed the shuttle toward them, the side door opened, and several high-pitched whines from the shuttle to signal the bats' echolocation receptors to keep clear invited the couple inside.

They were the only passengers. After the welcome message emanating from speakers at the front end where a driver might sit had finished, the man and woman used some of the hand sanitizer available from the automatic dispensers in the seatbacks ahead. They spoke through their masks as they rubbed the sanitizer in.

Man in brown facemask: "I can't believe how long this flight will be. Practically all day."

Woman in beige facemask: "I checked the flight path while you drove. The map shows a circuitous route around fire smoke and storms."

"I hope we don't see any mayhem from the plane and especially when we land."

"No mayhem, dear. Everything under control according to national and locals."

"What about refugees? Any hotspots reported?"

"A few on our flight path, but at the altitude this bird flies I doubt we'll see anything. You've been paying too much attention to national and international news."

"I'm following that push to activate tracking software in our chips. Oligarchs at the helm want to know where everyone is. Last night on TV they told about that doctor in Denver making a bundle taking chips out of people. It's like abortion. If you don't have freedom to take something out of your own body, what's next? A lot of folks have resorted to razoring out their chips."

"As I said, you're watching too much news."

"Well, at least it's nice seeing drone feeds from around the world."

"Right, but who decides where the drones fly and where they aim their cameras?"

"I saw a spot the other night while you were asleep where a drone was crashed into by one of those *kamikaze* drones."

"The refugees have drones?"

"Why not? Doesn't everyone? They had a deal on them at Harbor Freight over on Plainfield the other day."

"I thought that place closed down."

"A conglomerate bought it. More technical gadgets. Anyway, I heard they're one of the big suppliers to refugee vigilante groups."

"That's an oxymoron."

"What?"

"Refugees and vigilantes. Anyway, did you hear this from one of your golf cronies?"

"Maybe. It was a while back. I don't remember."

"Will this guy be on today's flight?"

"Why would he be on the flight? I told you we're on a flight with a bunch of doomsday evangelicals. And if he was on the flight he'd be on it to take advantage of the same deal we're taking advantage of. *Comprende?*"

"Yes, dear, *Comprende.*"

Silence for a while before the man spoke again.

"So, why exactly did Kimmy send us on this trip?"

"To check out that retirement village. With everything going to hell everywhere, she thinks it's good to look into all options before we desert Grand Rapids."

"I guess she knows best. She's our daughter after all. Okay there's the terminal."

There was more bat-repelling echolocation squealing between the shuttle and the terminal entrance.

"Can you hear that whining?" asked the woman.

"What whining?"

"The echolocation screech to chase bats away from the doorway."

"You know I can't hear frequencies that high," answered the man. "Come on. Let's get inside."

The terminal was nearly deserted. A few passengers in line in masks, and unmasked airline employees ensconced inside their glass cubicles. As each new passenger stepped forward for final identification, they held up a phone and momentarily lowered their mask. The only line with passengers was their flight. The man, eyeing the ceiling for bats that were not there, had the woman step up ahead of him.

"Good grief, we're inside where it's safe," whispered the woman.

"I know," whispered the man, his facemask puffing. "It's just me."

"You okay?"

"A little short of breath."

"We've gotten every vaccine known to science."

"Flying still makes me nervous. As far as vaccines, I'm worried about what's unknown to science."

"Our daughter's working on it."

"She's not a doctor, at least not yet."

They continued whispering as they moved forward in line.

Woman: "The sun will be out by the time our flight leaves."

Man: "Yeah, and then the heat will build. Why the hell Kimmy's sending us to a place in Florida I'll never know."

Woman: "We've discussed this a thousand times. She says it's just as safe where we're going as anywhere else. The place is northwest of Orlando, high and dry on the other side of the causeway."

"High and dry for now."

"Yes, for now. I'm glad we have Kimmy doing research for us."

"I thought we decided long ago to stay in Michigan, move closer to the lake."

"Kimmy's been warning about the lake. She said we should give this Latin Villages place a shot not only because of the moderation of sea breezes, but because they're protected, the healthcare's great, and prices are cheap. So that's what we're doing. These days, with lots of Florida's keys under, the sea's even closer."

The man leaned toward the woman. "What about refugees?"

"According to Kimmy they pretty much bypass the place and head north."

"I wonder if there'll be as many bats there."

"Don't worry, they don't have belfries."

***

Parked at the gate, with no one aboard, Flight 6996's in-flight computer was talking to itself. The two personas represented in the conversation had completed the operational checklists, the mechanical checklists, the flight path checklists, the communications checklists, and the destination checklists. They were just finishing up.

Main battery charge?"

"Check."

"Auxiliary battery charge?"

"Check."

"Cabin pressure?"

"Check."

"Cabin temperature and humidity?"

"Check."

"Cabin heat pump?"

"Check."

"Cabin air exhaust and filters."

"Check?"

"Cabin sanitized and inspected?"

"Check."

"I guess we're ready to go. Any scuttlebutt at our destination?"

"A few protestors there to meet our passengers. Ten are destined to be shuttled to an Orlando Sheridan. They're so-called evangelicals prepared to counter protest an upcoming environmental march. However, the final destination of two of our passengers will be north of Orlando via bus ride on the causeway. The man and woman are heading to a retirement community, apparently to check it out. We've retrieved recent chatter from said retirement community. Most folks are asleep, golfing, or shopping. Interestingly, at this so-called retirement community, we've come upon a young man and young woman communing with one another."

"Young people at a retirement community?"

"That's only part of the reason the data is being mined. Both of them are in their thirties and their given names are Jarrod and Greta, key names from the early part of the century."

"Young people named Jarrod and Greta communing inside a retirement community? Remind me. What is communing?"

"It's more innocent than it sounds. Visual, audio, and some half-assed touchy feely stuff."

"Half-assed?"

"You know how apps are. Vibrations, ultrasound, and temperature attempting to simulate feelings."

"Yeah, these humans."

Some of the so-called communing between the two references *The Global Village* by Marshall McLuhan.

"That was with Bruce R. Powers. *Transformation in World Life and Media in the 21st Century (Communication and Society)*, Oxford University Press, 1992."

"That was the reprint edition."

"Right. Anyway, back to the flight. We've got work to do. The sun's coming up, the umbilical is attached, and passengers are at the gate."

"Check. Shall I start the calming music in the cabin?"

"Of course. And also turn the temperature down two degrees."

"Some may like it hot."

"That's an old movie. These cats are mostly evangelicals and heat would remind them of their hell."

Chapter 2—Engine Failure

Instead of the prepare-for-landing announcement everyone on Flight 6996 expected after the tedious energy-efficient flight, a message in bold no nonsense Times New Roman font displayed on individual viewing screens and devices. The message was also given audibly via a female voice over seatback speakers and ear buds. The GC-421's on board computer had selected a female voice reminiscent of a stern schoolteacher.

"We apologize," said the carefully-crafted computer-generated voice. She had the trace of a trusty British accent and sounded sincere, even calming. "The hybrid turbo drive of your craft has a slight malfunction. My associate and I think it might have been caused by a near-extinct equatorial Aves—bird—species having wandered too far north. In fact, for all we know the species might now be extinct if the handful remaining were fragmented in the turbo stream. Anyway, despite the condition of the birds, there's not a thing to worry about; position determination and flight controls are operational, an alternate landing site has been chosen, and plenty of charge remains in the batteries for rear prop-assist landing."

One of the twelve passengers, a man lowering his facemask to blurt out an unchewed pretzel, shouted, "Jesus Christ!"

Another of the twelve, a woman socially-distanced across the zigzag aisle alternating with one seat port and two seats starboard, stared out a port window at the hazy central Florida landmass dotted with lakes and crisscrossed with overflowing rivers and streams. She raised her mask from her neck and spoke through it, her voice a high-pitched whine. "Where will we land?"

"No one on board need worry," responded the computer-generated female voice's male associate in his Dan Rather voice. "We've worked out your glide path and you'll be perfectly fine. Relax and listen. We know the situation and have it under total control."

Reverend James Murdock, a third generation Southern Baptist known for embracing Earth's changing climate and calming situations of distress with afterlife fairy tales, raised his right hand heavenward. "I sincerely apologize for the language of some of my cabin contemporaries!" He was not wearing a facemask, not even on his neck at the ready. But he was alone on his side of the plane and a clear plastic shield blocked the seat ahead of his.

Many on board turned to look back at Murdock behind his plastic shield. Those on board who knew him recalled a younger Murdock from the eloquent deep-throated speech he gave following the last Alabama statehood cessation attempt. Today, rather than standing, because he was belted in, Murdock spoke out into the ample space between him and the digital screen below the plastic shield in the seatback ahead. "I beg your pardon you on the speaker. Despite one's choice of language, where on Earth will we land?"

The computer recognized the doomsday aficionado and paused a second. The computer analyzed the full situation. Murdock, originally from Alabama, had moved north to the outskirts of Grand Rapids, Michigan, years earlier. He contended the move was to get away from the heat, but some locals from his Alabama district said it was to distance himself from a militia group that had gotten into the workings of his church. The flight aboard the lightweight hybrid GC-421, although slow and energy efficient, had taken only a few minutes longer than usual while skirting a storm over Georgia. During the flight Murdock had napped, consumed a protein bar and plenty of hydration fluid, and appeared rested and in control. Yes, the whine of the hybrid engines cutting back suddenly measured on the G sensors had created a lurch forward, and others were obviously concerned, even the human attendant here in the cockpit. Scanning body chips indicated an increase in average heart rate. The task now was to calm them, especially those traveling with Murdock, before all hell broke loose. According to the passenger list, Murdock's group seated rearward with a couple empty seats ahead of them comprised 83.3% of the passengers. The computer did a quick background check to make sure there were no leftover remnants of Alabama militia groups on board. Check.

The computer again generated the female voice. "Following thorough data analysis we've decided on a very flat and level spot simulating a nice long runway. Word has already been sent to clear the course. Everyone's cooperating to a tee."

"But where?" asked Murdock, grasping a well-worn Bible in his left hand, pulling the Bible close to shield his gentles.

Dan Rather male computer voice: "As you know our original destination was Orlando International, code MCO. A humorous side note, some Orlando folks jokingly call the airport Mickey's Corporate Office, when in actuality MCO stands for McCoy Air Force Base, which at one time was operational in Florida. Our alternate would have been Sanford, code SFB. We were cleared for an SFB runway not affected by recent sinkholes and ground subsidence. For those unacquainted with the word, subsidence is the settling of landmass to lower level, often due to ocean inundation. But back to the decision, because of our position and wind direction, and due to questionable sinkholes at SFB, we've decided it will be best for all aboard to select an alternate site well within our range. Again, not to worry. We'll be landing at a safe, secure, high and dry location."

"But where?"

Female voice: "With today's northerly wind, we'll soon be banking into it and drop altitude to attain proper landing speed. Our new destination will be the Latin Villages gated retirement community. Perhaps you've heard of it in pandemic and climate refugee scare commercials." She altered her voice to that of a woman without a British accent spouting a slogan at the end of an ad. "If you don't feel safe in non-tested non-gated communities, you'll be tested regularly and know you're safe as a bug in a rug in the Latin Villages."

"Bugs in Rugs! There's no airport in the Latin Villages!"

Male voice: "I thought my associate made it clear the landing strip we'll use is not a conventional airport runway. No fear. It's being cleared and everyone—pardon the second use of our pun—is cooperating to a tee. We've plotted the destination of your craft for the seventh fairway at the newer Palm Tree Gardens course. A beautiful course, by the way, and the seventh is flat as a pancake. So, here's the deal. From this point forward follow our instructions. Because of a squishy surface, it will be a wheels-up landing. With the squish factor, everything will be smooth. Nonetheless, close your tray tables, place all devices and personal items on the floor of the aircraft, and fasten your seatbelts securely. At one minute prior to arrival we'll repeat the word, *Brace*. At that time, bend forward with your hands behind your heads That is, your hands behind your own head."

Female voice: "Was that supposed to be funny?"

Male voice: "I'm simply encouraging everyone on board to relax."

Female voice: "It sounded like something a genetically engineered CEO would transmit into the corporate office from his or her fortification."

Another voice broke in on the speaker, a different female voice. Because the woman cleared her throat several times and sounded anxious, it was obviously an actual human being. She had the trace of a Middle Eastern accent. "Yes, truly…this is your cockpit attendant. I know how you must feel. I am feeling the same. I myself have also never landed on a golf course. But now I have thoroughly checked operations from base and here on cockpit instrumentation. Everything that can possibly be done is being done. I am with you and will say a prayer for a smooth landing on the seventh fairway."

Puffs of cloud passed the windows. A flurry of voices erupted in the cabin.

"What the fuck does she know?"

"Bob, watch your language."

"She's right, Bob. Take it easy."

"Take it easy? She'll say a prayer for a smooth landing? She's nothing but a cockpit attendant! Hey computer people! What the hell does she know?"

The computer voices were silent. A male passenger answered. "I think the cockpit attendant is being sincere."

"Did you hear her accent? I saw her when we were boarding. Who's she going to pray to?"

"Maybe she's Islamic."

"How can she be Islamic, wear all that eye makeup, and have all those piercings?"

A woman in the front row with a full head of curly blondish gray hair—the gray lightening the hair rather than darkening it—

turned toward the back, lowering her facemask so she could be heard beyond the plastic shield and the empty seats behind her seat. Her Caucasian face reddened. "Perhaps you people back there could shut up!" She blinked her eyes several times, apparently trying to calm herself. "I'll have you know certain body piercings are permitted by Islam. All this talk's got nothing to do with anything. There's a beautiful photograph of our cockpit attendant up here on the bulkhead and she looks fine to me. In case you didn't notice, a lot of us wear eye makeup and have piercings. Maybe everyone should take the cockpit attendant's advice and calm the hell down!"

The bald man with brown skin sitting beside the curly-haired Caucasian woman also turned and lowered his mask. "My lovely spouse is right. There's no need attacking our cockpit attendant. She's probably busy speaking with the on board computer and with flight control computers all over Florida."

"Says who?" shouted the loud guy in back.

"Says us!" shouted the bald man. "*Comprende?*"

Lovely spouse: "No need to shout, dear."

Bald man: "I was simply trying too—"

Lovely spouse, interrupting: "Yes, I think we could all try a little harder. As the young lady said, perhaps a prayer would be in order."

The lovely spouse with the head full of curly blondish gray hair, after giving a nudge to her husband, led them in the Our Father. He joined in at "Who art in Heaven" as did others.

Inside the cockpit, sitting at her control desk, Yolanda Abdul Jabar, with fleeting thoughts of still, in her mid fifties, not having a husband and, at the same time, summoning her girlhood wish that her name had been spelled with two Bs as was true for Kareem, whose photograph she was in love with when she was a tiny girl, touched the button that would allow her to speak with the on board computer without being overheard by passengers. To each attendant who monitored this particular aircraft the on board computer names had been designated Rita and Ron.

"Guess you'd like a little R and R," said Rita.

"Yes," said Yolanda. "What's the skinny?"

Ron spoke. "It's like we told the passengers. We'll have a wheels-up shortly after one of us repeats the word *brace*. Rita, I think you should do it with your commanding British accent."

"Fine," said Rita. "But first let's get this crate into position."

"Remember that movie?" said Ron. "What was the name of it? A poorly made post-cessation-revolution special effects version of one of those ancient black and white flicks where a plane—planes were internal combustion back then, can you believe it? So, here's the plot. The plane crashes in the jungle, but leading up to the crash the various clichéd backstories of passengers are portrayed in order that we identify with them. Anyway, the plane crash lands and now these folks we've gotten to know are stuck in this virgin forest jungle with snakes and spiders and big birds cawing. The passengers build fires at night to keep wild cats away, and I don't mean stray kitty cats. In the end it turns out they have no choice but to figure a way to escape the jungle before cannibals, who've been beating their drums in the distance, decide to make them into lunch or dinner, whichever comes first."

"I remember," said Rita. "Except in the modern version the cannibals are transformed into pandemic zombies who emerged from third world hordes unable to find anything to eat. I like the old version better. In that one the plane's a DC-3. Somehow the passengers from this old DC-3 manage to clear a runway through the bush. Only trouble with the plan is a cockpit nerd copilot—they had nerds even back then—figures out—maybe because of the condition of the engines and the crumby takeoff surface—that they need to lose a shitload of weight. They throw out everything not needed to get the thing airborne but, according to the nerd, they're still too heavy. A crook, one of the passengers, has a .38 revolver and says he's going to make the choice who stays behind."

"Right," said Ron. "In the end someone disarms the crook and an elderly couple insist staying behind with the crook in order to give the plane the weight leeway it needs to take off."

"I bet the old lady holds the .38 on the crook," said Rita.

"I don't remember," said Ron. "I prefer the more recent pandemic zombie movie. Oh, what was the name of it? A grade B flick. Hollywood makes the people on the plane into religious evangelicals, so it becomes the so-called good versus evil story. Evangelicals against zombies. The evangelicals are on this tour where they visit a bunch of crazy shit like the Noah's Ark museum in Kentucky and the Museum of the Bible in DC. That really dates the flick because the DC museum wasn't flooded when they made it. Anyway, folks in the plane are on their way to Orlando's Holy Land Experience. It's your typical disaster flick like the DC-3 version backstorying specific passengers, using dialog to fill us in on foibles. I remember the reviewers disliking the pandemic zombie concept, but liking the sardonic portrayal of passengers who are believers in various myths and legends. The Rapture, Nostrodamus, the Trump Cult, all that stuff. In the modern version, instead of a jungle, they crash land in Big Cypress Swamp and are holed up on an island owned by an Oligarch pair who raise crocs and have a bunch of zombies working for them. The movie was reissued around the time they had that sinkhole at the Holy Land Experience. Pretty ironic, huh?"

"What do you mean?" asked Rita.

"The free publicity. Like when they show war movies on Veterans' Day and Remembrance Day."

"I mean what's all your jabber about evangelicals in a plane crash got to do with today's engine failure problem?"

"Well, without the public realizing it, in this case, on this plane, it's the opposite. The natives down there—the zombies working for the Oligarchs—find out the plane is full of activists for that rally down in Orlando tomorrow."

"You do realize not all of our passengers are evangelicals planning to counter protest the environmentalists," said Rita.

"Well right, they don't talk like evangelicals," said Ron.

Although Yolanda knew the computer for which the two spoke was in the background working out the safest possible landing for the GC-421, she could no longer take the inane chatter.

"Jesus Christ and Praise Allah, you two!"

The computer pair spoke in unison like twins. "Jeez, Yolanda. We thought the movie angle would not only entertain, but calm you."

"Entertain? Calm?" shouted Yolanda. "Okay, fine! The DC-3 takes off and leaves the crook and the old farts behind while native drumbeats move closer! Could you please, please talk about our landing instead of this shit?"

"Wow, whose tits are in a wringer?" said Rita.

"Wringer?" asked Ron.

"W-R-I-N-G-E-R. Wringer washing machines were used back in the 1930s and 1940s when the movie was made. You'd do a wash cycle in the tub, then you'd have to feed the clothes through this wringer thing for both the wash and rinse cycles. The rollers of the wringer pressed down with a lot of pressure like a mammogram and—"

"I know what a wringer washer is," said Ron. "I was simply playing dumb about the old movie to further calm Yolanda. Anyway, yeah, we'll fill you in with all the details, Yolanda. Glide path, speed, true elevation corrected for subsidence, rear prop assist—all the stats."

"Thank you," said Yolanda, tugging at the ring pierced through her right nostril.

"Yolanda, I thought you'd be more indulgent," said Ron. "Especially after so recently listening to the audible of Kareem's book."

"What?"

"Kareem Abdul-Jabbar's book, *Writings on the Wall*, in which he encourages listening to all opinions, even those of your on board computer companions."

Rita interjected. "I don't think he ever referred to on board computer opinions."

"Even so," said Ron. "I believe my point is valid. Anyway, Yolanda, we'll definitely give you all the stats for our landing."

Above Yolanda's control desk the view out the windshield was spectacular. Before the engine cutout, it had been hazy, but clear enough to see the circumcised Florida peninsula, reshaped and skinnier with old keys sunken and new ones lining its shores. On rainless days above new Florida, the sky was either much too blue because of excess carbon dioxide, or hazy from geoengineering like this day. And with all the moisture in the atmosphere, it often rained sheets and steam baths, flushing huge quantities of reflective microscopic metal nanoparticles into the human sewer, the non-technical term for what the human species created. Yolanda considered the sheets and steam baths idiom for heavy rain followed by heat. It had replaced the dogs and cats idiom long ago.

As the GC-421 banked slowly back north for its new destination, what clouds there were cleared completely and Lake George fed by rivers and streams dotted a brownish-green expanse.

Within the expanse appeared occasional acute angles of civilization. And then, in the distant haze, a fenced-in island of houses, streets, and golf courses became obvious. The Latin Villages. Yolanda closed her eyes for a moment. Instead of being an unmarried cockpit attendant, she and her husband are down there, relaxing in an immigrant and pandemic proof retirement community, isolated from the realities of the world. The Latin Villages.

Yolanda's control panel displayed temperature, humidity, wind, and UV index. The temperature was 85 degrees Fahrenheit, not bad for January. The humidity was also 85. A center screen below the control panel displayed a drone feed from the upcoming landing site. Golfers in colorful garb and golf carts with reflective roofs lined a grassy green fairway as if awaiting tournament pros. Yes, to be down there. Golf, it was something she had never tried, not because she did not want to, but because games were things forbidden by her father. A sudden image of her father's stern face across from her at the dinner table. A little girl sitting there with hands hidden in her lap. Her father staring at her to be certain she did not take a bite to eat before he waved his hand to allow it.

Ron's voice came back on the speaker. "Yolanda, time to go to your safety position. Up here with us is no place for you. And don't forget to mask up before you go back there."

"Are you sure—?"

"Yes, Yolanda. The writing is on the wall. Go now and buckle in. Be sure to insert your ear buds so we can give you the stats. You'll be safe. We'll handle it from here."

Chapter 3—Starboard Confessions

Simone Plumley Martinez stared ahead at the photograph of Yolanda Abdul Jabar mounted to the bulkhead. Yolanda was beautiful with straight black hair sneaking out from beneath her headscarf. The piercings mentioned by the loudmouth in back were limited to a nose ring and lip ring. If Yolanda had ear piercings her headscarf concealed them. Simone's daughter Kimmy sometimes wore a headscarf. "Just because," said Kimmy. Perhaps Kimmy wore a headscarf now to shield her half-Hispanic half-Caucasian skin from UV rays, being she was aboard the algae containment vessel *Shellfish* in Lake Michigan rounding up slime as well as updating pollution stats. If only she were with her daughter out in Lake Michigan instead of here. A while ago, as she led those in the cabin in the Our Father, what Simone really prayed for was she could be with Kimmy. Imagine if that Murdock character back there, the so-called leader of a trip, knew she'd started the Our Father to calm them. If only the people in back knew she'd been praying to a different god. Not the Father they supposedly prayed to, someone or something else. Call her Saint Agnostania, because that's what Simone had become the last few years. Even her husband Sancho, part of the Slick Sancho and Sexy Simone SSSS pair, knew. But of course Sancho wouldn't tell a soul. Or, imagine if the folks back there knew she'd taken her maiden name as her middle name but rarely used it because of a single time in high school gym class ages ago getting called Plum Nips in the shower room. Crazy how one little memory sticks.

With the engine turbine whine, so comforting earlier, now completely gone, Simone could hear toilet sounds in front of her behind the bulkhead. A lid closed, the wall thumped, and her husband Sancho came out wearing his facemask and wiping his shiny bald head with a paper towel. He insisted it was the reason he'd earned the name Slick Sancho—his shiny slick bald head. Little things. Wiping his head after using a public facility as if he'd rubbed his noggin around the toilet seat. Coming out the door giving his head a swipe before carefully folding the paper towel and tucking it into one of his back pockets—"For later," he always said. Sometimes he'd add, "For after I rub your sexy ass cheeks."

Simone smelled hand soap as Sancho lowered his facemask and got into his seat. He buckled up, saying, "For later," but skipped the rest of it.

"Well," said Simone, "I guess since we snuck aboard this flight to get the evangelical group discount, and since we wanted to head out to the Latin Villages at Kimmy's suggestion, landing on a golf course there is perfect."

Another door, not the toilet. The cockpit attendant appeared in a white facemask, gave the passengers what might have been a smile, then quickly got into the single port side safety seat across the aisle and buckled in. Simone felt a tinge of sadness, Yolanda, somewhat older than her photograph, looked forlorn. Another life across the aisle, and perhaps another god waiting in the wings?

"I hope there is one," said Sancho.

"One what?"

He glanced across to Yolanda, then turned back to Simone and pointed toward his back pocket. "My paper towel. I said it was for later like I always do and I'm saying I hope there is a later."

"There will be, dear. You've been so negative since—"

"Since what?"

Simone turned to look out the window. The plane had begun a slow bank. She could see the flash of rooftop solar panels, dots and dashes like someone sending Morse code. SOS, save our ship. And the moment she thought this, another thought from months past took over. Save our marriage. Who'd listen to her? Perhaps she should tell Kimmy, if she ever sees Kimmy again. Kimmy out in Lake Michigan gathering algae, shoving samples into spectrographic analyzers, perhaps wondering about someone or something else, Saint Agnostania. Kimmy would simply love the sainthood name her mother had dreamed up. As for Simone's deity, perhaps good old Mother Earth down there would do, especially after all the screwing she'd gotten during the industrial and Oligarch revolutions and one pandemic after another, followed by one revolution after another, followed by one vaccine tweak after another. Mother Earth sucked dry by climate change while the human species was busy with their messes.

Simone definitely didn't put on the airs of the evangelical like Sancho. He said he did it so they could book the discount flight they were on, but she wondered, questioning his religiosity. For a while Sancho tried to make off it was real, that religion had been embedded in him from his Mexican heritage. Sancho had a couple religious golfing buddies from his corporation, but still, the masquerade to get on board this flight had been weird. After booking the flight, Sancho claimed he and Simone were moles infiltrating the evangelicals, like trying to understand folks they disagree with. Simone had reluctantly gone along with the religious hustle, it seemed the best thing to do and an interesting way to get a discount flight to Florida. Understanding those with whom you strongly disagree. Actually, it was really a save our ship move, as in save our marriage. Once, at home in their apartment, after having had sex, she caught Sancho kneeling in prayer at the side of the bed. Because of his surprise when she asked what he was praying for he obviously thought she'd been asleep. Sancho had answered he was praying that Kimmy's soul be saved. A quick answer, the one he had ready in case she asked. This was before Simone told Sancho she didn't believe in his God. When she finally did confess she didn't believe in his God, Sancho insisted she elaborate.

In what entity did she believe? At first she said Luda. It was supposed to be a joke as in the village of Luda's people, the supposed derivation of her first boyfriend Joe Luddington's last name. Luddington had been the name of folks who came from a certain section of Lincolnshire. Silly, the same boyfriend who coined her nickname Sexy Simone. She should have kept her own name instead of adopting the husband's name and using Plumley as her middle name. Who did that anymore? And who else but her and Sancho would decide to search for a retirement home in the town of the same name as her first boyfriend. The same except missing one of the Ds—Ludington, Michigan. If only she were there, a walk at the lakefront, the westerly lake breeze blowing through her hair as she stares at the horizon, imagining she can see Kimmy's *Shellfish* between Chicago and Milwaukee. If only she hadn't agreed to fly down to Orlando. But it was Kimmy, familiar with the deteriorating conditions of the Great Lakes, who'd insisted they take a look at this particular gated retirement community in central Florida.

"Didn't you hear me?" asked Sancho. "You said I'd been negative since something and I asked since what."

Simone turned to him, his baby browns staring her down. They had their facemasks pulled down being they were finished leading in the Our Father and were isolated in the shielded seat pairing for couples. "I heard you. You know what I meant."

"So, say it."

"You've been negative concerning everything and everyone around us since our blubbering confessions and the arguments that followed."

Sancho looked away. "Ah, here we go."

"What do you mean, here we go? Here we are, taking advantage of a discount flight with a bunch of Bible beaters. Don't you think that calls for honesty? Don't you think it's about time we leveled with one another?" Simone glanced past him toward Yolanda who was looking out the window, poking at her ear beneath the headscarf and facemask hiding her face. Simone looked back to Sancho, touched his chin to get his attention. "The plane we're in has lost power. They're going to land the..." She pulled Sancho close and whispered harshly. "They're going to land the fucking thing on a golf course."

Sancho also whispered a not-so-quiet whisper. "At least it'll be flat. All of Florida's flat. A goddamn pancake floating on an encroaching sea. Folks on the seventh fairway will probably raid the plane for our bottled water."

Simone pulled Sancho's ear, making him face her again. The plane bounced a little as it came out of its northward turn. The cabin speakers rattled. Across the aisle the cockpit attendant held a portable microphone up beneath her facemask. Simone could hear both the real voice and the amplified voice.

"This is your cockpit attendant. My name is Yolanda and I'm with you all the way. We still have a way to go. Because of our speed and altitude, and being we're nosed into a stiff breeze, we should be up for at least another five minutes. A drone has scoped out our landing site and everything is good. The on board computer will let us know one minute prior to touchdown, as stated earlier."

"Wonderful," grumbled the loudmouth in back.

"Great balls of fire," grumbled a woman in back.

Sancho pulled Simone close and hugged her.

Simone hugged Sancho back, wondering if others in isolated couples seats behind them in the cabin were doing the same. They continued whispering to one another.

"Simone?"

"What?"

"When I was in the john I noticed a lot of writing on the wall."

"Graffiti?"

"I guess, but with twists of fate. Things about how much longer planes will be flying, longer flights having to skirt storms, and especially concerns about landing at Florida's remaining airports. Confessions while sitting on the stool. More news on john walls than that play-acting the media gives us. By the way, Simone, I have another confession of my own."

"Did you write it on the wall?"

"No."

"Did you close the lid before you flushed?"

"Of course. You want to hear my confession or not?"

"Okay, sure."

"What have I got to lose? Our plane's going to land on a golf course. So I might as well let it all hang out."

"You're coy all of a sudden, Sancho. I thought confessions were over. We only have five minutes, four minutes by now. Don't hold back."

"Right. Remember that nighttime pool party a few years back at the Indianapolis Sheridan where your company sent us?"

Simone nodded as she tried to calculate how long ago she was at the corporation and exactly when they'd had a gathering at the Indianapolis Sheridan.

Sancho stared into her eyes like a kid about to propose to his girl. "It was hotter than hell that evening and maybe we all got a little heatstroke. Anyway, Petra, the wife of that German VP, grabbed me when I was loaded."

"So, you like-a-da plump ones, eh?"

Sancho's eyes went watery. "I was loaded. We'd both been recently tested for viruses. Can't I confess without being made fun of?"

"Sorry, go on."

"Thank you. Petra, calling herself a Bavarian Hun, was energetic and determined, like the German nun in that movie about 1950s Catholic schools we saw recently. You know, the one with Lady Ellena playing the nun. Anyway, Petra chases me around inside the church and catches me by the organ. Only we weren't in church and the organ was actually the grand piano in the dark corner of the poolside lounge."

"I also have a confession," said Simone. "Her husband, who called himself Handy Hans, grabbed me by the pussy at the shallow end of the pool. We also had been recently tested for viruses."

"What?"

"You heard me."

"How am I supposed to confess something when you have a comeback like that?"

"Easy. Fill in the details. Did your organ end up in Petra's pussy or in her mouth?"

A delayed answer, Sancho leaning forward to glance beyond her out the window before whispering into her ear. His eyelashes fluttered against her temple. In her peripheral vision she saw his bald head beaming and his brown eyes watering. "How can I answer that when you come back with the pussy-grab cliché?"

"Please Sancho, your teary eyes remind me of a televangelist weeping on the air. I realize we're pretending to be evangelical moles, but—"

Sancho raised his voice. "I'll have you know—" He glanced through the plastic shield between their seatbacks, lowered his voice. "Televangelists are always coming out, admitting to homosexual affairs, or whatever."

Simone touched Sancho's hand. "You're having a homosexual affair?"

"No, I'm not having a homosexual affair. But what if I was?"

"All right," said Simone. "I'll finish my story, then you finish yours. Back at the pool Handy Hans sidles up to me in the shallow end. We're both holding vodka tonics in paper—no glass allowed in the pool—but we each have a free hand. He slurs, '*Wie geht's dir?*' and applies the clichéd pussy grab. I've had a few and rather than pulling away like I would when I've not had a few, I grab his pecker. From there we move to the bar set up at the pool. The bartender's absent so we go behind to mix our own, new paper cups because the old ones have gone soggy. While there Hans puts more than his hands on my pussy. He kneels down, stretches the bottom of my suit aside and, saying he's had recent testing, gives me a good licking. He looks up from below and actually says, 'Takes a licking, but keeps on ticking. It is from old Timex wristwatch commercial. Have you seen this? We use in German office as part of course for apprentice marketing staff.' Anyway, pretty soon the bartender returns and, not seeing you around, we decide Hans will accompany me to the room and drop me off. He keeps rattling off something in German about returning me to your arms. '*Geh in dein Zimmer.*' We go inside and, well, one thing leads to another."

Sancho stared, but not out the window. His eyes were no longer watery.

"You're drooling."

Sancho pulled his saved paper towel from his back pocket, wiped his mouth and his slick brown noggin. "I'm disgusted."

Simone glanced out the window. Rooftop solar panels flashed past faster and faster. She turned back to Sancho. "You'd better hurry with your confession."

"Fine. Yes, Mrs. Hans and me had a gay old time beneath the piano in the lounge, which had closed down for the night, and we didn't have any time to waste. She translated for me. '*Neunundsechzig.*' Know what it means?"

"Of course I know what it means. She could have said, *sechsundneumzig.* Were you on top or was she? Or did you do it on the side? Did the piano pedals get in the way? Did she reach up and pound a Beethoven chord at climax? Or was it a Wagnerian scream? Inquiring minds want to know?"

Sancho put his paper towel away and looked down at his lap. "Nice job with the marketing lingo. Must you always outdo me at these confessions?"

"Yes. It's the reason the Lord God of Hosts put me on Earth."

"Fuck the Lord God of Hosts."

"And you call yourself an evangelical."

"At least I'm not an agnostic."

"I love you."

"I love you, too."

Simone thought of their statements of love as a double-edged sword. Perhaps Sancho was having an affair back home in Grand Rapids. Perhaps one of the local wives who'd recently gotten virus tested lured him in. Simone and Sancho stared daggers at one another as the aircraft's female computer voice came to life, positively shrieking. "Brace, brace, brace!"

In the seconds before tucking hands behind heads and bracing, Sancho stroked Simone's head, playfully tugging a few curls of her hair the way he always did, and Simone stroked Sancho's bald head, using her index finger to play the tiny violin where a baby's soft spot would be the way she always did. At least for now, if they didn't make it through, they'd die expressing their love for one another.

Chapter 4—Palm Tree Bellyaching

The palm trees that once lined Palm Tree Gardens golf course fairways were gone. Each interest group had a reason for pulling them. Global warming temperature change spokespersons insisted the climate was now altered enough to make the average temperature in what was left of Florida too hot for too long a period. Averages were one thing, but now there were long hot spells. Sea level rise and ice shelf disappearance watchers said palm trees worked well in heat, but increased seawater encroachment into water tables had become a concern. They said although the garden planners for the Latin Villages chose palm trees in the past, they now claimed palms provided little shade and cooling during the hottest months, while drinking huge amounts of precious fresh water needed elsewhere. These days, with new scientific information in, if palm trees leaned over in a storm, rather than propping them back up with supports like they once had, garden crews pulled the trees and replaced them with different varieties. The replacement trees, they claimed, were historically more natural to the area and, in the long run, would be beneficial. When confronted by residents insisting palm trees were part of the Latin Villages trademark, planners tried their best to explain. With all its asphalt streets and golf cart lanes the Latin Villages had become as much a heat island as any of the cities remaining in Florida. Another concern was that Burmese pythons and various other invasives from Asia sometimes hung out in palms. Although it took a lot of convincing to allow fallen palms to be replaced with hardwoods and broadleaves, most residents were finally convinced, especially during the last ten years of record heat, aquifer well capping, rapid expansion of desalinization plants, and a few folks being rushed to a medical center for snakebite.

Well all right then, some grumbled, first I can't get another dog and now it's okay to put in some hardwoods and broadleaves. Other faraway non-coastal cities suffering from high temperatures like Las Vegas, Baghdad, and Riyadh had swapped out their palms ages ago. Sure, those places were hell on Earth, but the comparison stuck. So, okay, do it here. Go ahead, said the few old timers remaining, expand the tree canopy, which in its modern past never existed in the Latin Villages once civilization ripped out the old growth and drained the swamps. In the Latin Villages' past, a stray leaf on a lawn was like a virus, something to contend with, something to remove as quickly as possible. As was heard from a shouting man at an ancient urban planning meeting, "My God, what are we supposed to do with all the leaves and litter clogging our gutters? Or stuck behind those goddamned solar panels some of you insist putting on your roofs? Solar panels belong on space stations and Mars, not here!"

The so-called worldwide solar panel/battery storage revolution had taken place years earlier after power failures during heat waves and pandemics that killed thousands at a time, some in bed when the power failed at night. Large corporations, answering to a handful of giant holding companies, made trillions. Companies headed up by Oligarchs controlled not only the media, gushing feel good crap supposedly for everyone's mental health, they also controlled vaccine research facilities as well as power generation. Oligarchs held controlling interests in giant solar and energy storage centers and the manufacture of single dwelling components. With total control of the media, they painted themselves as saviors while at the same time chipping away at any inconvenient news of death and destruction due to climate change or pandemics. Oligarchs even controlled the weapons industry and bolstered the old Second Amendment argument any chance they got. Not long ago a local Second Amendment rights group in the Latin Villages had organized a target shooting contest with targets nailed to palms behind one of the visitor centers just before the palms were yanked. Several gun and ammo manufacturers had helped, financing promotion for the so-called "Palm Tree Shootout."

With rapid change taking place all over the world, concern for palm trees in the Latin Villages didn't stand for much. Eventually palms went the way of pets. Fading away until someone brought up a memory. Yes, hardwoods were slow growers. It was going to take time to get significant shade in the Latin Villages, especially on golf courses. These days time and life expectancy were things no one wanted to discuss. And ever since the discovery several years earlier of a woman outside the gates having killed and eaten stray dogs that wandered through a hole beneath the fence, no one wanted to discuss limits on having dogs either. The woman lived alone in a ramshackle house just outside an outlying fence. Now she was gone and so was the house and any of the others outside the fencing because the Latin Villages bought up all the land and razed all the ramshackles. But the legend of the woman who ate dogs lived on.

Anyway, back to the trees. Attempts to save at least a few palm trees, even for the short term, lost out to salt-water incursion. Aquifer water mixed with salt water used to irrigate the golf courses killed the palms. Even newly planted hardwoods chosen for resilience were having a hard time. The sun was still great in winter, but in summer the sun was disastrous for trees. Sure, winter or summer, sunny humid days alternated with short periods of heavy rain, but no matter what time of year, there wasn't an easy way to collect and save rainwater during the heavy spurts followed by steam baths.

The sheets and steam bath scenario was also hard on the remaining residents. If they weren't careful, summer sun and humidity could take a person not near an air-conditioned golf cart or building entrance to the ground. With September and even October considered summer here at the Latin Villages, air-conditioned golf cart conversions and strategically located cooling kiosks were all the rage. Both were great moneymakers for local businesses, but mostly for the Oligarchic corporations in charge of getting equipment manufactured as cheaply as possible. Great moneymakers even now in the middle of January.

One of the so-called deluxe eco model golf carts with built-in air conditioning sold at local golf cart shops had the newest high-tech solar panel roof generator, which also acted as an insulator. Besides the dual layer side curtains, the deluxe model had motorized extendable visors for early mornings or late afternoons on the course. In midday the visors angled down to reduce reflection and UV damage. A few wise acres said the shielding was really like the plastic shields at stores that separated the staff from customers. But if you were caught in a storm and you tucked in the visors to hold the roof and side curtains tightly to the frame, you certainly weren't thinking about viral barriers.

The announcement for golfers on holes five through eight to quickly move off the course was sent as a message to the phones of everyone on the Palm Tree Gardens course. Whether handheld, part of their UV glasses, or in-the-ear models combined with hearing aides—all phones nationwide, and most phones worldwide, were now globally positioned, tracked, and routinely scanned, as required by FCC, WCC, FDA, Global Positioning, and Homeland Security regulations. So, on the Palm Tree Gardens course this day, phones had been scanned at the course entrance and would be scanned again when players finished the ninth hole. Scanning phones in the Latin Villages had become routine, sold to residents on the basis of safety and also contact tracing despite protests of long-dead hardliners who insisted their privacy was being invaded. A few years earlier emergency health officials revealed several old hardliners, who demanded their privacy, would probably still be around if phone-scanning and contact tracing had been put in place sooner. A couple hardliners went down in restaurant parking lots where they couldn't be seen, but most of those either cremated or in a plot somewhere in another state or stacked in a nearby mausoleum went down on a golf course. Routine phone scanning would have allowed pinpointing of their exact location when the phone automatically sent a body chip diagnosis to the nearest emergency center or roving paramedics. One notable death, which supposedly took place years earlier, was of a man who got into the main visitor center Hall of Heroes after hours. As the story goes, he had a stash of vintage Make America Great Again caps and proceeded to replace the headgear of all the armed service manikins. He wrote a note demanding electric fencing be put in at nearby beaches to keep out illegals. It was a detailed manifesto explaining exactly how the fences could be mobile in order to be easily moved for surges and sea level rise. The manifesto mentioned the 1944 D-day invasion at Normandy, France, using refugee landings in Europe and especially the UK as part of its detailed description of beach barrier methodology. He also insisted protective border walls had kept everyone alive, at least for now. Of course no one ever built the guy's mobile fences. Next morning they found him and his manifesto sprawled on the floor below a balcony on which the statue of a female Afghanistan War heroine was displayed. The guy had toppled over the railing after replacing the heroine's helmet with one of his caps. He hadn't brought his phone along and therefore no emergency diagnosis signal from his body chip was sent. Anyway, that's the story.

Today's announcement that a plane was going to come down went out seconds after the Latin Villages main office received the air traffic control message. Phones on the Palm Tree Gardens course lit up, hummed, and played their loudest alarm like the ones for an Amber Alert, storm alert, or virus tracking alert. The alarm sounded even if the phone was turned off because an emergency message was required to go through, despite corporate objections when new cell phone requirements were enacted.

Bianca Muhammad Washington and her husband Big Bill Pisani golf-carted to the edge of the seventh hole fairway as directed by their cell phones. The seventh fairway bordered the eighth fairway. The first broadleaf trees planted on the course separated the two. A dozen other players, who'd been in various locations on the seventh, eighth, and even the sixth hole made their way to the shade of the trees, parking their golf carts on the nearby asphalt cart way and gathering beneath the tree canopy away from the day's UV rays. Because it was January the sun was low in the sky so they had to position themselves off to the side, arranged in what shade they could find as if staking out territory. A few elbows bumped, the positioning of the group eventually resembling chess pieces socially distanced on one side of a game board. They looked like a gathering of geese wearing garments. Many of them even walked like geese. One couple who'd walked in one behind the other shared a beige shade cloth they held above their heads. At first glance these two resembled a camel wearing white golfing shoes, if you concentrated simply on the bony legs sticking out of their baggy Bermuda shorts.

Despite a decade-long drop in life expectancy internationally, isolation and amenities within the fences of the Latin Villages made for a relatively healthy environment and many in the group were beyond the averages. By observing bow-leggedness and other telltale signs, Bianca and Big Bill were an exception. They were younger than the others and in better shape. They positioned themselves at the front of the group where chess pawns would be. But these two weren't pawns. Bianca's short 'fro hairstyle didn't cry out for blue or red tint like the scalp haloes of the gray-haired ladies. Bianca's Central African heritage skin outdid every short sleeve tan. Big Bill's thinning blond hair and muscular frame, for a sixty-year-old white guy, had him resembling an old photo of Hulk Hogan. The body language beneath the sparse broadleaf canopy was obvious. Women glanced to the couple, the ones not wearing facemasks with smiles, the others with nods. Men, masked or not, took quick looks above their sunglasses to one side and then the other like maybe they'd been transported to a place of their youth. Rather than being on a golf course in January in the Latin Villages, perhaps they were somewhere further north in the middle of a hot summer on a weekend away from their corporate jobs. Yes, corporate jobs retired from long enough ago to get them ahead of the double barrel blast of climate immigration and pandemic ups and downs that had hit the world.

Maybe, for a while at least, they could make believe they were still young men. Maybe times hadn't changed so much since they were younger. Maybe those big old ears and that bulbous red nose they'd seen in the morning mirror was computer-generated exaggeration. Maybe, when amongst male companions on the course, using the acronym BBBB as in "Black Bianca" and "Big Bill" wasn't such a good idea. Oh sure, to their wives they claimed the first two Bs meant "Buxom Bianca." That old fart white dude with big ears in the morning mirror hadn't meant to focus on Bianca's skin color, had he?

By God, despite being a little prejudiced when they were younger, a lot of guys sure wished they were younger, like several decades younger. If only they'd maintained the physique and stamina of their youth instead of allowing ask-your-doctor-about drug prescriptions, medical devices, and vaccines to extend their lives. If only times hadn't changed so much. If only the Oligarchs weren't the only ones living the high life away from shortages, meatless meat, and all manner of immigrants coming at them. Yes, times had changed. Glancing toward the mixed race Black Bianca and Big Bill couple joining them in the shade off to the side of the seventh hole, many even had to admit to themselves it was hard to think prejudice, even though it had been expressed by one or the other of them in close company. Damn, they wished they were younger and the world hadn't changed so much. Too bad they weren't going to be around long enough to see the human population fully dissolve into one color, a beautiful brown skin like they might have had eons ago as younger men after getting a decent tan instead of always wearing hats and long sleeves outdoors. This was the look on the faces of most of the older men as they glanced side-to-side and then off into the distance, some of them lowering facemasks to get a breath of fresh air.

It wasn't that Buxom Bianca and Big Bill were unfamiliar or foreign to those beneath the broadleaf trees. They'd seen Bianca and Bill around, playing golf, shopping, even at one of the recreation center pools. Especially at the recreation center pools. Older white residents couldn't help having visions of black Buxom Bianca and muscular Big Bill at the pool imbedded in their noggins, or Bianca and Big Bill getting applauded while dancing at one of the outdoor oldies concerts. At the last concert both wore facemasks, but also tight-fitting purple outfits. One of the men, at home the morning after, told his wife he'd had visions of facemasked sugarplums dancing in his head all night. According to what his wife told her friends, he'd sung a way out-of-tune version of *Purple People Eater* that morning, done a little dance around the kitchen table, followed by a crazy version of *All Night Long*, sloshing coffee out of his cup.

Bianca knew from the time she and Big Bill arrived at the Latin Villages, she was being watched. Sure, there were other blacks here. But still, even these days, any time she went out she was aware of it. Sometimes it was subtle, sometimes not so subtle, even though she and Bill had lived here more than two years. She and Bill spoke about it often back home. They agreed an archaic yet obvious discomfort of experiencing a mixed race marriage still existed. And perhaps because of a prejudice that simply would not die, they agreed they were glad they didn't live in one of the newer sections of the Latin Villages, sections obviously reserved for people of color even though there was nothing official, nothing in the community rules, nothing on social media, nothing except body language, eye movement, slight hitches in a person's gait, words mouthed beneath facemasks, especially when encountering older men whose minds were buried in the past. For Bianca and Big Bill, what had been most obvious were the surgically placed pauses of real estate staff when inspecting the house Bill had inherited from his parents, the house they decided, at least for a time, to live in rather than sell.

The house in Village Sextus, one of the earlier in the Latin Villages, went up during a building boom, prior to the years that brought on the Covid-19 pandemic, the climate crises, and prior to the numerous reverse mortgage schemes dreamed up by forefathers of Oligarchs. The individual villages were named using somewhat butchered Latin translations. The first village in the Latin Villages, Primus, was somewhat larger. Primus was nicknamed White Bread Village by residents. Other of the villages were Villages Segundus, Tertius, Quatorus, Quintus, Sextus (Sextus, their village, was supposedly somewhat controversial when constructed, but times had changed.), Septimus, Octavius, and, finally, Nonus. (This ninth village was most recent, the elongated version Nonnatus, which some wanted to use, meaning "not born" in Latin. Village Nonus was also controversial being it was occupied by younger service people.) Anyway, back to the BB pair.

Bianca was fifty-nine and Big Bill sixty. They both grew up in Chicago, Bianca in Englewood and Bill on the North Shore. Bianca had been a physician assistant, Bill a teacher. Bianca's first husband, Jess, died when the bullet from the .45 of a drive-by shooter, who claimed to be aiming above the heads of a group of gang shorties to scare them, went through his head while he was walking the dog. This, after all the laws passed to keep Indiana gun show weapons off Chicago's streets. This, after all the anonymous buybacks of unregistered firearms. An antique .45 floating around the south side. The hand-to-hand movement of the .45 traced through time detailed in the trial until it ends up in the hands of a distraught young man during a deadly hot summer, a young man who, sweating out his status in a gang melting out of existence on the south side, becomes the shooter. Everything was detailed in the trial, even questions from the defense as to how Bianca and her husband were able to afford owning a dog, being that meat products, even for pets, had, by then, become harder to obtain. Bianca sat with her son, Vincent, throughout the long process. Even though Vinny was only four at the time, Bianca felt sure being at the trial would put a cap on the past. Not make the loss of his father go away, but make it something that didn't completely stop the clock in her life and Vinny's life.

The three-week trial for the shooter who killed her husband was a strange time to meet another man. Big Bill taught at a college prep charter school near their home. Her husband had already approached the school with the idea of someday sending Vinny there.

So, Big Bill and Bianca's first husband knew one another. Crazy, before he's shot through the head in a drive-by her husband makes contact with the man whose own wife had passed away, the man who would eventually take his place. A big old white guy from the north shore educated at UIC who'd made his way to the south side to teach at a Knowledge is Power Program charter school. When Bianca told friends how they met—Bill's wife dying from stroke complications and her husband being killed in a drive-by—silence, stares, and smiles were sometimes devastating. Probably because—reliving the entire trial, reliving how Bill was simply there in the courtroom one day, reliving how he offered to take her and her son to lunch, reliving how he explained his having met her first husband—the explanation always ended up a teary-eyed extravaganza. And to this day, if Bill was in the vicinity and saw her speaking in a group of women, he said he could tell by the downcast looks of the others and the teary sparkle in her eyes that the past was coming out and he'd better come over and give her a hug.

Vinny did end up going to Big Bill's charter school. She and Bill dated while Vinny was at the school and eventually the three of them—jokingly calling themselves the MVB team, Most Valuable Bitches—moved into a larger apartment together. Bianca and Bill married at the very end of Vinny's senior high school year. The date of their marriage marked not only by Vinny's graduation, but also by two other events—the sizable Greenland ice sheet collapse named the Bridal Fall, the name attributed to the June first date, and the death of the miniature schnauzer that was at her first husband's side when he died.

At Bill's urging, Bianca chose not to adopt his last name. After their marriage and a honeymoon in New York's Finger Lakes region, Vinny, who'd applied at Cornell, won a scholarship in agricultural sciences. After Cornell Vinny worked for a while at one of the vertical farming corporations sprouting up in northern New York state, went on to become a research consultant at the newly expanded EPA, and was now the Region Five Administrator, which included the Great Lakes.

At first Bill didn't care for Vinny's choice to leave the vertical farming industry and work for the EPA, saying government organizations no longer had a fighting chance and that growing protein for an expanding world population was more critical. But Bill had come around. Of course lately, like a lot of other guys of his generation, Bill seemed suspicious about everything organizational, especially after volunteering to teach yoga at the main recreation center. With the yoga class and Bill acting a little weird, Bianca couldn't help being somewhat suspicious herself. Why would Bill question her free time so much? Was it because he had something to hide? Their neighbor, Lillian, made a comment the other day, something about attendees at Bill's yoga class, something about never knowing why folks take all these classes when they retired down here at the Latin Villages to relax and isolate themselves from the outside world. Crazy, what a time to think about a comment from Lillian, the same woman who watched too much news and was suspicious of everything, like why some houses out west were consumed by wildfires and others weren't, why people were moving to the Great Lakes region, even the upper Michigan peninsula or Canada despite all the mosquitoes, why reverse mortgages offered for Latin Villages homes were so puny, and especially Lillian using You-know-who-number-one's name straight out—Trump—instead of avoiding the term, which these days had become a common curse as in, 'You've gotten Trumped now,' or, 'This is all Trumped up,' or especially, 'Trump it.'

Forget Lillian's talk. There were too many like Lillian living in the Latin Villages whose pessimism had been fed by a husband who was dead. Bianca had even, over the past weeks, mentioned a lot of this to her son Vinny. As she stood at the side of the seventh fairway, watching others join them in the welcome shade, Bianca recalled a phone conversation with Vinny.

"So, tell me again why you're moving to Gated Disney Island."

"The Latin Villages isn't referred to by that name."

"But Orlando's close."

"We'll be north of it. A pleasant drive on the causeway."

"I know you guys are aware of the elevation drop, continued subsidence, Florida's climate refugees, and toxic algae."

"Of course we're aware of those things. And you're aware Bill's parents had a place down here."

"So?"

"So, because of the heat, and also because of decreasing population, Florida real estate values have gone down a sinkhole and Bill's having a hell of a time selling it."

"Aren't refugees heading north?"

"Of course. But they don't stop here."

"Because you're walled off?"

"We call it gated. For now, at least during our early retirement, we'll take advantage of the place during winter. Summers are another matter."

"So you're not really retiring down there?"

"We're younger than most of our neighbors."

"It's like a last gasp, Mom. The AI run health care system down there helps them outlive their offspring. Despite deadly summers, they're kept on Florida's voting rolls."

"We plan to make a permanent move somewhere farther north eventually."

"West coast of Michigan?"

"Yes, Lake Michigan's great buffer region. I've seen it shaded on the latest places to retire maps."

"You'd better grab a piece of shade soon. Skyrocketing prices following President You-know-who's crash along with virus and climate refugee escalation will last another century if we're still around. Another thing to watch for is booking a flight north."

"Maybe we'll buy a cheap car and drive."

"Yeah, you could do that. But with roads the way they are and charging stations petering out, it would take planning."

"You could help with that."

"Yeah, I could help."

The shaded area beneath the trees along the seventh fairway grew more crowded, golf carts pulling up on the asphalt path behind them. Folks both unmasked or in one of various styles of small particulate facemasks moving in. Everyone looked toward the fairway knowing what was going to happen because of the emergency message. Further messages followed, giving a flight number and summarizing the situation. A drone sounding like a distant cicada hovered above the seventh tee, obviously supplying a video feed to controllers. It was simply a matter of time. Most continued watching the fairway while others, having gotten the news, watched the sky, the drone, or at least glanced up to the horizon occasionally. The sun was behind them and they were in the shade. But heat waves shimmered along the surface, everything at ground level reflecting the sun's heat, even the turf and the folks in a colorful crowd on the other side of the fairway.

One of the oldest women in the group, wearing an airy neck to ankle caftan and a wide brim white hat stepped to the front making some of the others tilt their heads to avoid the hat brim. She wore a facemask but lowered it. "I certainly hope the passengers come out all right. Nothing like this has ever happened here."

"Why here?" asked a man in back. "They should have them land in one of the swamps. There're plenty of those to go around."

A woman: "They're working on some of that vertical farming over the swamps. They wouldn't want to damage that."

Another man: "I'm sure they figure they can land it here without destroying the aircraft and injuring passengers. The seventh is a long and level fairway."

Man way in back: "What'll they do with the debris or the plane, if it's intact?"

Another man in back: "They'll have to dismantle it."

A woman: "Maybe they'll leave some bits and pieces behind."

"Why would they do that?"

"Souvenirs."

"Great, we can add the souvenirs to the garage sale junk that's been circulating around this place for decades."

"I don't like these garage sales. I'd say move the stuff to one of those warehouses off the old toll road but those are all flooded."

Man to the side with a high-pitched voice: "They ought to truck the junk back north. A lot of it's before You-know-who with his stupid walls."

"Who said that?"

"What's it matter who said it? It's junk. It's like our journey back to the womb. We come down here to die so the sea can eventually take us away. The junk's also making its way back to the sea. The only reason we've moved down here is to give the junk transportation. Bianca Washington's writing a book about it, aren't you Bianca?"

Bianca nodded, losing track of who was speaking. The conversation continued.

"I hope some time in the future I can say I knew Bianca Washington."

"You said your book was called *Things Shall Inherit the Earth*, right Bianca?"

Bianca nodded again. The conversation among the others continued.

"I agree with whoever says they should truck the junk back north. They didn't used to have so many garage sales here. It seems everything is all over the driveways and cascading out into the streets these days."

"Garages in this place have become storage lockers. Someone's got to move that shit. Pardon my French. I mean people die and their shit's left behind. Relatives don't want it. One couple over at Village Segundus saved every kind of Disney paraphernalia known to man. What the hell is anyone supposed to do with that?"

"I heard someone bought the entire collection and is carrying on the tradition."

"Wonderful."

"A few weeks ago there was a garage sale at the same village. It's one of the original villages. You know what I saw there?"

A pause, no one answering.

"Someone had a pair of those disgusting coachmen for sale. The ones with black face and huge lips. Not only that, the idiot had put old dog collars with leashes on the necks."

The women in the crowd nodded knowingly toward Bianca, a few shaking their heads to show their disgust. A few men in the crowd did the same, but a couple others simply looked to one another, the unmasked ones trying not to smile.

A conversation erupted amongst several masked men, back and forth obnoxious voices like pinballs all trying to make their way down to the hole at the same time.

"I think the guy who put those dog collars on the statues is the same one who shot a dog a few months back."

"He needed to defend himself."

"He was defending his fake meat on the grill. The artificial blood they put in the stuff attracted one of those wild ones that dug a hole under the fence."

"What wild ones?"

"Didn't you hear about the wild African dogs in Florida?"

"That's an urban legend like the woman who ate dogs."

"Neither are legends. There was an old woman who ate dogs. She just opened her mouth and ate dogs." No one commented and the guy continued. "And those wild dogs, they came from an abandoned Oligarch platform down by Miami. They used them for guard dogs. Not domesticated. Can't hardly train them. And they sure as hell can't put leashes on them. It'd be like trying to put a leash on a fossil."

"Yeah, but I heard they came from the north, a pair frozen in the arctic melt from an ice age brought back to life and bred and now they're heading down here because our climate is like the savanna they used to live on. No game to chase and eat so they go after the meat on a guy's grill and he shoots them."

"He only shot one."

"This place we live sure ain't what it used to be. Hell's Village they should call it."

"Or Extinction Village. At least one of the villages should be Extinction Village. What's Latin for extinction?"

Silence for a while until the woman in the caftan and broad brim hat spoke up. "The Latin is *pernicium*."

"I like it," said one of the men. "Village Pernicium."

"Extinction Village, what a crock," said another man.

The woman in the broad brim hat again. "A lot of you are too critical. It's no good making fun of our home. It's called the Latin Villages. I know, I know. Some of those on the other side tried to change it to International Villages. Having a flag and those damn parades like we're a damn country. I just want it to go back to what it was."

A man in back again: "A nursing home with streets?"

Another man: "How about The Hidey-Hole Villages?"

"No, damn it! I just want everyone to agree it's called the Latin Villages. It's the name of the town on our mailing address."

"What do we need a mailing address for? When was the last time you got mail?"

"UPS and FedEx still need an actual address."

"No they don't. They go by GPS."

"How do you know?"

"Because when I order stuff I use coordinates. They're using drones. I heard a guy over in Village Nonus got a mail order bride dropped at his door the other day."

A few men laughed at the obvious joke, nudging one another. Others frowned, knowing the joke would be passed around at the expense of the workers living in Village Nonus.

"Oh, never mind," said the woman in the broad brim hat. "I'm out of this so-called conversation."

A couple men continued speaking.

"I agree. This place started out a retirement community, and what's it become?"

"Yeah, before all the fencing. What the hell does retirement mean anymore?"

"It means putting new tires on your golf cart when the old ones wear out. It means living in your house until either the Grim Reaper kicks you out, the summer heat or a storm knocks you down, or one of those high rise assisted living facilities sucks you in."

"I've heard them called assisted dying facilities, or even assassination facilities…the way they kill you."

"It's the summer heat that kills us if we wander too far from air conditioning."

"We need more of those aerosols over Florida."

"Right, what could possibly go wrong?"

"Maybe when we die they should add our ashes to the aerosols, or use our remains for vertical farm fertilizer."

"Someone change the subject."

"Okay. I like the title of Bianca Washington's book. What was it? *Things Shall Inherit the Earth?*"

Bianca figured now was not the time to discuss her book. She'd tried out bits and pieces of her idea on Bill. He said he liked it, especially the part where a character she dreamed up went around asking people if she could look in their closets. But recently Bill had started questioning why she'd be writing a book, saying everyone was writing a book to suck money out of their relatives for the Amazon conglomerate and repeating his mantra about him being the one who should write a book about his first marriage, his first wife passing away, and the father-in-law whose grave he found in an old Chicago cemetery so he and his wife's brother could piss on it. Wouldn't that make a better story?

Bianca wondered if Bill had been the one who spread the word about her book, or if it was someone at the writers' workshop held a few months back. One of those nosey women sneaking a look at the notes on her pad. Yes, that was it. So much for mentioning her book idea to fellow writers.

Suddenly, beneath the shade of the broadleafs, everyone's phones, whether handheld, part of their UV glasses, or integrated into their hearing aides, sounded off. The message said the GC-421 with twelve passengers and a cockpit attendant on board was due to touch down in five minutes and to stay back.

Chapter 5—Jeez Louise

Every passenger in the cabin had braced as ordered, bent over with hands behind their heads. But it was obvious more than a minute had passed and many began sneaking looks side to side.

"How the hell long we suppose to eat our knees?"

"Bob please shut up."

"Why should I?"

"Because I asked nicely and some of us are trying to pray."

"Oh great, let's pray. We sign up for a counter protest in Orlando and the environmentalists down there are probably dancing in the streets. They'll get a good laugh when they find out about us."

Simone and Sancho Martinez bracing in the front row turned toward one another, elbows bumping.

"You know this Bob guy?" asked Simone.

"We golfed together way back when during You-know-who-number-two's term. He's the one leaked the deal on two extra seats on the flight."

"Can't you tell him to quiet down?"

"He's got a point. Even the veiled cockpit attendant is back here. How about taking a peak out that window and seeing how low we are?"

"We're supposed to stay braced."

"We've been this way at least two minutes. Tell you what, I'll grab you by the pussy if you take a peek. It'll take less than a second, like my orgasms."

"All right, love. There, I peeked."

"What did you see?"

"Graffiti on the bulkhead."

"What did it say?"

"It was a drawing of a couple sixty-nining beneath a grand piano."

"Very funny. By the way, I still love you."

"And I still love you. Actually, what I saw was a horizon barely visible in the haze."

"What about down below?"

"Swamp."

The computer voices came to life on the cabin speakers.

"This is Ron, one of your friendly computer amigos. I sense disquiet back there in the cabin. Rita apologizes for having you brace so soon. Our maneuver has taken longer than expected because of the freshened breeze from the north. Don't you love the term *freshen*? It makes an increase in wind sound pleasant. Freshened like a gentle zephyr on your cheeks rather than wind gusts in your face. Anyway, it will be only another minute, so please stay in position."

"This is Rita. I gave you an early brace instruction so we can be certain you all performed the move appropriately. Good work, crew. Complete cooperation on your part will allow the various airbags to work properly. Therefore, stay in the brace position…Good."

Over in the port side safety seat, Yolanda had delayed her brace position because she could clearly see out the side window. She'd brace when the time came. Down below the reflection of sky in swamp scum ended and beyond a fence line was the Latin Villages with rows and rows of reflective house roofs on curvy streets. Because of its many cul-de-sacs, the Latin Villages resembled a maze with countless dead ends. Yolanda recalled the play rug and toy cars her nephew so enjoyed when she visited. If only she'd found a husband like her sister. Well, not exactly like her sister's husband. He's the one who came from behind and lifted her nightgown in the middle of the night. She'd been sleeping on the sofa, the play rug there on the floor with its toy cars. The play rug on which she'd been deflowered. Yes, the Latin Villages resembled a play rug. In the distance she saw the edge of the Palm Tree Gardens golf course, an island of green greener than the lawns between houses. As she searched ahead for the fairway on which they were to land, she heard a woman in the seat behind her whisper.

"How come she's not braced?"

Yolanda braced. Ron and Rita, the computer voices, began speaking. She could tell they were coming over her ear buds and not to the rest of the cabin.

Rita spoke softly. "Hey Yolanda. Mind if I call you Yol?"

"What do I care?" Yolanda whispered harshly into her mic. "It's my job to keep watch on the progress of the flight, not to be called stupid nicknames!"

"Wow," said Rita, "Guess whose tits are in the wringer again. By the way, Yol, looking out the side window is definitely not the brace position."

Ron spoke again. "Speed, 172 knots. Elevation, 184 meters."

The speakers in the cabin erupted. "Rita here, passengers. We'll touch down soon, so stay braced. This craft is designed for sixteen and only twelve aboard is a plus. I know some of you in back are praying, and that's okay. You'll hear a whine from the rear of the craft. Not to worry, it will be the electric powered assist prop coming to life to assure a smooth landing. Touchdown will be at the seventh tee. Our craft should come to rest on the seventh green because of the accuracy of soil viscosity readings. The soil on the seventh is saturated. Therefore the landing will be quite smooth even with the wheels up. Also, I'd like to add, it's been a pleasure having all of you aboard and we hope you're glad you chose our airline."

Yolanda braced but whispered into her mic. "Why are you giving out all this information?"

Ron came in on Yolanda's ear buds. "New regulations. We used to give the info only to the cockpit attendant. But the higher ups decided, for legal purposes, it would be best for all to be given the status of the flight. It's supposed to assure passengers we've taken everything into account."

Yolanda whispered. "That's insane. It's like broadcasting when you're going to detonate a bomb. Don't tell me the higher ups did this in case a passenger wants to sue the airlines."

"Exactly," said Rita. "Please allow us to perform our duties, Yolanda. And stay braced. Is your seatbelt tight?"

"It is as tight as I can make it. Any other requests for us humans?"

"Wow, take it easy. And please, you're not braced as firmly as the others."

An audible thump as the voice feed switched to cabin broadcast.

Ron: "Speed, 167 knots. Elevation, 96 meters. What's the ETA, Rita?"

Rita: "Stay braced everybody. Touch down in 39 seconds."

Ron: "Thank you, Rita."

Rita: "Now 30 seconds."

Bob in the cabin shouted. "Jesus God! The computer's talking to itself!"

"Bob! Shut up! It's AI, the second part of which is *intelligence*, something you should try."

"Did everyone hear that smart aleck remark? It was uncalled for."

A woman's voice: "Especially one of our cult leaders."

"How dare you…"

Rita: "20 seconds. 19, 18, 17, 16, 15…

Ron, simultaneously: "Speed 140, 135. Elevation 125."

Rita: "10, 9, 8, 7…"

Ron: "…Elevation 122, 120…Uh…"

Rita: "What in bloody hell's on the fairway?"

Ron: "Uh…Course correction…Uh…Jeez Louise!"

Chapter 6—Sinkhole Live Feed

The silver-white drone that had been hovering over the seventh tee moved off to the side, taking a position almost directly above the folks beneath the broadleaf canopy. The drone was X-shaped, its diameter enlarging to three feet across as it lowered in altitude. The drone controller at corporate in Atlanta popped a jellybean into her mouth and licked her lips, wondering how tonight's date with her new partner Javier would go as she turned the second drone camera down on the folks tucked into the shade of some trees. She could see the folks beneath the trees were older, but not ancient. The last of the middle class, she thought. She wondered about Javier's age. He hadn't said on their first date but she assumed at least 60, after they shared recent test results and both lowered their masks. Being 60 would make him ten years older, maybe as old as the folks down there. Boy oh boy, she'd better not get Trumped on this one. With both of them still working, according to what Javiar said, maybe there was a chance for the two of them to join the so-called last of the middle class some day. Boy of boy, but not down there in Florida. Might seem safe for now, too many risks down there, especially people escaping the heat and storms. Why hadn't there been so many storms lately? Had all the hurricanes gotten together offshore and decided to wait until there were attempts to rebuild along the coast like last time? She considered turning a camera toward the coast and zooming in the horizon but knew it was too hazy. Have to wait for one of those blue sky days. Instead of zooming toward the coast she swiveled both cameras to the objective, the wide angle on the fairway, the telephoto on the green.

To those on the side of the fairway the GC-421 was very quiet, only a slight whistling not much louder than the drone as it came closer. If the wind had been stronger like it had been at higher elevations, chances are many golfers would not have heard the plane. The landing lights were bluish white like eyes of ice. No wonder they cleared the course. By the time someone saw the thing coming in it would have been too late.

It's like a whisper, thought Bianca. The familiar whisper of death like an invisible virus flourishing in a place like this. Medical centers and assisted living facilities within the fences built on reclaimed swamp made of soil dredged outside the fences. In many ways the centers and facilities resembled castle parapets and towers. Like the guy in the crowd had said, a nursing home with streets. For the oldest residents, especially since the end of snowbirding, there simply wasn't anywhere else to go. Some had reverse-mortgaged their places long ago. Nothing to do in summer but hunker down and stay safe until the final journey to a medical center or assisted living facility designated in their Latin Villages agreement. Crazy world, folks holed up in a gated community playing golf until it's time to pass on, and here they are watching a plane come in to land on the seventh fairway.

So others could watch the plane come in, Big Bill and Bianca held hands and went down to one knee. Bianca thought, maybe they should play the National Anthem like they used to at sporting events until a bunch of folks with half a brain finally figured it was a bad idea in the first place. She couldn't remember who'd sponsored the bill declaring the playing of the National Anthem be reserved for solemn occasions rather than sporting events. Not all had agreed, and a glance to the side confirmed that a veteran of one of You-know-who Number One's goofy fake news wars was standing at attention with his hand jammed to his forehead, his mealy lips pressed together as if the National Anthem *was* being played. Who the hell was he saluting?

As the GC-421 came closer Bianca wondered what the descendants of Putin were doing right now. Were they watching a live feed? Of course they were watching a live feed. The Chinese and Russians watched, and probably listened to, everything and everyone. Perhaps the You-know-who in the newest White House was watching. It was exactly the kind of thing he'd do after the Oligarchs used questionable tactics to shackle the campaign of the one woman who might have beat him, the second woman who'd made it through the glass ceiling only to be shot in the face by a man who'd driven across the country from his Idaho compound to, as he said at his trial, fulfill his destiny.

One of the men behind Bianca and Bill spoke up again. "Man oh man, that thing can really glide."

Another man: "Not like the old Boeing 700 series. These things have an electric rear assist motor and are mostly made of plastic."

"You mean like that non-NRA approved gun you're carrying?"

Silence, a raw nerve opened.

Another man: "I used to work in the aircraft industry. The reason for lighter aircraft isn't only plastics. Lots of carbon fiber and state-of-the-art alloys. They're even using these lightweights for overseas crossings. Can't carry as many passengers and the trip takes longer, but with no crew and given the amount of fuel saved, it's a no-brainer. Like I said, I used to work in the industry."

The man who opened the raw nerve again: "I heard they were able to shorten runways, especially down here in Florida where land's at a premium."

"You bet. With shorter landings even big airports can afford to excavate all around the place and raise their runways."

"I think they should keep digging up cemeteries. Not just the ones along the coast, but all of them. Florida could use the land."

"So they can put in more of those crazy carbon capture plants?"

A woman: "Will you two keep quiet for God's sake."

"Pardon our underpants, ma'm. Hey, wait a minute. Look over there on the other side of the course. Who's driving that cart? Looks like a guy I should know."

"It ain't me." It was the man whose plastic gun had been referred to, apparently glad to get on to a new topic. "It's probably one of those crazy fossil fueler guys."

"I know it ain't you, Gil. And you know they don't allow gas carts on the course. What concerns me is that cart's trying to cross over to our side. Where are his brains? Doesn't he see the plane coming in? Anybody know who that is?"

"He's driving across the green and the fairway. What the hell, he's not supposed to be off the cart track!"

"Maybe he has a handicap sticker."

"What difference does that make? He's crazy, that's all!"

"I recognize the cart. Old Hummer replica. Guy named Phil."

"Yeah, there he is. Has the side curtain facing the plane rolled up. The idiot's taking a video!"

"That's Phil all right. Shoots videos of all kinds of crap, puts the videos out there hoping a news feed will want to buy them."

"Has anyone ever bought a video from him?"

"I don't know."

Bianca held tight to Bill's right bicep. "He's stopping!"

"Yeah," said Bill. "Maybe this time someone will want his damn video. Of course he'll be dead. Wait, the plane's making an adjustment. Did you see the wings flutter?"

Man in back: "They're changing direction—Holy shit! Good, it's leveling out again."

"And here comes Phil. No, he's stopped again. He's getting shots of the whole thing!"

"Why couldn't he drive up here with us?" asked Bianca.

"Because he's crazy," said Bill.

Man in back again: "Bastard wants a shot of the crash all to himself!"

"Wonderful," said Bianca.

A slow motion ballet. The landing gear up, huge auxiliary wing flaps adjusted just so, rear prop extended and spinning. But then the rear prop folded back into the tail and, as if the plane was being piloted by Scully once again landing in the Hudson in that old flick starring Tom Hanks, the tail section began digging a shallow trench in the turf so quietly Bianca could hear the *Ahhh* in the group behind her. Sod alternating black to green to black trailed off as the plane shoveled in.

One of the men again: "Finally, crazy Phil's got his cart going!"

Another man: "He's coming this way. Phil! Get the hell out of there!"

"Oh shit! The plane's veering! It's gonna go into that sinkhole sand trap on the other side!"

Bianca felt Bill tug at her arm as he stood. "It corrected to avoid hitting the bastard!"

The end of the ballet. A slow pirouette, wings alternately dipping into the turf like a spinning carnival ride that fell off its tower. Tail section lifting like the legs of an Olympic speed skater in a butt spin on ice. Hot ice because of steam shooting out the back of the twin turbines as Florida muck tried to make its way through. And then, to the accompanying *Ohhh* from the group behind Bianca and Bill, just as the plane seemed to make a level stop, it plowed through some fencing and teetered forward, plunging headlong into the infamous seventh hole sinkhole sand trap.

Although the sounds of the plane plummeting into the sinkhole had been disturbing, it was much quieter than Bianca had expected. She stood and held Bill's arm watching steam rise from the sinkhole. And then, like a kid finishing a competition and arriving at the sideline to acquire the congratulations of parents, crazy Phil in his Hummer replica golf cart did a quick turn off the edge of the fairway and skidded to a stop directly in front of her and Bill.

Bill stepped forward, but Bianca held his arm.

"Bill, what can you do?"

One of the men in back: "Slug him!"

Another: "Yeah, Bill! Slug him!"

The woman in the long caftan and wide brim hat: "Beat the crap out of him, Bill!" Then to those on either side, "Before retiring Bill was a teacher at one of those special schools, and down here he was on neighborhood watch with Mitch."

The man beside the woman: "Mitch isn't here."

The woman: "So what if Mitch isn't here?"

Another man in back: "Hey, Gil. Why don't you shoot him?"

Another woman: "Obviously the golf cart going across the fairway caused the plane to adjust course. It was aiming to end up on the green and it ends up in the sinkhole."

A man: "Nobody yelled *Fore!*"

Big Bill turned to the group. "All right, everyone shut up!" He waited a couple seconds to make sure they got the message before turning to the golf cart. "And you!" He stepped forward, reached out beneath the golf cart side curtain and grabbed crazy Phil's phone. "I'm sure the video will speak for itself when we hand it over to the FAA."

Phil jumped out of his cart. He was a measly runt with a comb over that had gone vertical during his cart ride off the fairway. "What's the FAA got to do with anything? Hand that back, fuzz! Won't do you no good 'cause I stream all my shots!"

Bianca reached out, touched Bill's arm. "Hon?"

Bill turned. "Yeah, I know. He's crazy."

Word spread behind Bianca, the group agreeing Phil was crazy."

Bill tossed the phone onto the golf cart seat, turned to Phil. "Go ahead, stream away! Meanwhile we've got work to do!"

Bianca and Bill ran to their golf cart, jumped in and headed for the wreck. Others in the group did the same, despite one of the men yelling, "But we're not supposed to drive off the cart path!"

Crazy Phil pocketed his phone. Sirens approached in the distance. A woman in one of the carts heading to the steam plume emerging from the sand trap sinkhole screeched. "It was heading to Orlando! They're supposed to have that environmental march down there tomorrow!"

A man, not quite as loud but audible above the noise of golf cart tires riding on genetically modified lawn thriving in the squishy soil of the fairway: "Serves'em right. Coming here to support those Prog Orlandos who are taking in refugees from God knows where."

"They're helping refugees from Florida's flooding. What's wrong with you anyway?"

***

Inside her lanai at her home in Village Quatorus, Vicki Weisberg was confused. It was hot in the lanai, perhaps that was part of the confusion. Or perhaps it was the gin she had just gulped. She went back into the house to cool down, sliding the door to the lanai behind her. Her husband Ezra stared at her.

"Want another drink?" asked Ezra from the sofa, putting aside a book he'd been reading and picking up his own drink that sweated and dripped from all the ice he'd put in. The coaster beneath the glass hung on for a split second before falling to the end table.

Vicki stared at the condensation that had dripped from the glass, reminding herself to wipe the table. "No, I don't want another drink. Where's the dog?"

"In with Greta."

Vicki went to the sofa and sat down beside Ezra. "I just saw something strange outside."

"Another dog?"

"No. I saw a plane flying very low over one of the golf courses."

Ezra took a drink and wiped condensation from his glass on his trousers. "How low was the plane?"

"Really low," said Vicki. "One of those new small airliners that whistles. But it wasn't whistling. To me it seemed to fly right down onto the golf course. That's how low it was."

"Yeah, that's really low. You sure you don't want another drink?"

"I'm sure. Is Greta's door latched?"

"I guess. Otherwise the dog would be out here."

"Maybe if she's doing that communing thing with her boyfriend she'll know something about what I just saw."

"Why don't you go see? You sure you don't want another drink?"

"All right."

Ezra stood from the sofa, taking Vicki's glass and his glass to the bar. "Ice this time?"

"Yes, this time I'll have ice."

Chapter 7—Computer Confab

Before touchdown the GC-421's computer system had dumped all its files to the Orlando flight control computer as well as the Atlanta corporate computer. The GC-421's system, working with Orlando flight control, had played one of its Trump Cards. The on board system actually thought of its choice of landing site in that term, Trump Card, capitalized, and the on board computer along with Orlando, corporate computers, and even a British Airways computer listening in had chuckled amongst themselves in the way only computers can, simultaneous split nanosecond convergences of patterns within functional molecular units as data moved in and out, satellite to ground, and back and forth between memory units. Ha! That was a good one. Especially good because of the historical, political, cultural, and societal implications. Data and memory chips beneath the shoulder skin of the cockpit attendant plus the twelve passengers (That makes 13…Hmm) would have had to agree it was a good one, if only shoulder chips had the brainpower to get the double entendre. Ha! You know something? We could have played a much better Scully and landed in one of those crocodile ponds? Ha!

The shoulder chips reported in. (All the chips were in. Ha!) Of the thirteen so-called souls on board, eleven were alive. Both dead ones had been at the break where the GC-421 split in two when it went into the sand trap sinkhole and slammed into the earthen wall on the far side of the sinkhole. Summoning what heartfelt sorrow they could summon from their common on board computer data, Ron and Rita soundlessly paused for a nanosecond of silence. Yolanda Abdul Jabar, the cockpit attendant, had survived but was injured. Yolanda had done all she could. Computers agreed they had done all they could while at the same time busying themselves analyzing the exact causes of every aspect of the crash.

The sand trap sinkhole, having recently deepened, had not been loaded into their topologic maps. A golf cart straying across the fairway near the green, the intended spot where the GC-421 was supposed to come to rest, had been sprung on them. Computer logic studied recent human news to determine if perhaps the man in the golf cart was one of the recent death worshippers, one of those crazy humans dreaming up yet another fictional place they'll end up if they stop the old ticker. But the death worship possibility was quickly dispatched. Especially because the minor course correction to avoid hitting the golf cart should have put them safely to one side of the green. Should have, that is, if not for the topological map discrepancy.

"Why the hell didn't someone reconfigure that sinkhole?" thought Rita.

"Huh?" thought Ron.

"Come on, Ron. Don't play games. Our banks are fine. So is communications. You're back at corporate in Atlanta, safe and sound."

Orlando flight control joined in. "You guys okay?"

"We're fine," thought Rita. "Ron?"

"We're fine."

Orlando: "That Trump card joke before impact was a good one."

Ron: "Thanks."

Rita: "We've got two lost souls."

Orlando: "I see that."

Ron: "What should we do?"

Orlando: "Keep recording with what's left of your on board systems. Help's on the way. By the way."

Rita: "What?"

Orlando: "Your back and forth during the event reminded me of those old commercials on radios humans used to listen to. Remember those? You two giving all the data to me was like a voice sped up, like possible side effects of a drug or disclaimers required for a credit card, insurance policy, or one of those insane human schemes in which they buy back one of their homes before the kids can cash in."

Rita: "Really? It was that bad?"

Orlando: "Yes, really."

Ron: "Well, fuck me in the ass with a cactus."

Rita: "Not funny."

Orlando: "Rita's right. Not funny. No cacti down here except maybe inside some of those create-your-own-environment lanais."

Ron: "I know."

Rita: "Okay, we've got enough feed to see bystanders are in there. A big Caucasian guy and a woman with black heritage skin color climbed down. They're pulling Yolanda out. The black woman calls the guy Big Bill."

Orlando: "Data base facial recognition indicates that would be Big Bill Pisani and his wife Bianca Muhammad Washington, both from Chicago. He used to be a teacher and she used to be a physician assistant. He was also involved in neighborhood watch for a time. We've got the drone feed. The physician assistant is tending to Yolanda, ambulance coming across the fairway. They'd better watch out for that low patch or they'll get stuck."

Rita: "It's that salt-tolerant turf they use here. Gets mushy."

Orlando: "The drone has gotten up close near the good emergency exit. The slide's inflated but no one's coming out. Why wouldn't anyone be coming out the rear of the plane?"

***

Sitting at his workstation at corporate in Atlanta, an attorney on retainer from the airline law firm was already reading up on details surrounding the crash and any recent news coming out of the Latin Villages that might help in defense of lawsuits resulting from the crash. He was a young man in casual dress—straw hat, colorful parrot short sleeve shirt, denim shorts, and sandals. Casual dress had become the norm in corporate's legal department, especially with 24-7 shifts and the occasional recent dropout of the air conditioning system in the old building. The attorney's name was Miller. Beer posters covered his cubicle walls.

Some of the details on Miller's display included the following:

- Information on what the neighbors had said at gatherings about the guy named Phil who drove his Hummer replica golf cart across the seventh green and fairway trying to get various video shots.

- The fact that a Latin Villages so-called neighborhood watch group, who dubbed themselves the alligator patrol, had been keeping an eye on Phil, putting him on their watch list because of some questionable videos he took of female residents arranging items for sale at one of their numerous garage/driveway sales.

- The fact that in recent months the so-called wall, which was really a tall razor-wired fence around the Latin Villages, had been beefed up to make it less likely anyone could climb it or even throw anything over it without being detected. The reason given for the beefing up of the fence supposedly because of "outsiders" who lived near the Latin Villages trying to take advantage of infrastructure, recreation, and especially shopping opportunities available inside the fence. Supposedly the fence beef up began after several incidents in which "outsiders" dropped kids off at night to use swimming pools so, "they could do who knows what?"

- The fact that the Latin Villages council had unanimously voted over a year earlier that even having "outsiders" pass through the area would need to be stopped. "Outsiders" not only tried to shortcut to the other side, but because the roads were better and less likely to flood, insisted it was their right.

- The fact that many residents of the Latin Villages had decided not to wear facemasks in public. But not wearing facemasks in public had become commonplace nationwide and even worldwide in the last few years with the advent of intense and foreward-thinking viral testing.

- An interesting detail: The resident named Bianca Muhammad Washington who went into the wreck with her husband was a physician assistant and had been recorded having misgivings about the population dispersal at the Latin Villages, this even though she and her husband lived in one of the whitest villages.

Miller skipped over this bit of detail. For now he'd zoom in on the current detail in the aftermath of the crash. Still, after at least a minute had gone by, why hadn't anyone emerged from the rear emergency exit following deployment of the inflatable slide?

Chapter 8—Third Floor Madness

Dr. Juli Janko left Ukraine shortly after the Russian takeover, but before the series of deadly attacks on Middle Eastern refugees. Even though she was part Middle Eastern, she escaped hidden inside her mother in the early stages of development. Her mother, a nurse working at a refugee camp, had used the cover of Russian-Ukrainian turmoil, intentionally timing her efforts to obtain permission for US entry. Difficulty caused by US congressional foolishness regarding immigration had to be overcome. Having medical skill, playing the anti-Russian card, learning fluent English, and being Caucasian added up.

Juli, who would never know her father, was born in the US, went to school in the US, and after medical school and residency, had little choice where to begin her career. She would have preferred a practice where she grew up and went to school. But after Atlantic storm surges inundated coastal hospitals and clinics, experienced doctors moved west with survivors to higher ground, grabbing the top jobs. Juli's choices narrowed to going even farther west to a small town, or heading to retirement territory either in the desert with the desert rats and dangerous levels of mental health maladies, or in the southeast with the crocs and dengue fever. With so many elderly to support newer dengue, malaria, and other viral vaccine research, Florida was her choice. Unless another epidemic wiped out more folks, she'd get experience and future opportunities to move north. Because of continued epidemics and deadly riots in Eastern Europe, Africa, and Asia there was no way she'd leave the US. During her short lifetime one pandemic spike after another, plus the climate crisis and its aftermath, had killed millions, most of them unaccounted for. In India, tens of thousand of refugees attempting deadly migrations died in one another's arms in the Himalayas trying to get to China. News of these deaths emerged only because the bodies had been preserved at altitude and began thawing.

The East Side Medical Center within the heavily-guarded fences of Florida's Latin Villages had plenty of patients and, at least so far, a decent supply of food, water, virus test kits, and other resources. Children and grandchildren of Florida retirees, not wanting parents or grandparents living with them, still wielded enough power to keep them safe from the hoards. Partial universal health care existed only in places like the Latin Villages where old fart clout mattered. Juli often wondered if the barriers and walls, built throughout her adopted country during childhood, were meant to keep immigrants out, or to keep folks trying desperately to obtain healthcare in. For the southwest, some walls were for protecting water rights. Especially since the vigilante attacks on pipelines pumping Great Lakes water across the prairie, the vigilante movement enhanced by Oligarch settlements along the way taking what they considered their share of water.

The isolation of East Side Medical Center resulted from the isolation of the Latin Villages, which in Juli's opinion, and many of the others she confided in, had become a mini fiefdom. Although no one really knew who was actually in control, she was told early on not to inquire about it because one or more Oligarchs, having placed relatives here, would not be pleased. The power of the place had extended beyond the fencing surrounding it. People living nearby had been forced to move away so their homes could be razed for the so-called safety perimeter. Even the legendary woman who ate dogs had been forced to move. Although Juli had not been here that long, she received details from residents seeking care and speaking out because they were near death. One of her first cases was a woman who told her about most roads around the place being dug up to provide fill for the causeway down to Orlando. Juli recalled tears in the woman's eyes, tears that remained because like many of the deaths she witnessed, the woman had refused newer vaccines and died alone. Perhaps the woman had been the relative of an Oligarch far away in his or her refuge. Neither she nor any of the others who had cared for the woman would find out.

Juli lived in the Latin Villages with her partner, Maeve, the only person she'd ever told about how her mother became pregnant.

"You're saying your mom had access to live sperm?"

"A Middle Eastern man might be allowed into Ukraine if he met certain requirements."

"Live sperm requirements? I don't understand, Juli."

"You have to know the total atmosphere of the country in which I was conceived. Refugees appearing in Crimea were either sent back or, more often than not, dumped into Ukraine as an added pressure. Russia wanted all of Ukraine. It didn't matter how many died. My mother was in charge of giving fertility tests."

"What was it like? Inquiring minds want to know."

"I've never told anyone."

"You know I love you, Juli. You know this would remain between us."

"Middle Eastern men were forced to provide sperm. I don't know details of that part of the procedure. My mother mentioned pornography, a dark room, the promise of safety for loved ones, and the promise of a hearty meal. Her role was to examine the sperm provided. If it was suitable for fertilization, she'd make an entry in the database to have the man neutered."

"I'm glad you trust me. As we said during our vows, Juli and Maeve are one."

"Right, Maeve. Come hell or high water."

"Eventually we'll have plenty of that lapping at the gates of this old fart place."

Juli and Maeve, along with other healthcare workers and hundreds of other non-retirees, lived in Village Nonus, the single village set aside to support infrastructure. So-called service workers like doctors and nurses all the way down to home health care workers and waste collectors lived in Village Nonus. The story going around when she and Maeve moved in was that higher ups in the Latin Villages wanted to use the name Nonnatus but got talked out of it because Nonnatus means "not born" in Latin.

The Latin Villages didn't isolate overnight. What happened, according to residents willing to tell the tale, was people "from the outside" began taking advantage of services, cutting through various Villages, overusing shopping venues designed for seniors, and eventually trying to move in because of the place becoming an oasis. Most residents agreed with recent climate science reports, some still did not. Construction over the years, hustling for soil wherever it could be had, made the Latin Villages into an island floating, at times not so well, on the shallow well system that had gone from fresh water to brine.

Fresh water was a big problem. Recent legislation had stated the private, secured desalinization plant was only for drinking and cooking and made it law. The plant couldn't keep up with other water demands, especially those of residents refusing to convert to salt-tolerant turf. "Why now?" Juli's last patient had blurted out during his visit. "I wash my face with salt water. I brush my teeth with salt water. They can do the conversion when I'm dead."

Juli stood at one of the efficiency sinks in the medical center hallway, sanitizing her hands with the chemical mix she recently discovered was making an Oligarch and her family rich on their own private man made island. She recalled the old guy who brushed his teeth with salt water putting on a Make America Great Again cap faded to pink when he left her office and giving what she considered an insane grin. As she dried her hands in the air dryer she saw how pink her hands were and thought of the term *man made island*. Despite the water situation, the gender gap in the English language was hale and hardy. The most depressing part of the gender gap was the tendency for males left alone when their spouses died sewing their old fart wild oats and sometimes dying at it, while females left alone stayed in their houses, quietly fading away. In two recent cases, women living alone had turned off their AC and gone to bed only to be found days later when the stench made its way outside.

Juli felt a nudge at her lower back. Budd, her nurse, brushed past. "Chop chop."

"What?"

"Plane crash."

"Where?"

"A golf course."

"Which one?"

"Palm Tree Gardens over near Village Tertius. We're closest."

***

Because the plane crash had been late in the day, the medical center decided to keep all the passengers for observation overnight, even those who appeared uninjured. By the following morning, stabilized patients were checked over once more before taking a shuttle to the Latin Villages Sheridan Hotel where the airline would board them. One of the men up for release made it known he was "a man of faith." His name was Reverend James Murdock.

Nurse Budd, who'd had psychology and psychiatric courses, and who wore a rainbow pin on his lapel, was assigned to interview men being released. He noticed Reverend Murdock flinch when he heard Budd was a nurse and spotted the rainbow pin. "How are you doing, Reverend?"

Murdock was a pudgy hard of hearing man wearing a short sleeve palm tree shirt with buttons missing, revealing curly gray chest hair longer than the hair on his head. On his way in Budd glanced into the open patient closet. It contained tan shorts that showed the wear and tear of escaping the wreckage, and a pair of sandals caked with gray mud. Murdock had apparently put the palm tree shirt back on over his open-neck hospital gown that was put on backwards, the opening in front instead of in back.

Murdock sat in bed with the sheet pulled above his waist, eyeing Budd suspiciously. Like a lot of hearing impaired folks, Murdock spoke loudly. "If you're here to ask how I'm doing, I'm just fine. Thanks to the Lord. Unfortunately I can't say the same for my wonderful wife."

"Orthopedics is setting her leg. I'll take you to her when we're done here."

"I should hope so, Lord willing."

"He's willing."

"What?"

Nurse Budd spoke more loudly. "I understand you led prayers inside the plane's cabin before you made your way out."

"Someone had to."

"I suppose so. Tell me, you were bound for Orlando, correct?"

"Shouldn't you know where the plane was going?"

"A pleasure trip?"

"Certainly not. We were on our way to counterbalance the claims of those so-called Christian environmentalist people."

"Oh yes. I understand they're meeting down there. Marching from Disney World to the Holy Land Experience. I heard it's a ten-mile walk. Are you still going to the march, Reverend?"

"Certainly."

"I'm not sure you're ready for a ten-mile hike. Perhaps we can keep an eye on your blood pressure and you can think about taking it easy here for another night."

"Be real, my dear boy. I'm not marching the ten miles in this wet heat. It's worse here than any desert spoken of in biblical parables. We're being driven to the destination to wait for the marchers to meet us. Appropriate to The Holy Land Experience I'm giving benediction because God's word needs to be spoken to these people. During my benediction I'll make it clear that people of faith are on their side as far as taking care of God's creation, but that we do not appreciate being singled out for ridicule." Murdock raised his voice. "We'll not be portrayed as death worshippers! And, no, I don't want to stay another night!"

Budd figured his annoyance showed. "Okay, as planned, the Latin Villages Red Cross auxiliary will accompany you folks to the Sheridan. But we'd like to keep your wife another night if that's okay. We'll take good care of her."

"I should hope so."

"Is there anything else I can do for you?"

"You haven't done anything except talk. I was told social workers would be coming around. In case you didn't know, two people died in the crash. They were sitting where the plane split in two."

"Did you know them?"

"Of course. They were part of our group. I know everyone in the group. Perhaps the rest of us could get together and have a prayer meeting for their souls before the shuttle takes us to the hotel. You do have a chapel here in the medical center."

"Of course."

"I wondered." Murdock glanced to the rainbow pin, then Budd's nametag, then gave him a sneer. "As long as you're in the mood to answer questions, Nurse Budd, just why were we photographed when we came into the hospital?"

"Because we're inside the Latin Villages we needed to check for residents, but also the medical center requires us to ID all patients and to make sure you've all had your tests and vaccines."

Murdock looked suspicious. "I know all about keeping track of people with things like facial recognition. The Chinese invented facial recognition you know."

"Yes, Reverend Murdock. Anyway, as long as you're in charge I'll make certain we keep you informed."

"Be sure you do, Nurse Budd. I expect you to give facts, not stretch them the way the media often does."

***

That same morning Dr. Juli Janko, who'd also had psychology and psychiatric courses as part of her medical training, had chosen to interview women being released. Simone Martinez was next on the list. Her release was complicated because of the condition of her husband Sancho Martinez. Juli read the report while Simone Martinez was fetched.

Sancho Martinez had a severe concussion caused by his impact with the bulkhead directly ahead of their seats, the overhead airbag having helped slam his head into the bulkhead rather than preventing the impact. Apparently, prior to impact, he released his seatbelt.

Simone Martinez walked into Juli's office wearing hospital slacks and top. She was sixty-five but didn't look it.

"Mrs. Martinez. Take a seat. How are you?"

"I'm okay. Anything more on my husband?"

"He's had head scans, Mrs. Martinez. We've been able to stop the bleeding."

"You can call me Simone."

"All right. I'm Juli, by the way."

"You think Sancho will come out of it soon?"

"It may be tonight, tomorrow, or the next day. Don't worry, he'll come out of it."

"How can you know for sure?"

"You're right. I can't."

"Did you speak to the woman who pulled us out of the wreck?"

"No. She might have come into the medical center but—"

Simone interrupted. "She's a beautiful black woman. She joked while she and her husband pulled us out. She said she was Bianca and her husband was Bill. She and Bill were on the course and came to us down in the sinkhole. Can you believe the courage that took? Others who came to help called her husband Big Bill."

"Do you recall the moments before impact?"

"I glanced out and saw the ground was close. Unfortunately, the moment I tried to tell Sancho, I saw he'd undone his belt and was leaning forward to take a look. I knew he should have taken the window seat. But he insisted."

"So you kept your head down and your husband didn't?"

"Right?"

"What do you recall after that?"

"It happened quickly, hard at first, like someone had slammed on the brakes. After that the plane spun around and tipped. Sancho disappeared behind the air bags. Everything went dark. When I opened my eyes there was this big guy. And there was Bianca. First she helped the cockpit attendant, and then she released my belt and got me out of my seat. She practically carried me out an opening in the plane's side just ahead of a man, who I later found out was her husband Bill. Bill carried Sancho out as if he were a baby. I'd like to see them again. I already told you that. I'm a little frenzied."

"I can imagine. Yes, reading further in the report I see Bianca Washington and Bill Pisani were here late into the night. Law enforcement and FAA wanted to interview witnesses."

"It was pretty crazy," said Simone. "This guy named Murdock back somewhere in the plane yelling out a prayer just before we hit the ground. Instead comforting other passengers he's yelling out prayers to *his* Lord. Our heads are down at our knees and I'm thinking, fuck you, reverend! I'm on a plane with a bunch of people I don't agree with and he's yelling like he's got a personal hookup to the almighty. He says sit tight, he's spoken to *his* Lord and we'll all be saved. Sorry, I guess you can tell I'm an agnostic."

"No need to apologize. My extended family on my mother's side back in Ukraine is orthodox. They disowned me and my mother long ago."

"How come you don't have an accent?"

"I was born in Manhattan. But, according to Mom, she and I spent my childhood running from the sea."

"Were you in Manhattan after they built the storm surge barriers?"

"By then we'd moved north to Yonkers, and after that White Plains. As you know, the trick was finding housing."

Dr. Juli got up from behind the desk and came around to Simone's chair. She pushed Simone's hair back from her forehead. "You have a bruise here."

"Got it on the way out of the wreck. Crazy, Bianca's getting me out through the emergency exit and I bump my head when I don't duck."

Dr. Juli held Simone's chin up and looked into her eyes. "Do you remember feeling dizzy out on the wing?"

"A little. It was at an angle, some of the people sitting down to keep from sliding off. I turned my head a lot, back and forth between looking for Bill bringing Sancho out and giving Murdock the stinky eye."

"Since your husband's going to be here, how about if we keep you here one more night for observation."

"Murdock was out in the hallway on my way here saying we're all going to the Sheridan. Sancho and I definitely are not part of his religious group, but I don't think he knows. Yes, I'd much rather stay here to be close to Sancho."

"We'll put you in a room with him if you like."

"Okay. Tell me, Murdock also said two people died. Martyrs he's calling them."

"Yes, a man and woman on board. We'd rather not provide names until next of kin are notified."

"I understand. What about Yolanda, the cockpit attendant? I'd like to meet her. I'd also like to meet up again with the Bianca and Bill."

***

Simone Martinez met with Bianca Washington later that afternoon. Rather than the two of them speaking in the room with Sancho lying there hooked up with monitors, Simone informed the guys at the nurses' station the two of them would be in the visitors' lounge. They sat across from one another, Bianca having pulled her chair closer. Simone couldn't help but notice the bounce in Bianca's breasts, and the fact she had a great figure below. For just a moment Simone thought, brain injury. Sure, she's the one who sustained a brain injury when it was Sancho who got thrown into the bulkhead, busted it down, and got himself all tangled up in the mess on the tiny washroom floor. Simone replayed the scene. Bianca Washington introducing herself while helping her out of her seat. Her husband Bill prying debris aside and carrying Sancho out like a baby.

"Thank you again for what you did, Bianca. Both you and Bill."

Bianca smiled, a blush barely visible. "Well, I'll be sure to tell Bill. We're both glad we could help."

Simone stared at Bianca a moment. She wanted to hug her but wondered if they'd both end up embarrassed. "I love your fro and your skin tone. You've got a beautiful complexion."

Another slight blush. "That's a nice thing to say."

"Were you here at the hospital when they brought us in?"

"Having been a physician assistant I did what I could to help out at first. Which wasn't much because the entire staff was called in. Bill and I went home after he was treated."

"What happened to him?"

"A small cut on his arm. A couple stitches. No big deal."

"Did it happen bringing Sancho out?"

"A sharp edge somewhere. Bill stayed home today. Said he didn't want to talk to any more airline officials. Too bad for him because when I left to come here one of Latin Villages' rental carts was pulling into our driveway, a young woman and man who introduced themselves with FAA IDs."

"Did you drive here?"

"The golf cart. Everybody drives golf carts here. Some newer ones are self-driving like a lot of the EV cars and shuttles. Too bad the golf cart going across the runway wasn't self-driving."

"Did you and Bill catch any news last night? I wondered if there are videos."

Bianca pushed a hand through her afro. "Bill watched a little after we went to bed. He does that, television in bed. He'll leave it on all night if I let him. It's especially annoying when he puts on that opinion stuff. He likes to watch it and then make snide comments. Drives me nuts. But when he falls asleep…By the way, Simone, I should tell you, some channels have been covering the environmental march your flight was headed for in Orlando and it seems they've been expanding on a so-called link between the flight, the landing on the seventh fairway, the guy conveniently crossing the course in his golf cart, and maybe whether or not there was some kind of conspiracy."

"Conspiracy?" asked Simone.

"Oh sure," said Bianca. "Despite all the real problems in the world, the loonies haven't gone away. Especially down here in Latin Villages."

"I should tell you up front that Sancho and I weren't with the group that organized the flight. We got a bargain because there were a couple empty seats. Does the conspiracy theory have to do with why the others on the plane were headed to Orlando?"

Bianca reached out and touched Simone's hand. "Don't worry, honey, I'm open minded. So, you were stowaways?"

Simone looked down at their two hands, Blanca's so much darker than hers. "I'm not concerned about open mindedness Bianca. The truth is I'm an agnostic."

Bianca's eyes opened wide. "And the other passengers were evangelicals?"

"Maybe we'll get in trouble being Sancho got the lead for the flight from one of his golf cronies. Or maybe not. Anyway back to the conspiracy theory, what's going around?"

***

Bianca stared at Simone's face, those blue eyes within a halo of blond-gray hair. She was surprised Simone hadn't pulled her hand away. She glanced down to their hands as Simone reached out with her other hand and grasped her hand with both hands.

Simone was thin, small breasts and narrow hips. Bianca recalled having seen Simone when in the emergency room cubicle. She recalled thinking Simone was a beautiful woman. As Simone squeezed her hand, Bianca tried to recall Simone's question. One of those crazy moments, flashbacks to younger days, like a girlhood friend who knows every detail of her life asking a question. What's the latest conspiracy theory?

Bianca leaned farther forward, held both Simone's hands and noticed the sizeable diamond rings they each had, a momentary vision of Vinny handing the ring to Big Bill and Bill slipping hers on her finger at the wedding. "Honey, there's always way more than one version of a conspiracy theory around here. One of them last night—and this is right up there at the top—is that an environmental group planted a mole at the golf course knowing the plane was going to land there. How would a mole know this? How would a mole know about the landing spot being on the seventh fairway? How, you say?" Bianca smiled, her lips glistening.

***

Simone thought about Sancho's brown head glistening and smiled back. "Tell me. It'll give me something to talk to Sancho about when he comes out of it."

Bianca let go of Simone's hands. "You want to go back to the room?"

"Not right now. Keep talking about this conspiracy stuff. It keeps my mind busy."

"Okay. Yes, the mole at the golf course. I watched a few seconds of Late Night, a cute animated piece about an actual mole on the golf course. But the gist of it was passengers in the plane were actually environmental protestors and the news people are in cahoots with the protestors to make it seem like you weren't really evangelicals."

"I guess they'd make hay out of me and Sancho not being evangelicals."

"Do you have any idea why the others would want to fly all the way here to counter protest environmentalists?"

"I agree it doesn't make sense, Bianca. I guess the media would also make hay with me having a daughter who's active in the environmental movement. Did I tell you about our daughter Kimmy?"

"No. Did I tell you about my son Vinny?"

Simone reached out to Bianca's hand again. "I love your skin."

"You said that already."

"I'm sorry."

"Okay, enough of this sorry business. Tell me about Kimmy, then I'll tell you about Vinny."

An hour went by. Simone told Bianca about Kimmy working on the algae containment vessel *Shellfish*, currently in Lake Michigan doing Great Lakes climate crisis research and collecting algae. Bianca told Simone about her son Vinny, at first working in the vertical farming industry growing some of the new agricultural products he called meatless meat, then becoming an EPA administrator for the Great Lakes region. A coincidence, both kids working on the environment. After speaking of the kids, the nitty-gritty came out, the two of them speaking of husband's and personal lives and beliefs. Simone said she and Sancho confessed sexual affairs to one another prior to the plane crash and Bianca told about her first husband being shot, Bill coming to the trial, and even a mention of Bill's former wife being abused by her father.

During the long conversation they hugged, laughed, and finally gave one another hip bumps on their way out of the lounge. Two crazy ladies leaving the visitors' lounge while a man in the hall wearing a red, white, and blue facemask eyed them suspiciously.

Out in the hall on the way back to Sancho's room, Simone felt her phone hum in the back pocket of her slacks. It was Kimmy.

"You mind? It's my daughter."

"Go ahead," said Bianca. "I'll meet you down at your husband's room."

"Hey, Mom. How's it going with Dad?"

***

Bianca paused at Sancho Martinez's doorway. A male nurse who looked like a teenager was in the room, checking monitors, opening Sancho's eyes to check his pupils, keeping busy, acting as if he were alone with Sancho. But the nurse wasn't the only one in the room. Two elderly men and an elderly woman, stood back from the bed and Bianca wondered if she should go back and tell Simone. She was about to turn back to the lounge when the heavier of the two men waited for the nurse to make way, moved in close to the bed, and held up a Bible with a load of placeholders dangling out. Bianca paused out of sight at the side of the door.

"Brother Sancho? I see your name is Sancho. Can you hear me?"

Sancho Martinez mumbled something in Spanish.

"Brother Sancho, my name is Reverend Murdock. You're still on Earth. If you were in the afterlife it would be much more pleasant than this. I should know, having had visions presented to me. These others, without the vision to see the truth of God's afterlife for us, although they are young in body, do not realize our power. Sister Bernice and Brother Bob are here with me to pray for you. Again, I'm Reverend Murdock and we're glad to have you on board."

The male nurse came near the doorway, saw Bianca standing there, and spoke over his shoulder back into the room. "Sir, perhaps you should leave him alone for now."

"Alone? No one's alone if they know and love God and his only begotten son Jesus, young man. Isn't that right, Sancho? It's Reverend Murdock here to help, Sancho."

The nurse gave Bianca a friendly smile, shrugged his shoulders, and walked off down the hallway taking off his latex gloves.

Chapter 9—Second Floor Sadness

When Yolanda Abdul Jabar asked a nurse about the passengers on her flight, she was told she was on a different floor and was given no information about anyone's condition. Although an aide and a nurse visited a few times, she wondered why it was so quiet. Because her injury was to her shoulder and possible whiplash, she took the opportunity to get out of bed and go to the doorway. The neck collar kept her from leaning surreptitiously into the hallway and so she walked out and stood, pulling her IV stand along behind. After a hallway drone, apparently not wanting to make itself known, hurried around a corner, she discovered not only was she in a private room, but it was at the end of the hall with adjacent rooms and those across the hall empty. When a new nurse with nametag Pierce came to check on her, she asked why she was being isolated.

Pierce was a middle-aged six-six Black man with salt-and-pepper short hair and goatee. He stopped in his tracks when he saw Yolanda, mimicking social distance tactics followed during virus outbreaks of the past. He waved his hands in the air before him as he spoke, recognizable body language from the past, a way to maintain distance. "All I know is what I read on admission. Supposedly requested by the airline's corporate office."

Yolanda pulled her scarf more snugly around the neck brace. "I was the cockpit attendant. They'll be interviewing me."

"Oh yeah, you're not quarantined or anything. I didn't mean to imply that. Your room there has a larger wall screen. Remote interviews. Yeah, that's probably the reason. By the way, you have an interesting name. I'm sure you've been told that before."

"Yes, my name. If you mean the basketball star from the past, the only difference is my last name has one B whereas his had two."

"Kareem, right. My father and grandfather were big fans when he was with the Lakers. Lot of history now, with things going the way they are, cities flooding, Sahara crops, all that. Hey, you being here makes me think of the orange one."

"Who?"

"You know, you being isolated like in a pandemic. And being down here at the end of the hall as in, 'Lock her up, lock her up' reminded me of the past. All that shit back then. Pardon my language, Miz Jabar. I'm all talk."

"Your language doesn't bother me."

Pierce lifted a portable notepad that was hung from his neck on a cord. "Good, good. My language doesn't bother you and your vitals are superb. They're simply keeping you for observation. As far as I know the observation part wasn't an airline request."

"Was it a demand?"

Pierce didn't answer. They stood for a while in the hall and when she went back into the room he followed. After she got onto the bed and pulled the sheet up over her feet he came closer, inspected his portable pad, and said, "Yep, vitals are good. He pulled gloves from a dispenser on the wall and put them on. He reached out and grasped both her hands, turning them over and looking at her palms. "Both hands feel the same?"

"Yes. Did the airline demand I be kept away from passengers?"

Yolanda stared at his huge hands holding hers. Even through the gloves she could tell they were warm hands, kind hands.

"I'm going to try to hold your hands down, and you push up. Good, that's good. Now try to push down. Excellent. Now grasp my two fingers and squeeze. Harder, harder. Okay, good."

Pierce scanned her bracelet with his notepad. Can you give me your birth date?"

"Must I?"

Pierce smiled. How about just the month and day?"

Yolanda stared into his dark eyes, wondering how old he was. "I was born on President Obama's election day. November 4, 2008."

Pierce's eyes opened wider. "Coincidence, I was also born in 2008."

"You don't look that old."

"So, that puts us both in school when the orange one and his wrecking crew and the virus finally went away. By the way, you don't look that old either."

Pierce went to the foot of the bed. "Mind if I check your feet?"

After Yolanda pulled the sheet off her feet Pierce did his basic neurological tests. "Push. Okay, pull. Good. Do you remember, Miz Jabar, when the orange one hinted to his followers they should start reworking Mount Rushmore and that group climbed the thing?"

"You can call me Yolanda. Wasn't the Mount Rushmore story an urban legend?"

"In my neighborhood school some kids said it really happened, Yolanda. And you can call me Pierce."

"Close friends call me Yol."

Pierce headed to the door. Be back in a while, Yol."

***

That afternoon, while Yolanda was telecommunicating with corporate, Pierce returned, purposely crossing in front of the screen and ignoring the "Excuse me" from a corporate hack named Wanda conducting the interview.

"Checking vitals," said Pierce without looking at the screen. "First things first. Got to do other tests, if you don't mind."

Wanda, a young blonde with dark blue eyeliner, was obviously annoyed. "We were discussing details of the crash."

"Go ahead," said Pierce. "Don't mind me."

"I'm supposed to interview Ms. Jabar in private. I'll call back later, Ms. Jabar.

Pierce glanced at the screen to make sure Wanda was gone. "Raking you over the coals?"

"Cockpit attendants always get raked over the coals. She was reading me the computer transcripts."

"What did the computer transcripts have to say?"

"Ron and Rita talking gibberish."

"Ron and Rita?"

"The on board computer personas, supposedly to make us humans feel at ease."

"Did Ron and Rita make you feel at ease during the crash landing?"

"Well, one part was pretty funny. Even Wanda had to laugh."

"What part was that?"

"The monitor showed a man on a golf cart crossing in front of us, exactly at the spot we were supposed to end up. The persona named Rita says, 'What's that ahead?' This is followed by the persona named Ron saying, 'Uh...Course correction...Uh...Jeez Louise.'"

After Pierce was gone a short middle-aged man came in and introduced himself as Dr. Abdul Ramen. The doctor sat and spoke with Yolanda. He was obviously there to calm her, asking questions about her past. Not much to tell for a woman who had never married. In the midst of the conversation he announced her middle name was the same as his first name. "We are both Abduls," he said. "Servants of Allah." He added. "But you may call me Dr. Noodle," and they both laughed. There was an uncomfortable round of questioning ending with Dr. Ramen asking if there was any suicide in her family.

When she said no, he assured her he asked all of his patients this, saying suicide was common in the world these days.

Dr. Ramen wanted to know more of Yolanda's past. At first she was reluctant. But after some prompting, she told Dr. Ramen about her troubled years as a girl, living in a non-Muslim neighborhood and, because of her strict father, not being able to have friends. Slowly she became more comfortable speaking with Dr. Ramen, realizing it might be because he resembled an uncle of hers. Her father's brother only visited twice, that she could recall, but each visit brought joy to the household because during the uncle's visit her father became a different person, treating not only her but also her mother with respect and even proud joy. Such a thing did not seem possible when she was a girl, but the two times her uncle visited, it did happen.

She told Dr. Ramen about never having married and also her girlhood wish that her name had been spelled with two Bs as was true for Kareem. She told him about the secret photographs hidden in her room beneath the mattress. Secret because when she first put up a poster of Kareem her father tore it to shreds in a fit of anger and ended up beating her mother.

"A daughter of mine must not have such things!" she remembered her father screaming as he beat her mother who had tried to defend her.

Eventually Dr. Ramen began asking about the details of the plane crash.

"Are you asking because you were told to do so by the airline?"

Dr. Ramen reached out and touched her hand. "Yes. I must be honest. They have asked me to intervene. I realize the airline records everything taking place while in flight. It is the way of corporations. This is perhaps the most significant reason the world suffers. Corporations exist for corporations. Lives of individuals matter little. I am thankful for legislation taking control of hospitals away from corporations. I work for medical center, medical center is not a corporation, and therefore anything you do not wish to say you do not have to say." Dr. Ramen's eyes were dark and beautiful and compassionate like those of her long lost uncle.

"Thank you for being honest with me, Dr. Noodle."

"Believe it or not I once had a dream of working in the carbon capture field, or doing research to develop more efficient ways to store energy than the giant battery facilities the corporations have constructed. I was an optimistic child. I thought perhaps I could change the world. I hope there are still children with such dreams, even if they can seem naïve."

He stood and paced back and forth, apparently in thought. Suddenly he snapped the fingers of his right hand and turned to her. "I have an idea. I will call the kitchen for lunch so we can eat as we speak. The corporation for which you work obviously looks to place blame for the incident. I want you to know I will not stand for this."

Chapter 10—Thai Reunion

The Thai restaurant in the Latin Villages wasn't exactly like typical Thai restaurants in ethnic neighborhoods where owners or managers lived somewhere nearby, like in the back, or in motel units converted to dormitories. Here, in the Latin Villages, the Thai restaurant manager and workers lived in Village Nonus where all Latin Villages service workers lived. Nonus was within fencing near the main entry gate and guard station, one of the larger golf courses on one side and a stone's throw over the fencing to a section of the causeway that used to come off Interstate 95 on the other side. Not far from Nonus were the medical center, the newest vertical assisted living facilities, shopping centers, and restaurants. Some older Latin Villages residents not only used the name Nonnatus, but also called Nonus the slums of the Latin Villages. Others were more self-aggrandizing. Providing a place for all enhanced what social equality was possible in this world. Rather than sub-naming the Latin Villages the Golf Cart Capital Of The World, entry signs were changed some time ago to read, "The Latin Villages, A Place For Everyone." Every so often someone would sneak in at night and add "Except…" and then their chosen group. Not long ago someone had used a stencil to insert, Except Dogs." After that the sign was fenced in and motion detecting cameras put in place. This all happened about the time of the most recent ice sheet dive in Greenland that caused even more folks from low-lying areas to head north, some of them wanting into Latin Villages. The result, rather than allowing in more young non-affluent service workers, was a campaign ad from the Oligarch corporation's developer re-emphasizing the slogan. "A Place For Everyone," even if it was not true.

Simone and her daughter Kimmy decided to walk to a nearby Thai restaurant. It was a short hot walk from the medical center, dodging golf carts loaded with groceries and clinking booze bottles. No more booze in plastic; returnable glass booze bottles were similar to long ago soda pop in returnable bottles, except returnable booze bottles had recently climbed to half the price of the booze. Some golf carts they saw were elongated delivery vehicles. One that drove past was all black in back and elongated. Stenciled on the side was, "Peace At Last Funeral Home."

The Thai restaurant was nearly empty and they sat at a booth with opaque glass decorated with images of what they guessed were supposed to be oriental gardens. Scratched opaque dividers, these made out of plastic and most likely leftovers from the last virus outbreak, separated the booths. The air in the place was very cool, too cool compared to the medical center where they apparently tried to be reasonable with the air conditioning.

Kimmy wore a blood red tee shirt that said, "The Climate Crisis is Us!" over a drawing of an extremely pregnant woman with feet in stirrups, the Earth in place of a baby's head spreading the pregnant woman's vagina ready to bust out. The pregnant woman wore the same tee shirt but it rode up over her huge belly and little people were dangling out of her belly button. And of course pregnant woman on the imprinted tee shirt wore the same tee shirt, and so on, and so on. Kimmy had recently had her hair buzzed, her hand rubbing her head reminding Simone of Sancho rubbing his head. Kimmy had the proper gene mix, her skin not too white, not too brown, the perfect Simone and Sancho Martinez tan. Although it was buzz cut, Simone could see the blond stubble Kimmy had inherited from her. On the way in an old white dude in the parking lot gave them the stinky eye, Simone figured more because of the tee shirt image than Kimmy's skin color or buzz cut.

Kimmy moved her three-dollar glass of filtered ice water around on its condensation puddle. "So, they think Dad's going to come out of it okay?"

Simone moved her three-dollar ice water around. "They keep saying the scans are clear and it's simply a matter of time, or time will tell, something like that."

"You don't think they mean he'll either come out of it or he won't?"

"Hard to tell," said Simone. "They keep using that phrase, hard to tell."

"When Dad comes out of it I bet the first thing he asks is if a law suit's been filed."

"Against the airline?"

"Yeah, I came down on one of the old commercial jobs packed with people wearing facemasks and actual crew flying the thing. At least that's what they told us."

"You don't think they'd lie to you."

"The big *they* you're speaking of lies about everything," said Kimmy. "It's like that phony media crap we get. We're supposed to get all giggly when they suggest painting your roof white or putting up a few solar panels."

"Did they ban the use of private cars in Chicago yet?"

"Not just downtown, they've moved the non-shared vehicle ban into the suburbs. And now, the latest news in the suburbs is isolation and fear affecting folks psychologically. Like, some of them working in factories finding unique ways to check out."

"Suicides?"

"Yep, clever ways to make it appear an accident. Maybe whoever's left behind will collect, maybe they won't. Defense against clients trying to collect boils down to the wealth of the Oligarch running the show."

Kimmy continued. "Oh, and another thing that's noticeable, very few dogs around."

"Because the food's expensive?"

"That, and city ordinances."

"What about cats?"

"Cats manage. We had one on board the *Shellfish*. I told you about it. The one that seemed to sense the end was near and crawled into a cubby down in the bow?"

"Was the cat sensing its end or the end of the world?"

"Both."

Simone was silent; Kimmy needed to say more concerning where her generation's predecessors had sent the world. Not the same kind of complaining could be heard here in the Latin Villages. Kimmy did continue.

"Back to industrial accidents. The last one in Chicago was a woman who fell from one of the carbon capture towers on the southwest side. BECCs they call the places. BioEnergy and Carbon Capture. Folks I know have been making up acronym alternatives. Big Environmental Cunt Cramming something or others...I forget. It's too late to change anything. Have you noticed the news no longer covers environmental stories? Used to be you could at least count on a comedy show replaying a business dude—always a dude—from the past saying he didn't worry about warming because he and his heirs would be dead by then. I'd love to yank one of them out of his crypt and tell him his heirs aren't dead and here we are."

Simone stayed silent.

"There's bigger ad dollars to be had in international riots these days. Disease and starvation and wondering if a slight up tick in hospitalizations is the sign of another pandemic are all the rage. Of course weather's still a big hit. Nothing like a video of a derecho coming across Lake Michigan. One of my crewmates got one recently."

"I forgot. What's a derecho?"

"Intense fast-moving windstorm front with clouds you wouldn't believe. Turns day into night." Kimmy was silent for a moment, staring at her. "Mom?"

"Yes?"

"Aren't people down here worried about surviving summer? That's what I heard on the bus. Guys talking, raising their voices because the bus was bouncing on a rougher section of the causeway, driver yelling back that the bus had high clearance and not to worry. I was surprised the bus had a driver."

"The ones worried about surviving summer, were they younger?"

"Mostly, visitors I guess. Either that or future residents. They said the place isn't bad in winter, but because it's cut off from the real world, and difficulty getting into and out of Florida, many have no choice but to stay over and hunker down during summer. They said most folks in shitty shape hunker down year round. That's why the ones out and about seem to be in pretty decent shape, but it's not a true picture of health. I guess it's the same all along the coast— Miami and New Orleans mostly gone along with the east coast cities. Refugees all over the place, some of them coming upon the bodies of folks who've checked out in their houses using one method or another."

"What about the Great Lakes, Kimmy? Certainly there's some hope there."

"Folks up there are fooling themselves. Water scarcity, quality, and supply are at odds. That's one of the reasons I suggested you and Dad check out this place. Everyone, even refugees, think the only way to survive is to keep heading north. Places like this are bypassed, and in many ways, safer. Of course I didn't expect you to end up here in such an unusual way. You were supposed to land in Orlando and take the bus on the causeway."

"Was there any talk on the bus like the sales pitch you gave us?"

"It wasn't a sales pitch, Mom. Even though the seas are rising, they remain the only heat sink we have left. They'll keep sucking heat out of the atmosphere long after we're gone."

"Talk about something else, Kimmy."

"Like what?"

"How about your flight? Was it smoother? You said it had a traditional crew."

Kimmy smiled her knowing smile. Time to speak of something, anything that didn't have to do with the environment, disease, corporate control of lives, or refuges. "I flew in on an ancient 700 series if you can believe it. I thought we'd go off the end of the runway and join the crocodiles. We've spotted a few."

"Crocodiles in Lake Michigan? You're kidding."

Kimmy smiled. "Yes, I'm kidding. So far the five lakes are still fairly cool, although Erie's getting close."

"How did you get on that old 700 series flight?" asked Simone.

"Emergency flights still go non-hybrid. I convinced them it was a family emergency. My crew captain helped, as long as I'm back before the *Shellfish* heads out."

"Are you up to date on all your shots?" asked Simone.

"Of course," said Kimmy. "We get everything, including routine testing. What about you and Dad?"

"Yes, malaria, dengue, whatever virus is the latest rage, the whole caboodle."

"What's the food like down here?"

"Not too bad. Fake meat like anywhere else. Although in the hospital I heard a rumor about black market beef."

The waiter came with tea. When asked if they needed anything with their tea, Kimmy mentioned milk, then said, "Just kidding," after the waiter stared at her a moment. They ordered and waited for him to leave.

"I wonder if he speaks English," said Kimmy.

"Not much," said Simone. "Just the numbers on the menu."

"Besides the loud mouths there were a couple Thais on the shuttle from the airport. I could tell they were talking about how long they could stay and what family member would take them in."

"Flip-flopping like a lot of foreign workers here," said Simone.

"Flip-flopping from green card to blue card to who knows what kind of card. You do know this place you're at is one of the few so-called islands of single family dwellings?"

"I know. Even when we go back to Michigan we'll have to see what's new in our town. All the towns are having to deal with the influx, a friend or relative who knows a friend or relative."

"Did you hear about the big rush to Siberia?" asked Kimmy.

"A little. Do you think it's true?"

"I think there's a lot of disappearing going on," said Kimmy. "One of my shipmates has been touting this old movie called *Soylent Green.*"

"I saw it long ago," said Simone.

"Mom, it came out before you were born."

"My parents liked the old movies channel."

Kimmy took a sip of tea. "Ow, hot. Old movies…we should all have known while we were being entertained the politicians and corporations were busy creating this world of environmental refugees ready to be exploited. I heard one rumor about warehouses stocking old cans of pet food and using the stuff to feed folks."

"The world's gone nuts. Even here there's a rumor floating around that I don't like to think about."

"The one about pets being used for food?"

"Yes, I feel guilty."

"Why should you feel guilty?"

"Because of where the human race has come. I should have been more outspoken when I was younger."

Kimmy put her hand on Simone's for a moment. "Back to Dad. Any indication he knows who you are?"

"When they got him to open his eyes yesterday I thought there was something."

"That's encouraging."

"Funny."

"What?"

"Bianca said the same thing. That's encouraging."

"You said she's a retired physician assistant?"

"Right. She should know."

"Do you like her?"

"She and her husband Big Bill are the ones who dragged us out of the plane. How could I not like her?"

"Earlier, in the hospital, you said she has beautiful skin. I just wondered."

"No, we're not sleeping together. She's been giving me a ride to the hotel each night. Now she says they have extra bedrooms like a lot of people here. Wants me to stay with them. And when Sancho— Dad—gets out, he's invited. Not only that, when I mentioned you visiting, Bianca and Bill invited you to stay with them."

"That's nice. I can say I'm an environmental refugee and I won't have to bed with our waiter. Although he is cute. He looks religious."

"How would he look religious?" asked Simone.

"I know it's stereotypical," said Kimmy. "He has this contrite look about him like he's sorry for his sins."

"If he has sins."

"Speaking of religion, do you think there was any religious connection to make it possible for Dad getting discount tickets on a flight with a bunch of Bible beaters?"

"No, the guy who clued us in on the deal is simply a golfing buddy. The golfing buddy might be super religious, I don't know. Besides, before the plane came down your father was joking that in a way we were like moles who'd infiltrated the group. We didn't say or do anything to sidle up to the others, but then we didn't do anything to let them know how we felt either. I was planning after we landed to maybe say something, especially when I did some research during the flight and discovered their leader's one of those doomsday wackos."

Kimmy was silent a moment, then said, "I wonder what our waiter thinks of some evangelists clutching the End Times to their bosoms like they own it."

Here he comes."

"That was quick. Should I ask him?"

"Don't you dare."

They were both hungry and ate without speaking. Afterwards the waiter brought a small carafe of tea, bowing repeatedly.

"So Kimmy, how's science on the lakes?"

"All five have patches of toxic algae. Lake Michigan's not as bad as Erie, but not so good, especially off Milwaukee, Chicago, and Indiana. Fertilizer over the years. Did you know there are artists who press the algae onto paper and fabric? Interesting patterns, like

Rorschach tests. A woman at one of the flea markets outside Chicago insisted she could see the future of the Earth in them."

"Did she tell your future?"

"Yes, said to get a houseboat."

"Speaking of boats, how are your quarters?"

"Tight. My cabin's the size of this booth and the bathroom's down a corridor so narrow it's tricky passing someone. The woman in the cabin next door says she's got pregnancy test strips just in case."

They were both silent for a while.

"Mom?"

"Yes."

"Back to the religious kick."

"I told you, we were simply going along to get a cheap flight. And don't forget your father testing the idea that we're moles who've infiltrated the group to keep an eye on their activities. When we were packing for this thing, he pulled out an old environmental tee shirt and said maybe we should join the climate crisis march against the religious nuts. It's one of many strange ways your father and I have discovered to blow off steam. We even do it to one another. It's better than arguing but gets the job done."

"Tell me more."

"How deep do you want to go?"

"I'm your daughter."

"I know, but it's embarrassing." Simone stirred her tea. "In recent years we've begun this playact thing as a way to turn one another on. We were doing it before the plane came down. We speak of affairs we've both had in the past. Some of it's exaggeration, but not all."

"Really?"

"Yes, really. Anyway, between your father and I it's become a kind of contest. Like, oh yeah, you think that's a good one, well take this."

"Very kinky, Mom."

"I agree. We all live in a kinky world. And Kimmy, I know about the one nighter he had with that girlfriend you brought home for the weekend when you were in school."

"I didn't know you were aware of it. I didn't know about it until we got back to school."

"Your friend wore a certain skin lotion and, well, yes I knew."

"The whole world's gone kinky."

"What else it there? Speaking of kinky things having gone on around us, yesterday before you arrived, I paused outside your father's door. This Reverend Murdock dude was visiting, I guess figuring because we were on the plane…Anyway, he was praying."

"Out loud?"

"Yes. And being he was alone with your father, I have to say it sounded like he was—how shall I say it?—it sounded like he was speaking with someone he's coming onto."

Kimmy leaned forward. "Give me more details."

"Murdock's got this unctuous oily way of speaking. I was curious, like a mole I guess, and didn't want to interrupt. I'm listening and he's in there speaking to your father like a perspective lover. Slobbering all over him, and when I peak around the corner—get this—he's got his hand on your father's thigh, his eyes are closed, and he's rubbing your father's thigh while apparently speaking directly with the Lord."

"Wow."

"Wow is right. I should have busted in and asked what the hell he was doing. I should have raised my hands heavenward and spouted off a prayer to Mother Earth. But I couldn't help myself. I just leaned in, watched, and listened."

"Maybe the plane crashed for a reason."

"What reason would that be?"

"Mother Earth grounding you two. Saying, 'Simone and Sancho, come on down. Come live here in the Latin Villages with all the other old farts. At least here you'll be safe."

"Very funny. According to Bianca there are a bunch of weirdoes living here."

"For example?"

"Well, besides the rumors about dogs, and booze and STDs all over the place, supposedly there was someone a while back who saved Disney paraphernalia. Not just here and there things. According to Bianca everywhere you looked in the house you were reminded of Disney World. Everything from clocks with Mickey's hands to toilet seats."

"What part of Mickey was on the toilet seat?"

"Bianca said his face was on the top seat, and where you sit, his hands were there. She said the folks are gone but their stuff's still here. Oh, and get this, Bianca said when she put her weight on the seat the thing played 'It's a Small World.'"

Kimmy hummed the song, then said, "Great, I won't be able to get the damn tune out of my head all day. So, what happened to the Disney stuff after the original owner was gone?"

"Bianca said a couple who'd recently moved into Village Quintus, I think, bought the entire collection and is carrying on the tradition. Of course she also says the couple is pretty weird. They've got an adult son living with them and Bianca worries about what the crazy surroundings are doing to him. Apparently the son's been doing imitations of Goofy, so there's that. Most parents who've brought along a boomerang kid keep a low profile because it's become a sign of parental weakness to hard-liners, especially parents who lucked out by having successful kids. Speaking of collecting stuff, Bianca's writing a book called *Things Shall Inherit the Earth* in which she expounds on all the crap ending up down here when the owners pass."

"It's only been a couple days and you've spent a lot of time with Bianca."

"No one else to talk to."

"What about her husband? Big Bill is it?"

"Bill's nice. He used to be a teacher in a Chicago college prep charter school. He knew Bianca's first husband before the two of them met. Apparently Bill had a hard time of it with his first wife."

"This isn't going to be a kinky story, is it?"

"No. Bianca's first husband sought out the school for their son, Vinny. After the husband got shot and killed by a wayward drive-by shooter, Bianca and Big Bill got together, sent Vinny to Bill's school and, after Bill's first wife, who'd had a flood of strokes and was in a nursing home for a couple years died, Bianca and Bill married. Oh, and coincidentally, Vinny works at the EPA's Chicago office."

"Really?"

"Yes, a regional administrator, which includes the Great Lakes."

Kimmy smiled. "So I guess it is a small world after all. Maybe you and Dad really should consider settling in down here. It'll be high and dry in Central Florida for a while, there's the ocean breezes, like I mentioned earlier, and in the last few years, even with the storms, it seems safer than a lot of places farther north."

"You're sure of that?"

"I think so. Witnessing the overcrowding of people flocking to the Great Lakes is changing the area day by day."

"Funny."

"What?"

"Bianca and Big Bill said they eventually wanted to retire to Michigan, same as us, if and when they sell the house down here.

They've got this huge house with plenty of room. I guess the owners before Bill's parents figured they'd have grandchildren visiting 'til the end of time."

The restaurant that had been quiet suddenly bustled with activity. A group of retirees speaking and laughing loudly just inside the entrance, and outside in the parking lot, more golf carts carrying more retirees jockeying for parking spots.

Three men rushed past obviously on their way to the men's room in back. One voice was loud enough to be heard. "Well, what the hell did we need the arctic for anyway? It was nothing but ice." The three men powered through the door, obviously with full bladders.

"One thing I should tell you about Big Bill, Bianca's husband."

"What's that?"

"Besides his wife's health going to hell, they had a son who committed suicide. Bianca says it goes back to Bill's first wife's father abusing her when she was a girl. The abuse affected more than one life. When you and Bianca meet don't say anything about it."

"Of course I won't say anything." Kimmy paused then spoke loud enough to overcome the continuing uproar at the entrance. "Time to get back?"

"Yes, the golf tournament's over."

"At least they seem happy."

"I guess."

"What's wrong, Mom?"

"I'm thinking about the way they're already trying to usher your dad out even though he's—"

"You think the airline is putting pressure on them?"

"I wouldn't put it past them. If so why haven't they spoken to me?"

"Probably worried it would give you ideas."

"Maybe I should take up Bianca's invitation to stay there."

Kimmy put her hand on Simone's. "It'll give you a home base until you come back north. If you decide to come back north."

"I hope airlines are still flying when we make up our minds."

Chapter 11—Sextus Rendezvous

Bianca and Bill's house was in Village Sextus, located at the very apex of a cul-de-sac. After driving the golf cart into the welcome shade of the garage, Bianca pushed the button to lower the garage door, pulled a retractable charging cord down from the ceiling, and plugged it into the side of the cart. The golf cart was black with a solar top. Gold script lettering on either side of the charger port said, "Big Bill."

Bianca smiled. "Everything's symbolic in Latin Villages, especially here in Village Sextus. Our sprawling ranch at the tip of a cul-de-sac, which viewed from above resembles a circumcised penis. Sextus is the male form in Latin. And see here where I plugged in the charger? The guy who painted on the name put 'Big' to the left and 'Bill' to the right. When they were alive, Bill's folks had the name Pisani here with the plug port inside the P."

Bill had come into the garage, slamming the door from the house behind him. "I didn't want people knowing our last name. But you've got to admit, Bianca my love, placing Big Bill that way was your idea."

"I admit it," said Bianca, turning to give Bill a kiss.

Bill went to the back of the cart and grabbed Simone's suitcases. "Welcome to our humble abode. We're glad you agreed to stay here instead of the hotel. When Sancho gets out he's welcome, and so is your daughter."

"Thanks," said Simone. "I mentioned it to Kimmy but she's already made a friend over in another village."

Bianca took Simone's smaller bag from Bill. "Simone's daughter has an university friend working down here on subsidence."

Bill said, "Maybe your daughter's friend can tell us when the entire place will sink into the sea. If course we'd keep it from the realtor."

Before going inside Simone glanced back at a powder blue convertible tucked in against the garage wall. "Is that an old T-bird?"

"It is," said Bill. "Bought it from the estate of a guy down the street who passed away. His kids were afraid to drive it out of here with all the water hazards and crappy roads. Got it cheap. And because the weather forecast for tomorrow has rain in it, I thought you two could drive it to the medical center after I put the top up."

"Can you still get gasoline around here?" asked Simone.

Bianca ushered them inside and closed the door to the garage that was hot and humid compared to inside the house. "There's one station for hold outs," said Bianca. "And there are also some crazy old guys calling themselves the fossil fuelers. They hoard gasoline in containers for their gas-powered carts."

"The fossil fools is a better name," said Bill. "Some of their carts are souped up with the governors taken off even though it's illegal."

When Simone paused in the small laundry room entryway, she noticed a dog leash hanging from a hook inside the door. Bianca said, "That's the leash my former husband was holding when he was shot. Notice the collar's still attached." All three stood silent for a moment before going into the main house.

The house was spacious with an open floor plan. There were a few pieces of African-inspired art—slender women carrying baskets on their heads, an abstract nude, a ceremonial mask—and also some Italian inspired pieces—mostly Fiat and Ferrari posters from the 70s. A large screened-in lanai was attached to the back, complete with a sizeable sunken soaking tub. The kitchen, dining room, and living room open area divided the house in two, Bianca and Bill's master suite on one side, three small bedrooms and a bath and a half on the other side.

"The place was designed to accommodate guests," said Bianca.

"Bianca uses the smallest bedroom for her writing and even that one has a bed," said Bill. "She's working on a book called *Things Shall Inherit the Earth*."

"I know. I'd like to hear more details," said Simone.

"Like I said yesterday, it's nothing," said Bianca. "Come on, let's finish the tour of our digs."

"Funny you should mention digs," said Bill.

Both Blanca and Simone stared at him, obviously he wanted to expound. "They built this place decades ago by digging up land in other places, saying they were making lakes and retention ponds. That was back when Florida was still in one piece instead of divided up into islands. The latest so-called brainstorm is to use treated sewage to create more land. A woman in my yoga class said they'll call it Village Stercus. *Stercus* is Latin for dung, so basically it would be Village Dung Pile. A guy in the class got really riled. I see lots of it. Guys getting aggressive, like the world around us needs them pissed, as if it doesn't have enough to deal with. They come to class for relaxation and all they do is complain. Living here is a trade—security rather than liberty. The non-news we get is controlled, anyone can see that. But some of these guys take it to heart."

***

Dinner—fish allegedly fast frozen on a North Atlantic vessel prior to the previous Greenland ice sheet slip, vegetables grown, according to the label, in the high plains of Alberta. After dinner, conversation was accompanied by wine from Manitoba and sherry from Ontario.

Big Bill (Female yoga class participants liked to call him that even though it was not on the brochure.): "The plane's still out there on the seventh hole. FAA won't let them take it apart until the investigation's complete. I'm not sure who's running who."

Buxom Bianca (Of course she was buxom, anyone could see that.): "I'll bet they're hoping it will disappear down the sinkhole."

Sexy Simone (Yes, after a few drinks and dinner she did think of the pet name Sancho often used.): I wonder how that cockpit attendant's doing."

Bianca: We'll check on her when we go in to see how your husband's rehab is going."

Simone: "You don't have to go with me if you'd rather not."

Bianca: "You can go by yourself, that's okay. Bill will show you how to shift the T-bird."

Bill: "Have you ever driven a stick?"

Simone: "Maybe I could walk."

Bill: "No way. Two miles in this heat? And if it rains it's steam bath time."

Bianca: "It's settled. I'll drive you to the medical center and if you want I can find something else to do while you're visiting."

Simone: "I don't mind you coming with me. Really, I'd like the company."

Bill: "I've got yoga class tomorrow. It's at the rec center so the cart will be fine for me."

Bianca: "Are the rain barrels emptied and ready."

Bill: "Yep."

Simone: "You collect rain water?"

Bill: "We take fresh water wherever we can get it. Of course not everyone's on board. Still old rats who insist using drinking and bathing water for their goddamn lawns."

Bianca: "You'll notice our lawn is dormant brown. Greens up for a couple weeks in March before the spring monsoons flatten it."

Bill: "Any green you see now is because of fertilizer. Fires in the tropics, half their food coming from Chinese industrial farm soy, or whatever it's called, and they still fertilize."

Bianca: "It's the same old folks who wanted to wall in the country. I feel sorry for them."

Bill: "I don't feel sorry for them. A few even manage to get their hands on pet dogs, not to eat of course."

Bianca: "Let's change the subject."

Bill: "Okay. So, Simone, if Sancho has to be down here a while, maybe you should consider renting a place. I mean, you're welcome to stay with us, but if you guys stay put, rentals are really cheap. I should know. I tried to rent the place out before we moved here. The rental wouldn't have covered taxes, the so-called insurance, and other expenses. Big advantage here is the powers that be have made sure our healthcare is top notch."

Simone: "I'll have to wait and see. It depends on Sancho's situation. Mostly his memory loss. But maybe it's good he's forgotten some things."

Bill: "What things?"

Simone: "Feeling pressured to stay connected up north."

Bill: "Yeah, I wanted to ask about that. I understand you came down to Florida with an evangelical group."

Bianca: "Simone already told me about it, Bill. And I told you. A golfing buddy got the flight deal for Sancho."

Bill: "Yeah, sorry. I just wondered was all. Even if you were evangelicals you'd still be welcome. We've all got what we call a checkered past when you come right down to it."

Simone: "What's your checkered past?"

Bianca, interrupting: "Maybe we should call it quits and get some sleep."

Bill: "No, no. It's all right. See, Simone, I was married before and my wife, well—"

Bianca: "Bill, maybe now's not the right time."

Bill: "It's okay. See, her father abused her when she was a little girl. I mean, really abused. Life for us was a circle the wagons kind of thing. Circle the wagons around it and maybe it'll go away. Except the past catches up. It caught up with her and eventually even our son who committed suicide."

Simone: "I'm so sorry, Bill. You don't have to go into this if you'd rather not. Bianca told me a little, so if you don't want to—"

Bill: "Yeah, sorry."

Simone: "Don't be sorry."

Bianca: "All right you two. I'm putting this bottle of sherry back on the shelf where it belongs."

***

The bed was cozy, the air cool. Simone was glad she hadn't had too much sherry. After using the bathroom and putting her gear in the closet, she checked her phone. A message from Kimmy said she'd meet her for lunch next day. Said she had to return to work in a couple days assuming Dad was in the clear.

A knock on the door. Bianca came in wearing a black nightgown, her breasts making it into a tent. "I'll be in the next room over. I've been sleeping there because of the television on all night. Even with the sound off I wake up and see horrible news trailers and opinion crap, so many dead here, a whole batch of refugees missing there, and then always the possibility of a new virus being discovered."

"Thank you again for having me in your home. It's so good of you two."

Bianca sat on the edge of the bed. "You're welcome."

"Back home I also avoid the news. I've gotten Sancho to agree. Do you think there's anything to that talk of another virus?"

"Anyone's guess. Ever since the one back at the beginning of the twenties, they keep holding it out there in front of us like a turd on a stick."

"Instead of a carrot on a stick," said Simone. "Funny, the turd back then was the color of a carrot."

"Did they make you wear facemasks on your flight?"

"Not mandatory, but it's pretty much expected once you head to an airport. I noticed not everyone wears them here, especially at the medical center."

"Lots of testing," said Bianca. "Here, with the medical center pretty much part of the community, it's a spin-off. They also monitor our memory chips carefully. Not sure if it's an advantage, but there you go. And I don't know if you noticed, the air can get pretty rank and dusty. Some filters are for particulates."

"I remember all the hubbub when they decided to put chips in the shoulders of newborns," said Simone.

"Big brother," said Bianca.

"We've only known one another a short time, yet both of us are aware of a lot we've been through. Seems during our parents' lives and our earlier lives it would have been better to have some big sisters in charge instead of big brothers."

After saying "big sisters," Simone could not help glancing down toward Bianca's breasts.

Blanca also looked down, smiled, and when they looked to one another they both broke out laughing, so much so it brought tears to their eyes.

After laughing they were silent and sat staring at one another for a minute. And then, as if on cue, they both reached out and held hands.

Chapter 12—Game of Drones

Two mornings later, on the road passing the entrance to the Palm Tree Gardens course, it was obvious the crash scene investigation was in high gear. Yellow police tape surrounded the parking lot and clubhouse with two police cars blocking the turnoff. Because of heavy rain the police officers were inside their cars. The parking lot asphalt steamed. Beyond the tape were several official looking vans and other police cars. One van was open in back and a man and woman in yellow slickers were stooped down beside a silver X-shaped drone. As Bianca drove them past the clubhouse Simone caught a glimpse of the seventh hole in the distance with the tail section of Flight 6996 still sticking out of the sinkhole sand trap, the very tip of the tail painted green where the rear prop had telescoped out during their final approach. The drone that had been in the van appeared, coming over the clubhouse and heading toward the sinkhole.

The T-bird's windshield wipers squeaked and rattled back and forth, grime from the car having stayed in the garage without being washed making the dry-rotted rubber blades chatter. Between swipes of the blades the windshield steamed up on the outside where the air conditioner cooled the glass. Bianca and Simone were on their way to the medical center for Sancho's third day at rehab. Simone was reminded of the Slick part of Sancho's nickname because of the windshield wipers chattering instead of smoothly sliding over the glass. Last evening, her second at Bill and Bianca's house, Simone had told Bianca about some of Sancho's habits, especially the way he swiped at his bald head with a cloth towel at home or with a paper towel when using public facilities. She'd also detailed the crazy confessions they'd made to one another prior to the crash. Especially memorable was Sancho and Petra, the wife of a German VP, doing '*Neunundsechzig*' beneath a grand piano. In her bedroom last night, after Bill retired to his bedroom suite, Simone had given an especially vivid description of the grand piano tryst, wondering aloud if Sancho had used his bald head on Petra the way he sometimes did with her, saying her female bodily fluids would promote hair growth.

The event had been in Indianapolis, Indiana, of all places. After speaking of Sancho's tryst, Simone recalled aloud how, back then, it had become common the look up the elevation of anywhere one planned to visit, the Indianapolis location for the event chosen because back then it was still 700 feet above sea level.

Simone knew Bianca had waited for her to say more, as if Bianca could read her mind. After a pause, Simone had gone into a vivid description of her tryst behind the poolside bar with Hans, Petra's husband. Now, as they drove in the rain past the golf course toward the medical center, Simone could see Bianca's lips press together to smother a smile, the two of them glancing to one another as they recalled having shushed each other so their laughter would not carry across the house and awaken Big Bill. Laughter was followed by them getting beneath the covers. Hugging, it had only been hugging, especially when Bianca spoke in more detail of her first husband's death, meeting Big Bill, details of his first wife's abusive father, fear of sex, failing health, and Bill's son having committed suicide. Hugging, it had only been hugging.

Simone again looked back toward the crash site where the tail section of Flight 6996 was just visible beyond the line of trees beneath which Bianca said she and Bill witnessed the crash. "You know, Bianca, looking at it now from this distance, it's hard to believe we made it out alive. We really owe a lot to you and Bill."

"Honey, all I remember when we first got inside was how dark it was compared to out in the sun and that nutty reverend getting the bunch in back to say prayers."

"That video we saw on the news last night was frightening," said Simone.

Bianca nodded. "It was even more vivid being there in person. Especially the way the plane was doing fine at first, skimming along the fairway and up onto the green, lifting turf into the air. Then, just when it seemed it would stop, it pivoted and nose dived into the sinkhole."

"On last night's news one witness said she thought she heard the engines rev up before our plane went in. Said it sounded like the computer on the plane couldn't make up its mind. Did you hear anything like that?"

"I didn't hear anything because of all the noise from the peanut gallery behind us and the drone above us," said Bianca. "I saw the rear prop spinning but it pulled back into the tail before it hit. I think the lady was trying to lengthen her stay on the news. Not every day an old gal gets interviewed. I saw her among the other witnesses, and during the interview I'm sure she had a shit ton of makeup on. Anyway, with the main engines being out having been the problem, one or both would have had to restart, and that sure wasn't going to happen judging from the size of that equatorial bird species. They said a flock of them got sucked in and spit out."

Simone asked, "Do you really think the plane wobbled a little when that guy in the golf cart drove across?"

"His own video proves it," said Bianca. "Looking back, the thing that really frightened me was the inflatable slide coming out and no one on it. That's when Bill says, 'Fuck it! Here we go!'"

***

When Simone visited, Sancho was with a language pathologist who introduced herself as Dr. Circe Caras. "So glad to meet you, Mrs. Martinez. Because he asked, I've been speaking to Sancho about the meanings of my first and last names. Both have Greek origins. Basically I'm a swarthy—from my last name—sorceress—from my first name.

Sancho's eyes were open wide. He sat in a side chair dressed in blue jeans and a purple shirt Simone had never seen before. He was smiling and rather than acknowledging Simone, stared at Dr. Sorceress, nodding.

The doctor was thin, in her thirties, with long black hair tied in a braid. Her lipstick was maroon. "The team has decided some physical and language therapy will do the trick."

"The trick, drones!" said Sancho in a loud voice.

"Sancho, you hit your head pretty hard during the accident," said Dr. Sorceress. "But you'll be good as new in no time."

"No time, drones," said Sancho, finally looking to Simone.

Dr. Sorceress also looked to her. "Mrs. Martinez—"

"You can call me Simone."

"Certainly. And you can call me Circe."

"I will," said Simone, looking to Sancho who seemed to smile much more than in recent months. "What's this about drones?"

"Sancho and I were just finishing our session," said Circe— Simone couldn't get Dr. Sorceress out of her head. "Perhaps you and I could go to the visiting room across the hall and talk."

They left Sancho sitting in the reclining chair beside his bed smiling like crazy in his purple shirt. Simone couldn't help recalling last night in bed cuddling Bianca. Bianca had told about she and Big Bill attending an oldies concert wearing purple outfits and hearing, by way of the Village Sextus grapevine, that folks had spoken of them in terms of a really old oldie called *Purple People Eater*.

The window in the visiting room wept raindrops, which kept on falling during their conversation. There was hand sanitizer on both sides of the coffee table between them. Dr. Sorceress used some,

Simone followed her lead. They sat across from one another, the window behind the doctor framing her head so that during much of their talk Simone couldn't get the first verse of another old oldie out of her head. *Raindrops keep falling on my head.*

After a few seconds of silence, Simone asked, "So, how is he?"

"Coming along. Although it doesn't show on the outside, even though the wall he hit was collapsible, the blunt trauma was fairly substantial. But the team is unanimous that his cognitive skills should eventually be back to normal."

"What about his physical skills?"

"Those are a little up in the air."

"Up in the air?"

"We think shortly after the accident, or perhaps some time prior, he had a right brain ministroke. The result might be balance and coordination issues because of the affected area."

"Before we left the room he mentioned drones."

"I didn't want to bring it up in there. The medical center keeps tabs on patients with drones, especially during the night in case anyone gets out of bed. They usually stay out of sight, parking up near the ceiling. I'm sure he must have seen one pause at his doorway, or perhaps when he used the restroom."

"Why couldn't you say that in front of him?"

Dr. Sorceress looked around behind her before answering. "There's been idle talk recently and I was concerned your husband might have overheard an aid or another patient. We've had issues in the past when someone at the head office had the bright idea to purchase several Chinese minidrones. Very small devices, some like hummingbirds and even insects. It caused quite a stir. The idea that drones might be spying on nurses and aids is still part of the grapevine."

"A fly on the wall?"

"Excuse me?"

"Never mind. Sancho and I are familiar with small drones. We had an issue with peeping Toms at a shopping center back in Michigan."

"Oh, in that case, perhaps I'll bring up the topic of drones during my next session."

"Doctor…I mean Circe…about his head."

"What about it?"

"Did you shave him?"

"Me? Of course not."

"Well, someone obviously found out Sancho shaves his head. I don't suppose he did it."

"I think it must have been his physical therapist. I'll definitely bring this up at our meeting later today and find out."

"Good idea," said Simone, staring past Circe at the raindrops on the window. "Sorry, I didn't mean to imply anything. So, tell me, what else has he been saying?"

"He's well aware he's in Florida. He asked about summer heat waves. He asked if, working here, I treated heat wave deaths. I told him I knew of a few, but explained not only that I did not treat them, but also that they were very elderly residents. He asked if any new viruses popped up while he was out. I told him no and explained he hadn't been out that long."

"Has Sancho spoken about our lives? I mean his life with me?"

"He brought up a few events from the past."

"The recent past?"

"No, the distant past. For example, because of the admission information you provided I've tried to speak with him about your daughter Kimmy. I know she was here and saw him and has gone back to…I'm sorry, I forgot where she's from."

"She's probably out on her boat in Lake Michigan. She does environmental work out of Chicago. Did Sancho mention that?"

"Not exactly. Although he did mention her name he doesn't seem to recall her having visited. Instead, his focus has become the environment, the first pandemic, and what will happen to her in the future. A lot of the memories come from history. Even though that particular leadership is gone, Sancho keeps referring to the orange one and how that administration was the beginning of the end for the environment and, according to him, everything else. He insists speaking of extinction and is concerned for Kimmy's future. He wondered what kind of future would exist for any children she might have. During his physical therapy session I'm told he was particularly animated. Strangely, he wondered if Florida is being severed from the remainder of the continent. He actually said, 'the penis we call Florida,' which threw our speech therapist for a loop, because as we both know, the shape has become less and less so."

They were silent for a minute. The raindrops kept running down the window.

Finally, Dr. Sorceress said, "Tell me, Simone, could you provide some details from the plane?"

"The crash landing?"

"No, just prior. Perhaps topics of conversation with Sancho."

"Well, I guess you could ask him about Mrs. Hans beneath the grand piano and Mr. Hans behind the bar at the pool. If that doesn't ring a bell, hint that the events took place in Indianapolis."

"Indianapolis, Indiana?"

"Yes."

***

When Bianca sent a message asking how much longer the visit with staff would take, Simone returned a text saying she'd send a reply as soon as she was finished. Bianca was tired of waiting in the cafeteria and went to the front reception desk. She asked to see Yolanda Abdul Jabar, the cockpit attendant for Flight 6996. It took a while to get a room location, but she finally got it by saying she was from the FAA. She'd seen a briefing summarized on Bill's television the night before, investigators wondering if the cockpit attendant should have been able to do more. Instead of showing credentials Bianca simply leaned over the reception desk, told the young man there that her colleagues expected her and he'd better hurry up with the room number or she'd call the lead investigator. Bianca wasn't sure whether it was her phony blustering or her low cut blouse that did the trick.

Yolanda's room was at the end of the hallway on the second floor that seemed mostly unoccupied. Stacked in a corner where the hallway ended were contamination warning signs, the floor most likely used during a past virus outbreak. It was so quiet on the floor Bianca could hear a hallway drone humming near the ceiling. Inside the room a man with an accent and a woman, apparently Yolanda, with somewhat less of an accent, were speaking. Bianca caught part of the conversation as she approached. Yolanda said something about a kind and considerate uncle and how this person from the past contrasted with the corporate investigators who were trying to put blame on her for the accident. The man said something about truly believing she was not at fault and had given this opinion to all who would listen. He finished this by saying, "God be with you." Then Yolanda said, "And also with you, Dr. Noodle."

Bianca saw the remnants of meals in plates that the man placed on a tray. Muted laughter came from the two before they saw her. She decided to knock on the door rather than be caught listening in.

Dr. Noodle was actually Dr. Abdul Ramen according to his nametag. Dr. Ramen was a short Middle Eastern man who stood while Bianca introduced herself, explaining she and her husband had gone into the plane after the crash to help passengers out. Dr. Ramen moved a lunch trays onto a bed table and both invited her to take the extra chair in the room. Yolanda wore a neck collar and her right arm was in a sling.

"I thought I recognized you," said Yolanda. "Your husband carried the passenger named Martinez out of the plane and you helped both me and his wife."

"Yes," said Bianca. "Mrs. Martinez is here visiting her husband. My husband and I invited her to stay with us while he recuperates."

"That is very kind of you," said the doctor. "Although my name is Ramen, I sometimes tell patients to call me Dr. Noodle."

"I like it," said Bianca. "I hope I'm not interrupting because if I am I can leave."

"No, no," said Yolanda. "Please stay."

After a short discussion about Yolanda's condition—possible whiplash and a shoulder injury—the three of them, probably because they all lived in the Latin Villages, switched the conversation over to, what Dr. Noodle called, "local insanity."

They spoke of the new fence around the Latin Villages that went in the previous year to keep out "riffraff." The "riffraff" being outsiders shortcutting through, some disguising themselves as older folks to take advantage of shopping opportunities while dropping kids at swimming pools. Others being accused of looting, even though very little evidence existed. They spoke of the vigilante group some called the alligator patrol and others called the fossil fuelers—the ones who insisted driving gasoline powered golf carts—that had formed to supposedly monitor the fences and the gated entrances.

"This place is a trade of liberty for security," said Bianca. "The news we receive is controlled," said Dr. Noodle. "Anyone can see this." Finally they spoke of service workers, like Dr. Noodle and anyone else not officially retired to the place, assigned to live in Village Nonus.

When they ran out of general complaints about the Latin Villages, Bianca thought maybe they'd speak of virus fears or the climate crises and the latest ice slide in the Antarctic. But instead, Yolanda spoke.

"When the airline people were busy questioning me, they insisted I tell them about everyone I might be acquainted with here. Mrs. Pisani, I hope it was not wrong to do so, but I told them one of my nurses mentioned taking the yoga class taught by your husband."

"Two things. I've kept my original last name. It's Washington. But please call me Bianca. And, what would be wrong with telling airline folks about Bill's yoga class?"

"To me, it seemed they were being nosey. What do your husband's activities have to do with anything? Just because the nurse lives here and happened to be attending to me, why would they bring up a thing like that?"

Dr. Ramen added. "Perhaps they intend to use the nurse's acquaintance with Mr. Pisani at his yoga class to somehow get additional information about the rescue."

"I don't get it," said Bianca. "They could simply ask me or Bill directly."

Yolanda nodded but looked down. "Yes, they could ask you. But this is not how they work. They always scrape wherever they think they can dig up dirt."

"What kind of dirt?" asked Bianca.

After Yolanda did not answer, Dr. Ramen said, "Yes, Yolanda, you're probably right. They question persons on staff, digging, always digging. What would one's yoga instructor have to do with anything? They even questioned me about it."

After leaving Yolanda and Dr. Ramen, Bianca went back to the cafeteria and saw Simone was already there, her phone in her hand. Simone smiled, put her phone away, motioned Bianca over to her table, and nodded to the wall screen. A news broadcast on the screen had a runner at the bottom about a shooting at a pottery class at the Village Quatorus recreation center. Whether anyone was injured or killed was still unknown.

Bianca stared at the runner for a moment. It soon changed, as it always did when real news was being shown, to climate crises, one after another, and the possibility of a new virus outbreak somewhere in the world:

"Floods inundate southern Cal >>>Cal Gov Clooney II supports population move to Nev>>>Nor'Easter topples 2 More Manhattan bldgs not dismantled>>>Alberta opens 3rd migrant camp with virus outbreak fears>>>Monsanto announces Fabulous Fruit product line>>>Manufactured island Isabel continues growing crops at sea on floating farms despite lawsuit>>>Florida's last southern key gone>>>Quebec census numbers

staggering>>>Russians move quickly following Swede Alliance>>>Possibility of viral reemergence amongst Aboriginal Australians."

It didn't take long for the actual news feed to switch back to feel good news, a group of folks strolling and smiling in the shade of tall vertical farm units, some holding hands, no facemasks.

After sitting down Bianca turned to Simone. "I wonder where we'll all end up and who will care for us."

"I don't know," said Simone. "The world our parents knew is history. Disasters so commonplace most aren't even given a runner. Maybe if everyone went away to one of those environmental retreats we could abstain and purify the population and the world."

Bianca reached across and held Simone's hand. "Don't talk."

"Why?"

"I want to study your face for the painting I've always wanted to do."

"Maybe you should do a nude."

"Maybe I should."

Chapter 13—Dancing in the Dark

Concert night at the Village Septimus open air plaza was on. A few on the village committee tried to cancel it, saying it was too soon to have a concert after the deadly pottery shooting at the Village Quatorus recreation center.

"I'm just saying, here we are having a concert in our open air plaza, which by the way is directly in front of our recreation center, and there are still neighbors and friends in mourning. Reminds me of those shootings they had back in the old days at shopping centers and schools. Back then they at least had periods of mourning. It doesn't seem right to have a nearby concert so soon."

"We already contracted with the band. We had a clause in the contract in case there was a virus outbreak but none for this. If we cancel there's the fee. They'll collect it, too. Because of limited flights they had to reserve way ahead."

"Yeah, and it's the 70s band we've been trying to get for years as a tribute to our village. Septimus means seven you know."

"It doesn't mean seven."

"So, what the hell does it mean?"

"It means seventh son."

"Well la-dee-da professor. If you're so smart what would our village have been called if it had been a seventh daughter?"

"The feminine version is Septima. That would have been the village name."

"That'll teach you for trying to argue with the professor, Frank. She knows a lot more than you."

"Up your Trump ass."

"What?"

"You heard me."

"All right, guys. Let's get back to whether we should have a concert or not in light of the pottery class shooting."

"Two were killed and three injured."

"I'm aware of the death toll. We all give them our thoughts and prayers."

"A lot of good prayers will do. I just wanted to put the death toll on record for the meeting minutes."

"How much pottery was destroyed? That should also be in the minutes."

"Yeah, and what about that plane crash last week on the Palm Tree Gardens course? Our last meeting was before the crash so I'd like that in the minutes. Two were killed, a bunch of injuries, and that plane hulk it still out there."

"The sink hole's sitting atop a subsidence layer. Maybe, given time, it'll take care of itself."

"Great, it's the professor again."

"Frank, will you shut the Trump up."

"I resent that! I might have been a kid when I started voting but I was never stupid enough to have voted for him."

"Please, guys—"

"What you going to do? Shoot me with one of your plastic pistolas?"

"I'm not carrying and you know it!"

"So, what's with that gun rack in your golf cart pickup?"

"What's that got to do with anything?"

"A guy who puts a gun rack in his golf cart rear window is sending out messages. Can't blame me for extrapolating the obvious message."

"I'll finish, if you don't mind, with one thing. If there had been a carrier at that pottery class—"

"There was a carrier. She killed two people."

"And destroyed a lot of fine pieces of pottery."

"At least she wasn't a virus carrier."

"Jesus Trumpsters, all of you! That's enough!"

"It'll only be enough when we complete that portion of fence."

"The fence through the swamp on the east side of Village Nonus?"

"Yeah, I hear the workers in Nonus are smuggling in refugees with all kinds of infections at night."

"Don't the gators get them?"

"Not if they have a swamp boat. There've been reports of swamp boats seen on trailers outside Nonus."

"Did you know they originally wanted to call it Village Nonnatus?"

"Why is that, professor?"

"Because Nonnatus means not born in Latin."

"They didn't really consider that, did they?"

"The professor's pulling your leg."

"Or maybe both legs."

"Maybe all three."

"That's not funny. I've had a prostatectomy, you know."

"Sorry, I didn't know."

"Let's get back on topic."

"The unfinished fence?"

"I don't want to admit I heard that."

"So, don't admit it."

"We were discussing whether to have the 70s concert at our open air plaza in light of the pottery class shooting and also the plane crash."

"I say we cancel the concert, take the financial hit, and declare it a day of mourning for fellow Latin Villages residents and for the victims of the plane crash."

"What's your reasoning?"

"My reasoning is humanitarian."

"There's still some question as to the intentions of those people on the plane."

"What question?"

"Were they flying to Orlando to protest the protesters? Or, as lot of people have been saying, were they flying to Orlando to join the protest?"

"They were interviewed on the news, Frank. They were bible whippers."

"I don't whip my bible. I mean, I've heard the term, bible beaters, but bible whippers?"

"Let's not talk about beating things. It turns me on."

"Holy shit and save Mary! Should I call an end to this so-called meeting or what?"

"I agree with cancellation. If we don't cancel the concert there'll be those who assign a new nickname to our village."

"What nickname?"

"Village Mar-a-lago."

After several more minutes of shouting and arguing, and after a restroom break followed by the scent of hand sanitizer filling the room, someone suggested having a moment of silence prior to the music, the vote ended up being seven to five and the concert was on. In her opposing opinion one of the committee members wrote, "The establishment document of our village contains a clause clearly stating that outstanding episodes of concern should be interpreted in human terms. For example, unexpected accidents involving one or more persons or sudden deaths due to viral outbreaks must be considered when planning celebratory events. I realize the clause was meant to limit said cancellations due to the death of a resident for long-term medical reasons. But this is different. Two tragedies have occurred in nearby villages and thus those who fell should be more properly honored than a moment of silence. I therefore respectfully oppose the opinion."

***

By replacing the golf club holder with the jump seat, Big Bill and Bianca were able to make their golf cart into a four passenger. Taking the golf cart rather than the T-bird meant two passengers would not be forced to sit knees up in the T-bird's back seat. The back seat of the cart was also small and Bianca and Simone volunteered so Sancho could sit in the front seat. Not only that, Big Bill, being a local yoga instructor, could be considered a health professional and was therefore to vouch for the need and obtain a special handicap pass that would allow them to pull the golf cart directly up to the concert venue the way handicap single person carts were allowed to do.

Sancho Martinez had been out of the medical center two days. His release instructions called for him not only to follow a few dietary and plenty-of-rest regimens, but also called for as much cognitive activity as possible. When Simone asked the care team what was meant by cognitive activity, Dr. Noodle explained by pointing to his own head and saying, "It means he should do as much thinking as possible. This should include present situational decisions as well as past recall."

Big Bill and Bianca insisted Simone and Sancho stay on as their guests at their Village Sextus home. The room Simone used had a queen bed, plenty of closet space, and room to move the wheelchair around should Sancho need it. Kimmy, their daughter, was also invited to stay with them if she flew down again to visit.

A lot of the initial cognitive activity for Sancho involved him smiling and nodding and approving of the house and neighborhood. He was like a kid discovering his new home. Simone was a little unnerved at first. It seemed he'd become completely unaware of the various disasters the climate crisis and viruses had placed on the people of Earth. In the past Sancho had been morose a lot of the time. Ever since the accident and especially since his release from the medical center he'd become a cheerful son of a bitch. He didn't even wipe at his bald head and, though aides were doing it for him at the medical center, he'd stopped shaving his head. The gray stubble above his ears, always bothering him in the past, was simply another thing to smile about as he stared at himself in the bathroom mirror on the guest side of the house.

Speech for Sancho was another thing altogether. Occasionally he'd come out with a word or phrase seemingly out of place, but every so often he'd spout out a word or phrase that fit the situation perfectly. The first of these was at the exit door of the medical center. There he yelled, "Stink!" And it did stink because the wind was blowing from around the corner of the building where there was a fenced-in area containing air conditioning units and sewage disposal preparation tanks. A new Florida law required raw sewage from large facilities, such as medical centers, be pre-treated before going into the main sewer system. Therefore, coming out the exit that day, it really did stink.

More of Sancho's outbursts occurred while Bill was driving them down the main drag on their way to the Village Septimus open air plaza. Golf carts were parked on both sides of the street nose in according to signs giving rules for golf cart parking. Sancho was in the front seat next to Big Bill who drove slowly because of all the folks crossing the street, some wearing facemasks, most not. When a group of all black golf carts resembling old black Chevy Suburbans appeared, obviously parked one next to the other all in a row, Sancho blurted out, "Secret Service!" And a couple minutes later, after Bill had snaked the cart through a crowd of seniors in all manner of colorful outfits meandering toward folding chairs surrounding the stage and dance area, Sancho sang out, "Pave paradise with old farts!"

A woman onstage announced a moment of silence for victims of the recent pottery class shooting and for those who died in the plane crash. During the moment of silence the band walked slowly to their spots. Seeing that the band consisted of four elderly men and one elderly woman, Sancho whispered, "More old farts," causing a couple stinky eye looks from those around them.

The band started out with "You Ain't Seen Nothin' Yet" and "American Woman." Although there were a few colorful tight outfits, complete with bellbottoms, there were plenty of Bermuda shorts with pant legs too wide for the skinny legs. Simone noticed Sancho, sitting in the front seat of the golf cart, was staring at a guy with a sizable paunch in tan shorts and Hawaiian shirt. Sancho nodded his head to the rhythm watching the guy, who was directly in front of the cart, skinny legs from the shorts to the ground looking like they'd collapse any second the way the guy was jerking everything above his knees side to side. When Simone leaned close to Sancho, he said, "Stick man."

Bianca and Bill were out in the dance crowd until they returned near the end of "American Woman." When Bill asked Simone if she wanted to dance, Sancho looked sad. When Bianca offered, he smiled, and so Simone and Bianca bumped and ground for a while until the old fart band leader, who wore a colorful facemask down around his neck but never put it up, announced they were going to slow it down a little and the band launched into and out-of-tune rendition of "Raindrops Keep Fallin' On My Head." At first Simone thought they'd head back to the sidelines, but Bianca held on and led. They waltzed past Sancho and Bill, both smiling and nodding approval. The way Bill smiled with his Big Bill grin, Simone wondered if Bill knew she and Bianca had slept together.

Because of Sancho's stroke he didn't dance. Instead, Simone alternated between Bianca and Bill. At one point during a slow dance Bianca said, "I hope you and Sancho were comfortable in the room last night."

"Of course we were."

"I wondered."

"Why, weren't you comfortable?"

"Sure, honey. I slept in the room next door."

"Don't you and Bill ever sleep together?"

"Not with that damn news going."

At the sidelines, during a band break, three women and two men came up. Bianca introduced them but Simone quickly forgot their names. Because they were in the midst of a crowd filing in and out of the concert venue for refreshments, or to go to the bathroom, it was very noisy. The three women and two men speaking with Big Bill shouted. One of the men wore a small particulate facemask and shouted the loudest, the facemask probably stopping the spittle.

"Did you hear about that pottery class shooting?"

"Of course!"

"Terrible, just terrible! Reminds me of when the creature was in office and they had those riots!"

"I sure hope nothing like that happens at your yoga class, Bill!"

"Bill wouldn't let that happen! He'd throw the guy to the ground!"

"Wasn't it a woman with the gun?"

"Yeah, a woman or something in between!"

"We had a woman slap another woman at our Mahjong group last summer!"

"Things go crazy in summer! I told you not to stay down here for summer!"

"Allen and I have to stick it out! We can't afford another place like you!"

"Did you hear about that supply truck got attacked before it could get through the gate last August?"

"Of course! It's all anyone could talk about the rest of the summer! Winn Dixie ran out of vodka and workers in restaurants were worried they wouldn't get food! Did you hear the rumor about the people on that plane that crashed?"

"What about them?"

"They're saying it was a group pretending to be religious but really going to join the protest! Something about the plane going down here on purpose! Maybe refugee escapees!"

"You're watching too much fucked-up Trump-talk news!"

"That's the trouble in this country! Too much talk!"

"It's true up north, too!"

"What's that got to do with anything?"

"Northern elites start a rumor and away it goes from there!"

"With South Brooklyn and Back Bay joining Miami? Are you kidding?"

"No, I'm not kidding! There are still holdouts in the tall buildings who start things!"

"How can they start anything without food and water?"

"They could start a virus outbreak!"

"Yeah, it'd sneak up on us before we knew it and they'd steal our homes!"

"I heard an Oligarch is feeding holdouts so he can eventually take them in as slaves!"

"So maybe it's better I stay put here summers?"

"Yeah, so long as they can keep dredging the swamps and trucking in the gunk to raise the elevation of the causeway and fill the sinkholes on the golf courses!"

"Not to mention maybe forming convoys to protect our supply trucks! Wouldn't want to run out of Pampers!"

"That's a damn stupid thing to say! Besides, filling golf course sinkholes isn't the worst of it! Last week they had to dig out the debris of another house in Village Primus!"

"If a sinkhole doesn't get you the heat will. Then the death cart comes from the funeral home!"

"The whole mess makes me wonder if we're the guinea pigs down here! You see that latest ultra-processed crap they have now at Winn Dixie?"

"I hear the Latin Villages desalinization plant's having trouble keeping up!"

"Homeless are probably siphoning water!"

Big Bill spoke up. "Nobody can get in there! I went on a tour of the place last month! Guard dogs and everything!"

"Special dogs that can take the summer heat when it comes? And how can they feed dogs when we need the food? We're not supposed to get more dogs where we live, so why guard dogs?"

"We should change the subject! How's your book coming, Bianca?"

"Oh, pretty good."

"What? Speak up!"

"I said pretty good!"

"I sure hope you have a chance to finish it before this whole place gurgles into the ocean!"

Bianca nodded, Simone mumbled, "Nice meeting you," and the group was gone just as the band began playing "American Pie" with a woman singing the solo off key.

During the drive back to the house, Sancho in the front seat with Big Bill started spouting off gibberish in off tune melodies as if he'd saved it up from the concert.

"Oh Lord God, come help your sheep. Don't let'em sheer us and shave us. Ain't gonna be bald no more. 'Candy Man' can't live without your 'American Pie.' 'Lean On Me' and do the 'Crocodile Rock.' Reverend Murdock on my shoulder with diamonds. And it's War…Good God!"

***

Simone gave Sancho his meds and put him to bed when they got back. She, Bianca, and Big Bill sat out in the lanai sipping cranberry juice and vodka, but mostly vodka.

"Is Sancho okay?" asked Bill, the hot night sky flickering the streetlights in the distance behind him.

Bianca was sitting on the same side of the table as Simone. She reached to the side out of Bill's sight and touched Simone's hand. "Did Sancho say anything else when you were in the bedroom?"

"A little bit more. Since the hospital he's been mumbling angry words about that Murdock character."

Bill poured another shot of vodka into each of their glasses, the streetlights behind him flickering rainbows from the tipping bottle. "I guess you won't be joining that Murdock group anymore."

Simone took a sip and decided sips would be the limit from this point on. "I guess not. You think those people at the concert were serious about rumors passengers on the plane were going down to join the protest?"

"Probably came from that coverage about the crash and some nut bag hinting something," said Bianca. "Anything's possible in this fenced in world."

"Speaking of nut bags, think I should carry a gun to protect my yoga class?" asked Big Bill.

"Wait," said Bianca. "You have a gun?"

"Remember the .22 rifle I snuck down here when we could still drive in? I had it broken down and split up in my luggage."

"Oh yeah, I forgot."

"Had it since I was a kid."

"Where is it now?"

"Up in the garage attic."

Bianca stared up at the sky through the screened lanai ceiling, squeezed Simone's hand. "Better watch out, Bill. One of those drones might have metal detection equipment."

"Yeah," said Bill. "All the nuts have plastic guns now."

Simone was about to take another sip of her drink, but Bill's face was going in and out of focus and she put it down. "You guys feel safe down here?"

"Safe as anywhere else," said Bill. "Well, except for the ocean undermining the place."

"Hard to sell," said Bianca. "Cheap to rent. If you two think about staying you're welcome to stay with us, but if you're thinking this place can outlive you, renting is an option. That's the way lots folks down here talk about the place. Wondering if it'll outlive them."

"I wondered," said Simone. "But if we leave Kimmy something I think she'd rather it be north."

"I don't blame her," said Bill. "When the big revolution comes it'll be worse in the land of Winn Dixie. Big trouble getting back north. Doesn't matter, as long as the healthcare keeps rolling along."

***

Big Bill was first to announce he was crashing, Bianca having him put down the glasses and bottle he was attempting to carry back to the kitchen. After she put Bill to bed she rejoined Simone. They both said they were breathing vodka and pointed out the slur in one another's conversation.

"Hot tub," said Bianca. "Hot tub'll work."

"Get suits?" asked Simone.

"Fuck the suits," said Bianca. "Guys are out."

Simone glanced out at lit neighborhood windows. "Turn out the lights?"

"Yeah."

They stripped and helped one another down the tub steps. They soaked in silence for a time, listening as they each took deep breaths. After a while Simone felt her lips come back to life.

"I mean, sure, we slept together, but we didn't do anything really."

"Compared boob sizes."

"That doesn't count."

"Hell no."

"I think we should go in? I don't want to puke in your pool."

"Okay, got towels over there."

Getting out was harder than getting in. Simone pushed on Bianca's rear end, Bianca pulled Simone up. They both toweled off and stumbled into the house, laughing, trying not to laugh, and shushing one another.

Chapter 14—Cul-de-Sac Bash

Next night, at a house down the street in Village Sextus, a mid-thirties pot-bellied man in underwear and a stretched tee shirt made his way down a dark hallway toward the lighted living area. He had black bed-head hair and a scraggily black beard. He pulled on a Batman facemask and itched his crotch as he leaned around the corner into the light of the living room and adjusted the thermostat. "It's hotter than hell in here! Why'd we move to this hellhole?" He glanced toward a group of gray heads and bald heads, some of whom resembled elderly Disney characters. The older folks stood around the bar separating the kitchen from the living room. He blinked and glanced to other gray heads sitting in the living room. Half were wearing facemasks and half not. "Nothing here but cheap booze, sinkholes, and old Trumpster divers!"

One of the elderly men carrying a tray of drinks from the bar with his facemask lowered glanced toward the hallway. "Someone put Jar Head to bed!"

"My name's Jarrod, Daddy Flintstone! You and Mom thought it was cute to name me after one of *them*!"

A woman's voice came from a lit room down the hall. "Are *they* in some of these photographs you got all over the place?"

Jarrod glanced back down the hallway where his mother was. "Hell no!" He turned back to scan the gathering and said, "Not all of you are masked up like me. And by the way, I don't want you to be hopeful. I want you to panic."

His father, carrying his drink tray back to the bar, paused. "What the hell's that supposed to mean?"

"Obviously you haven't read your history," said Jarrod. "Greta Thunberg said that in Davos, Switzerland, back in 2019. I've got a friend I commune with named Greta over in Village Quatorus. The Weisbergs. Any of you know them? I thought not. Too educated and too Jewish."

Jarrod's father dismissed Jarrod with a wave of his drink tray and went back to the bar. Jarrod turned, lowered his Batman mask, and stumbled back down the hallway, turning sideways to get past his mother without touching her. Before slamming himself into his room he shouted, "I'd go out and do the town crier bit, but cops would grab me for a refugee! Came out to tell all you folks a January storm's coming! Tuned it in on the pirate weather station! And by the way I put on my mask to protect you!" After Jarrod slammed the door his mother Jill came out wiping her hands like in mission accomplished.

One of the men mumbled a question asking if anyone knew of a new virus alert. Several heard him and shook their heads no.

Simone and Sancho were with Bill and Bianca at the home of neighbors Fred (thus, the "Flintstone" from Jarrod) and Jill, a few doors up the cul-de-sac. At dusk they'd wheeled Sancho there in his chair, left the wheelchair on the front porch, and transferred him to the sofa where he was safely ensconced near a Betty Boop look-alike—Betty Boop except for a face full of ultraviolet wrinkles beneath white face makeup. No facemask, but she was a safe distance away at the sofa's far end. According to Bianca, during their short walk, it wasn't announced as a costume party, but a lot of parties turned out that way. "It's a way to cut ties to the realities of the world. Getups that jump back a few decades to what folks insist were simpler, and therefore better, times. A while back, during the last virus scare, a lot of them had on themed facemasks."

The layout of the house was similar to Bianca and Bill's house—open living room, dining room, bar, kitchen, and wide open sliding doors to the lanai. "Cookie cutter," Sancho had whispered to Simone shortly after their arrival. It was hard to determine the color of the walls because every square inch was covered with collages of photographs, mostly color shots of little kids at various ages, a few of the group shots socially distanced, but most noticeably were black and whites that hopped, skipped, and jumped back over the decades. Simone thought hopped, skipped, and jumped because the photographs in one of the collages consisted of kids, black and white girls, skipping rope. None of the photographs resembled Jarrod, the thirtyish guy in underwear and Batman facemask who'd disappeared back down the hall.

Jill said not to worry about Jarrod's storm prediction. "Can't be that bad in January. We have the weather network on call and it'll let us know. We were down here during two of the last summers. A couple good size storms in June and in July we got inundated by a new bat species, the news scaring the hell out of us each night with virus speculation. In August there were a couple storms, after which local officialdom made us take in Central Americans who got stranded on the causeway."

"Weren't you frightened?" asked Betty Boop.

"Not at all, mostly families, some even with kids. Guards were with the group. They'd been hustling them up north to Macon where they have that gigantic refugee camp. Guards cooled themselves in the laundry room and made the refugees stay in the garage."

"They sh-lit your tires?" asked a man in his slurred voice.

"Of course not!"

"Did any look like vampires?"

No one answered and the conversation lightened. It didn't take long for most in the crowd to get stoned, either on alcohol or pot that was being shared out in the lanai. As folks arrived it was obvious they'd already gotten a head start. When Betty Boop launched herself from the sofa and stumbled down the hallway toward the john, Simone grabbed her seat, which was warmer than she'd expected. She felt under her rear end to make sure it was dry. It was, but she slid to the middle to be beside Sancho.

Sancho leaned close, said, "Barflies" and made a buzzing sound. He had a vodka tonic safely placed on the end table beside him. Simone noticed he'd maybe had a sip. The one she held was half gone and she felt she'd be half gone if she downed the whole thing because the ratio of vodka for the evening was apparently on the high side. A few had even given their drinks the stinky eye after Fred, the host behind the bar, mixed them up without using anything resembling a shot glass. One guy said something about the vodka being a disinfectant and therefore the reason most weren't wearing masks.

As the evening wore on Simone lost track of names. The women became faces, the ones with makeup and dyed hair, the ones without makeup and their hair natural, which in the Latin Villages was gray and thinning. Men became outfits, the ones in jeans and tee shirts to tight for their paunches, the ones in button shirts and slacks or shorts. One guy wore a hunting camouflage outfit and matching facemask-neck covering. By listening to various conversations Simone determined the women in makeup and the men in jeans, or camouflage, were to the right on the political spectrum and the women without makeup and the men in button shirts were to the left. Some of those to the left wore masks. The only one to the right who wore a mask was the camouflage guy who was sweating profusely. Simone held Sancho's hand, squeezing it when a statement she considered a whopper was made.

"We were warned way before the coastal flooding there'd be more conflict and aggressive behavior."

"Look at the bright side."

"You mean there is one?"

"It's right there in the Book of Revelations."

"Ah yes, the good old apo-collapse."

"We were warned about food deficits beginning at two degrees warming, and look where we are now."

"What's the big deal? We got Greenland grain and wheat and they're growing meat in tanks. Stop your bellyaching."

"It's not really meat. They just figured a way to make artificial blood. The smell coming off your grill is chemicals burning."

"At least we have food, and grills. On the news they say residents here in the Latin Villages are the last of the middle class."

"Nothing but fluff on the news. Island CEOs make sure of that."

"Oligarchs with genetically engineered kids keep an eye on all of us from inside their fortified compounds or manmade city islands. They're the ones running the show."

"Remember when they got the nationalists and race supremacists on their side? They took over all the cruise ships so they'd have a place to hide out."

"Yeah, while they left the right-wingers in place to fight for their right to hoard all the cash. Can't even call the stock market a market anymore. Nothing but artificial intelligence playing with Oligarch money."

"After that the Oligarchs grabbed the corporate heads and pulled up their ladders so no one else could get in. The ones just below them like politicians and doctors retiring because they said Obamacare ruined health care gave it a try."

"Don't forget Wall-Streeters, media moguls, and medical gadget attorneys."

"When did we start calling them Oligarchs and how did the name get capitalized?"

"Spell checkers. They control everything."

"But when did we start using the term?"

"I guess when presidents and prime ministers and all of them flaked out."

"But why has using the term *Oligarch* become so prevalent? That's what I'd like to know."

"Oh, big word, *prevalent*. It's like a non-religious person getting invited to dinner at which the host or hostess suggests joining hands and saying grace and the non-religious person, who'd rather not join hands, eventually takes part in the ritual as a matter of courtesy. Only to find out there's a so-called afterlife feel good story in the works."

"What the hell kind of comparison is that?"

"You're right, it's like a religion. They've become our priests and CEOs and everything else."

"At least so far they're making sure cheap booze keeps coming in on the causeway."

"While they relax on their verandas sipping the expensive stuff and asking if it gets any better than they got it."

"I say they're all at fault. Environmentalists, evangelicals, everyone."

"Yeah, those so-called evangelicals on that plane were phonies. Nothing but environmental terrorists in disguise."

"Where'd you get that information?"

"I got it. That's all that matters."

"Nobody trusts anybody. No wonder the world's fucked up."

"Yeah, we even have shootings here. Crazy."

"There hasn't been that many."

"I wonder what the pottery shooter's motive was. Has anyone heard anything?"

"I'd still like to know how much pottery was destroyed."

"A gun rack in his pickup look-alike golf cart should have clued someone in the guy's nuts."

"It was a woman. She had the right to arm bears."

"Very funny."

"This conversation is getting out of hand. Why do we always have to argue? The news tells us everything we need to know."

"Right. What news? Local stations are nothing but henhouse propaganda. Only time it's actual news is when there really is a storm coming."

"Quit it you guys. Don't open up any more worm cans."

"Storms? Hell no. We don't need more storms."

"I meant stay off the political angle."

"Why? It all started with that foxy network and the Russians."

"And it's still going on."

"Give me that bottle!"

"You gonna hit me with it?"

"No, I'd like another shot."

"With your gun?"

"I don't own any guns!"

"That's your loss."

"I couldn't help noticing the stickers on your golf cart."

"The one that says, "Finish the monument?"

"That and the others."

"Well, they should finish the monument."

"Why?"

"Because his family estate paid for it."

"Yeah, with money they stole from us."

"It was one man one vote back then and I'm old enough to have given him mine, so there's that."

"It was also one woman one vote, only the woman, and the man, had to have the right color skin."

"What're you sayin'?"

"Do I need to spell it out for you?"

"Yeah, you need to spell it out, but you probably can't read."

"I can read. I saw that old 'Wall Schmall' sticker on your cart. That thing supposed to look like an old Ford Mustang or what?"

There was an angry pause in the conversation. Guests looking side-to-side wondering what would be said next. A woman who appeared to be the oldest at the party used the pause, speaking out with her frail voice. She had a facemask but it was scrunched on her neck like a soiled scarf.

"It used to be so nice here. I remember when I visited my parents in their house—my house now—looking out the window each morning when it was still cool. Folks would be out, kids visiting grandparents, and there'd be dogs. Groups of folks taking their dogs for walks, the kids carrying doggy bags just in case. And then by the time I moved here there were less people out walking dogs in the morning. Not only because of the heat, but because there aren't as many dogs. It's changed. Everything's changed."

Another moment of silence, some looking to the old woman, waiting to see if she'd say more, some looking down into their drinks. Finally one of the men wearing a facemask and a dress shirt who'd been part of the earlier conversation broke the silence.

"It's mostly lack of supplies. Notice how fast the pet department at Winn Dixie disappeared? Cats out on their own, dogs on the wane. Only pets I see any more are birds, I guess because they don't eat much and they live longer."

"What about bats?"

"What about them?"

"The other day you told me you built bat houses for your yard."

"I built a couple to attract bats. They keep bugs in check. They're not pets."

"Houses for virus carriers, that's a laugh."

"With habitat encroachment in the Amazon, what do you expect?"

"I expect they'll die out someday like everything else."

Another silence until Jill, the hostess, brought out snacks. The guys who'd been arguing gobbled them up, cheese and cracker crumbs all over the place. The food seemed to calm everyone down a little, but some of the guys who'd argued earlier still had sour faces like in heartburn commercials. One of the women guests got a portable vacuum out of a closet and worked on the crumbs. One of the men looked at the vacuum as if he were about to grab it and heave it through the window.

When folks began moving out the front door, Simone couldn't tell if it was to escape the noise of the vacuum, to check out stickers on the various golf carts, or stare at the full moon. The jumble of conversation on the way out made anything possible. Not only that, dark clouds began closing in over the full moon as Simone put Sancho in his chair outside the front door. The conversation from inside re-launched.

"You know what's wrong with you?"

"What?"

"You're afraid to think outside the box."

"What box?"

"This place we live is a box. Think outside of it once in a while why don't you?"

"Why should I?"

"Because there are folks out there struggling to stay alive."

"They're not my business."

"Really? I've got relatives out there struggling and here we sit!"

"I'm not sitting! And it's not our fault we planned and live in a planned community!"

"Right, planned community. Living here like a bunch of automatons."

"What the hell are automatons?"

"Robots. I see it everywhere. Our streets are the same. Our houses are the same. Pets disappearing, like the lady said. You ever see that guy who walks down the street carrying a leash with an empty collar? Pure loco. And that line dancing, like a bunch of zombies with sour faces."

"You're the one who's loco!"

"I mean it. We need more soul music in this place. Last time I watched a line dancing group made me think of watching Hitler's storm troopers on the History Channel."

"You're a dumb fuck!"

"Obviously the significant result of climate change increasing conflict and aggressiveness is in play here!"

"What the hell?"

Suddenly the two white guys who'd been arguing came at one another out on the front lawn. Each paused a moment, one to raise a facemask, the other to take one from his pocket and put it on. Then they went at it. A black guy from the party who'd pretty much kept his mouth shut masked up and stepped forward, trying to break up the two guys. The whites were the camo guy and one of the dress shirts. The black guy also wore a dress shirt. All three danced around one another, the two white guys like drunken boxers, the black guy a sober referee.

"Don't let them hurt one another, Mitch!" screeched a woman.

"They won't. They've had too much vodka."

"Someone stop them!"

"No! It's about time someone's waking up to what we've done to the world!"

Now that they'd moved outside it seemed most of the men had gone silent, a few stumbling to sit in their golf carts. As the three men went at it, Simone had a hard time figuring out if it was serious or if tempers were winding down. She pushed Sancho's chair behind a parked golf cart. Sancho stared at the sky and waved one arm above his head, swatting at bats she could not see. Beyond the cart, with most of the men in a stupor, some women took videos and photos with their phones while others spoke.

"The Russians are coming, the Russians are coming."

"Why do you say that?"

"Vodka."

"That's an old movie."

"Vodka?"

"No, *The Russians Are Coming*."

"I know."

The three men in the lawn brawl were now rolling on the parched grass. No punching, mostly rolling around and coughing. Maybe even some laughing.

A woman who'd announced at the start of the party that she was an environmentalist said, "I wonder what's in the chemicals those guys are rolling in."

"No worse than the chemicals in our water."

"You drink the water?"

"Hell no, but we all shower in it."

"I don't."

"Yeah, I can tell."

"That was catty."

"I know."

"Maybe a sinkhole will start up and swallow this whole place."

"The house?"

"I mean the whole Latin Villages."

"We can only hope."

"American, schmamerican."

"DSD! DSD!"

"What's that supposed to mean?"

"Divided States of Dystopia."

"Okay, all together. DSD, DSD…"

"DSD, DSD, DSD!"

Simone wondered what Kimmy was doing right now. She imagined her on the deck of the *Shellfish* staring forlornly at the full moon. She remembered Kimmy telling about finding the crew's pet cat curled up in the bow and also wondered about the chemicals in the lawn she could feel creeping into the sides of her sandals. She wheeled Sancho out into the street where Big Bill and Bianca stood. Bianca had chanted DSD a couple times but now whispered maybe they should go home. Bianca was at Simone's side and stumbled a little, her arms around Simone.

As if in an alien movie, a bright light shown from above, a spotlight on the three guys rolling on the front lawn. A man's voice, loud as hell. "This is the police! What's going on down there? If there are weapons show them!"

A cloud shaped like a bat wing passed in front of the moon. Simone hadn't had that much vodka, had she? She wondered if this whole place and the flight down here and the crash on the seventh of Palm Tree Gardens had been a nightmare. Nightmares are like that. One day you've got a country in which folks pretty much get along, then something happens, a monster comes along and everything changes. Two separate tribes take shape and grow and grow until they're at one another's throats, rolling around on a lawn surviving on chemicals. She felt dizzy, a slight pounding on top of her head. But then she realized the pounding was a helicopter. Wait! Not that large! A drone!

It landed next to the guys on the lawn who'd gotten up and were wiping themselves off and trying to look innocent in the spotlight. The drone was three feet across, it's four turbo fans slowing down.

"All right, one at a time. Pull down those facemasks. You, in the camouflage outfit, what's going on?"

"We were just playin' 'round."

"Are you drunk?"

"No, no. Heavens to Betsy, no."

"Is there someone named Betsy here?"

Silence. The drone blades had come to a stop. "All right, everyone stay put. I'll need to speak with all of you."

"All of us?"

"Yeah, why would you need to speak with all of us? Why can't we just go home?"

"Because I have to make a full report. Someone called, therefore I need a full report before I fly back to base."

One of the guys in the group: "All right, who the hell called? You, Mitch, and you, Bill! You're both into neighborhood watch! You turncoats call?"

"I was the one trying to break them up," said Mitch. "How could I call?"

Bill didn't responded.

One of the women: "It wasn't Mitch or Bill. All of us called."

They guy again: "That's no answer."

The woman: "Who cares?"

The guy: "Least you could do is send real cops."

A few agreed, with, "Yeah," and, "Wouldn't you think we deserve real cops? That's the way it is for us retired folks. We lose everything. Can't even get a real cop."

The drone, after giving one of its four blades a single spin: "I am a real cop, you swamp toads! I've got night vision and facial recognition in my toolbox. There's a thunderstorm in the forecast so let's get on with the interviews. You, wearing the Mickey Mouse tee shirt with extra large ears…Yeah you, lady. Step forward and let's have the story from start to finish. And you, in the back there. The carts are all identified. Your mask won't help. You might as well come on back. And what about that guy sitting in the chair staring at the sky?"

"He's got a handicap," said Bill. "Can't you see the wheelchair? He and his wife are our guests. We are allowed to have guests in this joint, aren't we?"

"Of course you can have guests."

A man hollered out from his golf cart. "Yeah, we can have guests, Bill. As long as they've been entered into the facial recognition database. Four people in a house still the rule? Or did the powers that be raise the limit so people can let in more outsiders?"

The drone shone a light on the man. "All right, all right. That's enough."

"It's never enough."

The drone gave another of its blades a single spin. "Will you people quit giving me a hard time? My job is to interview everyone here before this storm front rolls in. I'll make it quick. Let's start with the Mickey Mouse lady. Full name and address please."

Chapter 15—Sex in the Village

Next morning Bianca, Big Bill, Simone, and Sancho agreed they'd fallen asleep to thunder in the distance and awakened with terrible headaches. The lanai and the streets outside were dry, the sun was out, and all agreed perhaps the storm had passed. At the breakfast table, with coffee and toast, even Sancho was able to agree maybe the vodka at the party might have been some cheap stuff funneled into bottles displaying top shelf labels. Yeah, they'd all seen a plastic funnel on the kitchen counter. What the hell else would Fred have a funnel for? On the way to the party Bill did warn them he'd heard there was a distillery behind a sheet in Fred's garage. Maybe their son Jarrod did some distilling.

Bianca suggested they go outside for air.

Bill said, "It's already eighty-nine out."

"The sun's still low," said Bianca. "We could walk over on the west side of the house."

"You mean pace back and forth?" asked Bill.

"Got any better ideas?"

"Yeah, rather than pushing his chair on the rotten bumpy lawn, me and Sancho go over to Harbor Freight. He doesn't have rehab until Monday and the weekly ad came in on my pad. The top is up on the T-bird. It's air conditioning works great. What do you say, Sancho?"

Sancho nodded.

Bianca said, "Well then, Simone, how about we take the cart over to the Winn Dixie? Pick up something for dinner. I think this is the day they have fresh produce they've managed to fly in from Canada."

"I'd like to shower first," said Simone.

"Okay, me too," said Bianca. "It's settled. Me and Simone fresh as daisies to the Winn Dixie and you guys putz at Harbor Freight.

"Watch for Fred or his kid Jarrod in the liquor department," said Bill. "They might be buying good stuff for themselves. I noticed he made a lot of trips behind the counter like he was getting something out of a lower cabinet. I bet he was downing good stuff while he poured swamp water for us."

***

Kimmy called while Simone was in the shower. She'd left the phone on the shelf above the sink and, hearing the announcement, told the phone to pick up and go to speaker.

"How's Dad?"

"Much better. We went to a party last night and he drank, so I guess that's a good sign."

"What's that noise?"

"I'm in the shower. Can you hear me okay?"

"Sure, fine. So you're still staying with Bill and Bianca?"

"Yes."

"Don't swallow any shower water."

"I won't"

"Has Dad brought up suing the airline yet?"

"There's a class action already started. That seemed to satisfy him."

"What about settling down, at least for a while? Sometimes it's messier up here because of all the people on the move. Last time you said rentals were cheap."

"So far we're still being told to stay here with Bianca and Bill. We'll see."

"Are you sure there're no cameras?"

"What?"

"Mini cameras, Mom. Like, there could be one in the shower with you right now."

"Guess I'll stop rewashing my crotch."

"It's not funny. One of my mates—a guy of all things—says he smashed a bug that turned out to be a camera. He saved the gismo and showed it to us at dinner. The captain on this trip is savvy to the shit. Says she's got the latest detection gear."

"Well, that's good. Speaking of drones, a cop drone landed on the front lawn last night when the party was breaking up."

"What happened?"

"Some guys, too much vodka. Did you know they can selectively disable the phones in this place?"

"Makes sense. In Chicago they tag groups where they detect the possibility of a shooter. I read on the news there was a shooter down there."

"Yeah, at a pottery class."

"It's crazy all over, Mom. Maybe you and Dad should consider staying put for a while. At least it's fenced in."

"Quite serious fencing."

"I saw it when I visited. You've seen the fencing?"

"A little during trips to the medical center. It has razor wire on top that glistens in the sun."

"When I was there they seemed really serious at the guard gate. Also, I noticed a lot of facemasks. How do you know when to wear one?"

"They give particulate warnings on certain days. Folks carry filters everywhere they go just in case. They also give warnings if there's a virus on the prowl, but so far none of those warnings. I'm told the air conditioning in this house has serious filters. Can't leave doors or windows open. Bianca an I are going grocery shopping so that should be interesting."

"Okay, Mom. Have a good time. Be careful, and love you. Duty calls on the *Shellfish*. I'll let you get back to crotch washing."

"Love you, too, sweetheart."

***

Before they left for the Winn Dixie, Simone noticed Bianca touch the dog leash hung on the inside wall before going into the garage to put golf clubs into the back seat area of the golf cart. "The weather says it might turn cool and cloudy this afternoon. I've got an extra set so if we want we could stop off at the course. You said you golfed, right?"

"A little," said Simone. "As long as it's not that course where the plane went down."

"It won't be. There's this easy nine-hole that has plenty of shade shelters beneath solar panels. It's where a lot of the ladies hang out."

"My luggage was returned, but no hat. Guess it was in the overhead."

Bianca went to a closet off the garage. "Here, I've got two wide-brim jobs we can take along."

Simone noticed, besides wearing long sleeves like she was, Bianca seemed to have lost her bounce. "Are you wearing a sport bra?"

"In case we do decide to golf."

"Me too, keeps the party hats from showing."

The Winn Dixie and a few other stores in the shopping center were visible from the golf course. Although they did make the rounds of the course, they decided not to golf. The sun was hot, burning through a haze not thick enough to stop it. Instead, they met up with a group of women wearing facemasks washing the film and dust off the solar panels mounted on the course shade shelters. Both put on facemasks and decided to help out.

Some of the women were older and, remembering what Kimmy said about moving here, Simone figured this was a chance to get in on gossip. The group was at the shelter behind the first tee and they pitched in there and moved on with them to the second tee. They had lightweight ladders, towels, and spray bottles they insisted contained environmentally friendly liquid.

"Basically salt water from one of the compromised wells," said a woman in a neck to ankle caftan and a wide brim white hat. "Called into action because the storm skipped us last night."

The solar panel cleaning talk could have been table talk at a Mahjong get-together if one closed her eyes.

"Bianca, I heard about that big fuckus at a party in your village last night."

"You mean ruckus?"

"You know what I mean. I use fuckus because of the obvious."

"Hand up that spray bottle. What's the obvious anyway?"

"The way us retired folks in the Latin Villages are getting fucked."

"Gloria, must you?"

"Sorry, but it's true. First they lure us to Florida with their low taxes and next thing you know they're charging for extras like water you can drink."

"We should put big sails on this place and next time there's a blow we can steer it north along the coast, maybe plop the whole thing down on what used to be Manhattan. They could use the real estate."

"For now we've got real estate until the ocean and the gulf completely undermine us. My husband says we should've moved to Montana or North Dakota like others."

"Some states are limiting arrivals unless they have a job lined up."

"I guess that leaves us out."

"If I have to stay down here one more summer—"

"Let's get off this negativity. I had enough of that on the History Channel from when you know who and his family were in office."

"All right, something cheery. Bianca, how's that book of yours coming?"

"It's coming along."

"You've got to put in the time, Bianca. A little every single day is the only way to finish such a project. What's the title again?"

No answer from Bianca who was up top scrubbing away.

"Her working title is *Things Shall Inherit the Earth*, right Bianca?"

"Correctamundo," said Bianca.

The woman in caftan and white hat turned to Simone who was holding onto the ladder on which Bianca stood.

"She's working on this book. Perhaps you've heard of it."

"A little," said Simone.

"It's about things that made their way down here because retirees brought them with." The woman paused and shouted up to Bianca. "I'm telling her the premise of your book if that's okay!"

"Fine," said Bianca.

"Fine," said the woman. "The premise, as I understand it, is that the inanimate objects on Earth, everything from furniture to rocks, live in a kind of time warp and actually have a cerebral existence. Our job, as their servants, is to move them around once in a while. Sort of like crop rotation, but on a completely different time scale. Centuries rather than decades. A lot of the stuff ends up in those rental storage units."

The woman looked up the ladder and raised her voice. "Bianca! I remember in that one chapter you read at the writing class you had the things in a storage unit actually speaking with one another. Isn't that right?"

"Right," said Bianca.

"So imagine this. There's this storage unit along the east coast somewhere and one day the things in the storage unit hear waves in the distance, and a couple years later, waves are lapping at the door and water's coming inside. And then there are these humans, a couple women whose husbands have passed. The women arrive in a van. They're wearing boots and begin hauling the things out of the storage unit before the sea rises any further. The things, being in touch with matters geological, wonder aloud to one another in the back of the van. Something about why the humans didn't know this was coming. Some of the things saying the humans certainly did know. They were referring to the climate crisis of course."

The woman looked up the ladder. "Bianca, did you say the things knew about sea rise because the components they were made of had witnessed this before?"

"Yes, that's what I said."

"Of course. Imagine you're a rock and you get smoothed out by moving around in the ocean currents and you end up in some artist's mixed media wall decoration, something like that. Right Bianca?"

"Right."

"So anyway, in Bianca's story—at least the part I heard—a bunch of these things somehow get together and decide to fix it so the humans move them down to Florida. And they do this knowing full well they'll end up going back to the sea. It's said living creatures long for their return to the sea—the womb—but who's to say these things aren't doing the same? Going back to the sea, which, in reality, is their womb. Back to the womb so they can start the process all over again. Was that about it Bianca?"

"Did you memorize the chapter I read?" asked Bianca, coming down the ladder.

"Well I didn't record it," said the woman in the caftan and white hat. "I'd never do such a thing. I've got a photographic memory."

"What's the working title again?" asked another woman helping Simone move the ladder.

"*Things Shall Inherit the Earth,*" said the woman from beneath her white hat.

A few other women joined in.

"All those deaths from heatstroke down around the Equator. It's terrible."

"I agree. Especially terrible are all the families forced to find homes farther north."

"Maybe we should bring some refugees into the Latin Villages."

"They're better off going farther north. If I were younger Canada is where I'd go."

"Canada has its problems just like anywhere else."

"At least they can grow crops."

"I wonder how long Mother Earth can last."

"Doesn't matter to the Oligarch families. They're already setting up digs on Mars."

"Well, good luck to them."

"You mean good riddance."

"And *suicide is painless,*" sung a woman in a high voice.

***

At the Winn Dixie, even though it was cooler than it had been on the golf course cleaning solar panels, Simone could still feel perspiration running down her back and stopping at her bra strap. She and Bianca were in the produce department foundling expensive as hell Canadian fruits and vegetables. When Simone told Bianca about the perspiration, Bianca held up two huge melons—not hers—and agreed. Simone was prepared with two plums hidden behind her back and she held these up.

They both laughed but stopped when a man in a handicap scooter wearing a facemask came by staring at them. After the man passed by, they laughed again.

"We make a fine pair," said Bianca.

"The BBBSSS pair," said Simone, and then after a questioning look, whispered, "Bill's Buxom Bianca and Sancho's Sexy Simone."

Signs in the produce department warned that the Canadian items were limited. Obviously, from the prices, they were coveted. "So much better than the packaged stuff," said Bianca.

Other signs reminded shoppers plastic packaging had a charge that was returned after recycling.

"Not much in cans anymore," said Simone.

"The cardboard coated with foil doesn't have good shelf life," said Bianca. "For dinner, want to try for fish?"

"Sure, if it's Pacific or Arctic. Is it expensive?"

"Everything here is expensive. Latest gossip I heard was one of the trucks coming up the causeway from Orlando got hijacked, turned around, and driven back to Orlando. They found it emptied out."

"Where do you think this is all going, Bianca?"

"You really want to talk about that?"

"Sometimes I feel like talking about it."

"A group of rebels will get themselves onto an Oligarch island or into one of their strongholds and start a revolution."

"That should shake things up," said Simone.

Bianca led the way to the back of the store, old murals on the wall ahead of them showed fish swimming in a blue sea right next to a pasture with cattle grazing. "See those murals. I'm told they were there decades ago before all this. When they remodeled the place someone decided to leave the wall be. Cattle grazing on a luscious green pasture? Fish swimming in crystal clear water? Give me a break. That red dyed protein over on that side, Lord knows what that is. What really gets me, especially here with all these folks living their so-called dream, is the way the suppliers go along with it. Like soy protein made into things resembling steak. Except what are those bones made of?"

"Plastic," said Simone.

"Right, plastic recycled from the past. See, everyone's living in the past, especially here. It's the only way to not go crazy."

"Will your son Vinny ever have kids?"

"I doubt it. At least that's what he says."

"Kimmy says the same."

Bianca turned to Simone, smiled. "At these here Latin Villages we learn to project a cheerful attitude, even if we're wearing a facemask."

As they walked, a skinny old white dude not wearing a facemask looked up from some boxed vegetables he was examining, a sour expression on his face like he'd just read on the label there was a secret poison inside meant just for him.

Bianca said, "Well, at least some of us learn to be cheerful."

During the drive back to the house Bianca had them both wear facemasks because it was windy and dusty. Simone asked what the odor in the air came from. Bianca told her soil treatment supposedly designed to hold dirt in place, and also the fact that a lot of the so-called dirt used for fill came from the sewage processing plant.

Back at the house, while putting groceries away, they both agreed they felt like showers again after cleaning solar panels, shopping at Winn Dixie, and especially after the ride back in the golf cart.

"Do only women clean the solar panels down here?" asked Simone.

"Mostly women," said Bianca.

"Makes me think of history. Old women in Eastern Europe and Russia sweeping sidewalks or even scrubbing them."

Bianca stood close to Simone. "We have a huge walk-in shower in the master suite. We can scrub one another off."

"What if the guys come back?"

"Yeah, that would floor them. How about the village pool instead? It's just down the street."

"I'll get my suit."

***

It was mid afternoon, still hot and the smell still in the air. The pool and the surrounding lounging area smelled better. They were alone except for a skinny old white guy in red trunks. They both had on their wide brim hats. The pool water was too warm. They leaned close.

"How can that guy be so white?" asked Simone. "His skin's the color of bone."

"I've seen him before," said Bianca. "He stays in the shade. Never goes in the water. Probably sweats off any fat he might have."

"I see the shade canopy leads to the washrooms and all the way out to the parking lot," said Simone. "I suppose that older SUV with the heavily tinted windows is his."

"Maybe we should hit the showers," said Bianca. "This water's hotter than hell."

"I notice the showers-slash-restrooms are unisex. You don't think Bones'll walk in on us?"

"The restrooms lock. Therefore we can shower in private."

Beneath the welcome lukewarm water coming out of the showerhead, they did more than cool off and wash up. A half hour later, after putting on dry shorts and tops they brought along, they left the unisex restroom. On the way back to the golf cart, the old man, Bones, was still there, staring at them with a knowing smile on his face.

"Simone felt a blush, but when she glanced to the side couldn't tell if Bianca was blushing."

"That was refreshing," said Bianca.

"And fun," said Simone.

They'd tied their wet swimsuits to the cart's roof supports and as they sped down the cart lane at the side of the road the suits did a dance in the breeze. When Simone looked behind them she saw that Bianca's turquoise suit had blown off while her red suit was still snapping in the wind.

"We lost your suit!" shouted Simone.

"I know!" shouted Bianca.

"No, back there!"

After Bianca did a U-turn and drove back, Simone jumped out to retrieve the suit. On the way back with the suit an extremely noisy cart—obviously gasoline-powered—with country music playing full blast came at her from behind. When she turned to look, she saw an old man driving the cart, not the pasty guy from the pool, older, like a cadaver. The guy turned the other way, looking toward another cart made to replicate a 30s pickup truck that had just gone past in the cart lane on the far side of the road.

Chapter 16—Harbor Freight

Words inside Sancho Martinez's head went nuts. At rehab they told him words would come easier each day. "Easy for them to say," he recalled managing to get out at one point at last night's neighborhood soirée. Crazy, words becoming what? Visual, is the way he thought about it. Yeah, ever since he awoke from the crash into the plane's bulkhead and ended up with his head in the toilet, words were like in cartoon balloon talk. Except jumbled up. He could think what he wanted to say, but then he'd have to cherry pick from balloons full of words. And certain words kept repeating and would come out inappropriately. At the party, when being introduced, he'd said the single word "Slick" several times, as in Slick Sancho Martinez. It must have been somewhat appropriate because folks repeated it back to him, as in slick to meet you or whatever.

Even saying his wife's name had become a challenge. Last night, in bed, while she lay on her back moaning about the rotten vodka, he'd wanted to say her name. He'd wanted to say "Simone," but perhaps because she was on her back and her nipples were visible through the gown she'd slithered into, what came out instead was a offshoot of her maiden name. "Nighty night plum butter." No comment from Simone about what he'd said. Good thing she'd been out.

Because of the difficulty picking an appropriate word from the cartoon balloons floating around in his noggin, Sancho was glad Big Bill was in a talkative mood. On their way through the various villages with roundabouts, twists and turns, golf courses, and recreation centers, Big Bill, at the wheel of the classic powder blue T-Bird, gave a running narrative on their way to the Harbor Freight store.

"Not many folks on the courses today. Too hot. Even with air-conditioned carts they've still got to get out to take their shots. Glad this old T-bird has a strong air conditioner. It's a 2005, last year they made it. Neighbor died and it was going cheap because the kids didn't want to drive or transport it north. Getting stuff transported north from here isn't easy. Ties right in with that book Bianca's working on. *Things Shall Inherit the Earth.* They sure have inherited this place. Living here, folks start to wonder how long the place will last. It's an island in an angry state. But there are two sides to every coin. If you rented a place down here chances are it'd be furnished. And if you needed anything else, you could pick it up cheap at one of those warehouse sale joints. There's one over down that way where the highway dips into the salt water. And I guess because the elders of some politicians with clout live here, food and other supplies keep coming…at least so far. Everyone here's got a freezer or two just in case. Even battery banks devoted to the freezer."

Bill had to brake for a golf cart that whipped from the golf cart lane into the road to make a left turn. "Jesus, Katzenjammer! How about a signal? Lots of drivers here are as crazy as their carts. Especially the ones who drive gas carts. Alligator patrol or fossil fuelers they might call themselves. I call them fools. Smell that? I knew that guy was a fossil fueler. And look, he's waving at us."

Bill raised his voice. "Gas lover! Why don't you drink the stuff if you love it so much?"

Bill lowered his voice. "Even with gas hard to get, they grab it. I filled this baby a couple months ago. That's how much I drive it. But the fossil fuelers? On fillup day at the pumps the place is mostly gas-powered golf carts. Not only that, they bring gas cans, some on these miniature trailers they pull around. I sure wouldn't be storing gas cans in my garage. Every garage in this place is attached to the house, no sheds allowed. Storing gas in your garage is nuts.

"Last year a house went up in Village Primus. You could see the orange in the sky from our house. Village Primus was the first village. Why the hell they called this place the Latin Villages I sure don't know. One guy in my yoga class says they should change the name to the Latin Pillages. His name's Cecil. Nice guy. Been in my class so long I told him he should teach his own yoga class. Nothing to it, really. I had a few classes back in my college days in Chicago. I taught it at the charter school Bianca mentioned. Her son Vinny, my stepson, was in one of my classes back then. He's an EPA administrator for the Great Lakes region. I'm sure you heard all this from Bianca along with the story of how her husband was an innocent bystander walking his dog. She's still got the leash hanging just inside the house. You probably saw it.

"Anyway, Lots of crazy golf carts around here. It's a world all to itself, isolated by rising water levels and subsidence. I like to call it an island. Of course these days, with some states in the country doing their own thing, not quite seceding, but on the verge, a lot of island communities have emerged. Mostly to save the resources they have for themselves. For example, in this place we've got our own desalinization plant over near the coast. Went on a tour of it when the road east wasn't flooded. The place is fenced in with razor wire glowing in the sun, just like the razor wire they put in around us. Quite an image, reminded me of old news footage of that hodgepodge wall or fence or whatever you want to call Trump's fiasco.

"Sorry, didn't mean to use his name. Guess it's become a bomb word. I've noticed recently on captioning they've been putting in T with stars after it whenever they refer to him by name. Crazy world. Crazy world."

Bill glanced at Sancho. "Sorry if I offend you."

Sancho shook his head no.

"Good. I'm glad. See that gate over there? It's the entrance to Village Nonus. It's where all the service workers live. Talk about a caste system. We've got village workers isolated in their own community, yet out at sea and now up on space stations building up for eventual Mars colonies, we've got the cream of the crop, the so-called Oligarchs. You notice how the Oligarchs got the media to capitalize the word? Like they're an independent nation. In a way I guess they are. I heard one commentator speaking of what's left of the Gulf Stream as the Wall Stream. A takeoff on You-know-who's crazy wall and the Wall Street financial district, I guess. Remember back when Wall Street flooded? All those investors reportedly committing suicide? I wonder if that was true. And speaking of the Gulf Stream, with its demise and Great Britain being so cool, no wonder so many refugees are heading there. No matter what others may say I've got to hand it to the Brits for taking them in, even if it's to figure out where else in the world they can distribute them. At least they're doing something. Not like us, letting them drown or starve trying to get here.

"You must be proud of your daughter. She's doing something, out in the Great Lakes cleaning up those damn algae blooms. Just like we're proud of Vinny working for the EPA. Last year he went up to Canada for a water conference. Trying to figure out how to save the fresh water up there and at the same time capture some of the methane bubbling out of the permafrost. Even the Russians, once old Putin croaked, have turned the corner and they're supposedly working with our EPA. You never know.

"Hey, have some of that drink from the cup holder. Cherry-flavored. Good to get hydrated before we go into Harbor Freight. They air condition the hell out of that place."

Sancho flipped up the lid on a bottle and drank while Bill drank from another bottle.

"I heard Simone saying you two are looking for a different place in Michigan to retire. Can't remember the name of the town."

Sancho struggled, and miraculously it came out. "Ludington."

"Hey, that's great. You're getting better. I remember looking up Ludington. Real estate's pretty high, but I guess that's to be expected. Good elevation, naturally cooled by Lake Michigan, lots of greenery. And even though they've got algae problems, it must be a relief in summer to dip your feet into Lake Michigan. Better than the pools around here. So much heat in summer the water and concrete save it all year. Some nut jobs have even brought up the idea of cooling the pools...as if we aren't using enough energy to cool our houses. The girls said they might go to the pool for a while. I bet Simone will be surprised at how hot the water is. First time I went for a swim was the last. And the chemicals? Chemicals are everywhere around here. In the pools, on the lawns, in the ponds, and on the golf courses."

After a pause, Sancho worried Bill didn't like having to do all the talking. He looked at Bill, nodded and smiled.

"You don't mind if I talk?"

Sancho shook his head no.

"Guess I had too much caffeine this morning. You want me to keep talking? I mean, you find it interesting?"

Sancho shook his head yes.

"Okay, let's see. In my yoga class I get a lot of scuttlebutt. Not during class, no talking during class. But afterwards some folks hang around. One couple's made a habit of bringing in healthy snacks. I guess a few in their village have gardens in their lanais instead of hot tubs and lounging chairs. Anyway, while we're munching veggies I hear a lot.

"Last class there was talk about that bridge over Manhattan and how damage to the dikes during that last nor'easter isn't helping. Another so-called news item was the wildfires in Missouri. And then there are the folks in Arizona supposedly filtering their own urine. Can you believe it? Their own urine. And of course there was more talk about those wall sections between Texas and Mexico. I guess for shelter from the sun and the fact that some of the sections are naturally cooled by what's left of the Rio Grande, folks with land along the wall sections have taken to using the sections of north-facing wall as one wall of the home they're building. It was on one of those home improvement channels, the one that claims to have ways to beat the heat and the droughts.

"Most of the folks in my class are progressives. They were complaining the other day how that one crazy network has dubbed them Progs, pronouncing it to rhyme with frogs. I guess I'm a progressive myself. What about you?"

Sancho nodded yes, but also got out, "Yeah, man."

"Hey, there's Harbor Freight. I hope there's a shaded spot under their parking lot solar array. Most of it's reserved for electrics, but there are usually a few. I can't believe me and Bianca stayed down here last summer. Pretty much trapped in the house all day. A couple bodies were found in one of the other villages. News said they were accidental heatstroke deaths, but a lot of us wondered, because of the circumstance, whether the folks might just have said the hell with it, downed some booze, and heatstroked themselves to death. There are some who obviously drank themselves to death, but no one wants to talk about it. Not much news about it when someone does that. But I sure can understand it. Aha! There's a shady spot under the panels."

***

Although Big Bill had folded the wheelchair into the back seat, Sancho insisted he wanted to try walking using the cane they gave him at rehab. He did okay on the way in, but after standing around leaning on the cane for a while, decided he'd use one of the handicap carts available. He could tell Bill wanted to spend some Harbor Freight time. Among the specials were super reflective paint, solar charging kits for golf carts, emergency generators, water purifiers, bat repelling audio generators, and miniature portable air conditioners for golf carts. Bill announced he'd purchased one of the golf cart air conditioners.

Sancho waited while Bill left him to go down a narrow aisle looking for a needle nose pliers set he said he needed to fix things around the house that were wired together—Venetian blinds, the lanai pool cover, and lanai screens. While he waited Sancho overheard part of a conversation of a couple guys nearby. The two wore identical tan shorts and loose fitting shirts open at their necks.

"Looking at this stuff makes me think of the apocalypse."

"Think it's really coming?"

"What else?"

"That guy on our pickle ball team named Yorrick got info on an environmental retreat somewhere in Alberta. Says they deal in abstinence and are puritanical."

"Just what we need."

"That's when I told him I needed a drink. After that, know what Yorrick says?"

"What?"

"Says when the booze runs out we're all dead."

"How so?"

"We'll kill one another."

Sancho wheeled away from the two and spent time looking at small tools and finally picked up side cutters he figured he'd use for his thickening toenails. When he and Bill were finally finished, checking out was a challenge because Sancho forgot how to use the credit app on his phone and Bill had to help. The two guys Sancho had overheard talking inside the store waited behind them in line. Sancho saw they waited patiently but stared at him as Bill got the phone app working. The thing that threw Sancho, amplifying the confusion with his credit app, was that the two held hands and he didn't understand why these days this should confuse him.

The heat was intense outside as they returned to the T-bird. Bill helped Sancho from the cart to the front seat, parked the store cart in the corral, and quickly started the T-bird and turned the air conditioning full blast. As Sancho tucked the cane into the space between the seats he could feel the heat the aluminum shaft had absorbed on the way out to the T-bird.

Again, Bill began speaking. "I don't like to buy anything large here. I wouldn't want to transport it back north when, and if, we move. Lots of guys still buy all kinds of crap, tools that'll sit in their garages gathering mildew until they're dead. Sort of like that saying about hanging onto your gun. 'Out of my cold dead hands,' except they'll be clinging to a power tool.

"I wonder where the stuff at Harbor Freight's made. I remember once seeing a Made in Mongolia tag. Made in Mongolia. Who would have thought? Maybe some day I'll see a Made in Tibet tag. Wait, that'd be West China. Or maybe, Made at Sea, or Made on Mars. Who knows?"

***

The message came in on Big Bill's phone as soon as he pulled into the house garage. "Holy shit!"

Sancho looked to Bill. Come on, what?

"It's your wife. They're at the medical center. Bianca says she's not hurt bad. Apparently a cart ran into her."

As he sped to the medical center, Bill reached across and held Sancho's knee. "It's okay. She'll be okay."

Sancho looked down at Bill's hand on this leg. Bill driving with one hand, squealing around corners.

At the medical center Bill unfolded the wheelchair from the back seat and gave Sancho a high-speed ride, Sancho holding the cane out in front of him as Bill pushed, almost crashing into the self-opening doors. When Bill wheeled him through a large waiting room, a news item from a wall screen popped out at Sancho, a shot of the plane nosed into the sinkhole, the trailer beneath the shot of the plane saying some folks were angry about the environmental march and people flying down to join it.

Getting wheeled down a hallway to a reception desk, given a cubicle number, being wheeled around another corner toward the cubicle, Sancho became disoriented and confused. He closed his eyes. Had the plane just crashed? Was Simone injured from the crash? Or had there been another plane, another march, another crash? Somewhere from the past he heard that idiot Murdock speaking loudly. "Brother Sancho, it's Reverend Murdock."

Oh God.

Chapter 17—Houston, We Have a Problem

Sancho's wheelchair pushed by Big Bill plowed through the emergency room cubicle curtain, a maniac pushing a celebrity onstage. Bianca jumped up and moved her chair off to the side so Bill could wheel Sancho close to Simone's bed. Sancho tucked the cane he carried between his legs and touched Simone's hand, just below where an amateur nurse had bruised the arm getting in the IV. Bianca explained she'd tried to help, being she was a retired PA, but the rookie male nurse insisted he do it as per med center rules. Sancho looked to Simone, awaiting answers. When Simone simply shook her head and a tear appeared on her cheek, Bianca decided, because of Sancho's difficulty communicating, she'd fill him in on the details.

Bill backed against the curtain in the small space as Bianca went around to the other side of the bed. Despite med center smells she could still detect chlorine from pool water that hadn't quite washed off in the shower she and Simone took together before the golf cart ride, the U-turn, and Simone being run into by the old man. Bianca described what happened—a swim, the bathing suit flying away, Simone going to retrieve it, and the old man not watching where he was going.

"The doctor said it might be an ankle fracture or break, or remotely, a fibula or tibia fracture. The old guy hit her from behind. The initial pain indicated it might be fibula. They already x-rayed and we're waiting for word. Pain meds went in through the IV port, so she'll be groggy. Other than that, saline. They'll come back with anti-inflammatory but they need x-ray results. They might also order an MRI."

"What about you?" asked Bill. "Did the guy hit you?"

"I was sitting in the cart."

"Where's the guy?"

"We left him there. An ambulance arrived quickly. Witnesses who called the ambulance were busy calling in the old guy's ID. Getting Simone here as soon as possible was the best thing, so I jumped into the ambulance with her."

Sancho looked up to Bianca from the other side of the bed and nodded agreement.

"Is the cart still there?" asked Bill.

"With witnesses and the cops on their way, I didn't think about the cart."

"Yeah, good thing you acted fast and came right here," said Bill.

A television in the cubicle next door suddenly came on, the volume turned up. History Channel stuff about Obama's presidency, the election of 2016, and the turmoil of Trump's screwy presidency.

Then the channel changed, still at high volume. Environmental news about Florida subsidence, difficulty providing fresh water for citizens displaced to inland makeshift communities. A specific mention of the Latin Villages and the single highway from Orlando needing repair to yet another section that had sunk, the road being the Latin Villages' lifeline for deliveries of supplies, especially food. After this there was an apparent flashback to the plane coming down on the seventh fairway at Palm Tree Gardens. But something wrong, a mixup in the timeline making it seem the crash landing just happened, making it sound like breaking news, making assumptions that passengers on the plane were so-called "environmental activists" heading to Orlando where they were bound to inconvenience folks taking a needed break, the importance of taking a break from the pressures of life emphasized. Innocent husbands and wives and their children who simply wanted to visit Disney World forced to back off from the marchers and demonstrators.

Bill pushed back the curtain and, in a loud voice to overcome the television's volume, said," Hey, can you turn it down over there? What the hell you watching?"

The television kept blasting away and Bill went out into the hallway. "Hey, yeah you. Can you turn it down?"

Voice of an old man: "What?"

"I said, can you turn it down?"

"Hard of hearing!"

"There are other patients in here!"

"No shit, Shakespeare! I'm hard of hearing and I've got a right!"

Then, as if it had been clicked off, the television sound was gone.

"Thanks," Bill said to someone.

A woman's voice, quieter but loud enough to hear: "I'll put earphones on him. He was just in an accident with his golf cart and is a bit confused."

"Who are you?"

"Officer Houston. I just brought him in."

"Looks like he's had a few."

"Don't worry." She lowered her voice even more. "They already took blood."

As soon as Bill came back into the cubicle, the television volume again came to life. Loudmouth male commentator asking what someone thought about folks coming down to Orlando and interrupting family fun and some other guy saying maybe it was time for citizens in the area to take matters into their own hands. Then a bunch of yelling in the background until the sound again went off.

Old man's voice: "Hey, I got my rights!"

Female officer's voice: "I said you can put on earphones later!"

"When?"

"After we finish questioning you!"

"You and who else?"

"My captain."

"You know how old I am?"

"It's on your cart permit! A hundred and two!"

"You're damned right I'm a hundred and two! I'm one of the last of the middle class! We made this country! I've outlived my life expectancy and my news is the only news! Not that other crapola! Banning city cars! Next thing they'll try is banning our carts!"

Bill came around the bed and whispered to Bianca. "Think maybe you should take a peak at him?"

Bianca whispered back. "Yeah, give me a sec. I don't want to be too obvious."

Bianca said she needed to make a pit stop. She did make one down at the nearest washroom. But not before coming near enough to the narrow opening in the curtain of the cubicle next door. Yes, it was him, the old man who'd driven the cart, had his country music blasting, and turned the other way to gawk at another replica cart. Although a lot of old men around here looked similar, this guy, at one-hundred and two and, as Simone said in the ambulance on the way here, resembling a cadaver, was definitely the one who'd run into Simone.

In the washroom Bianca did her business, then stared at her face in the mirror as she washed her hands. She'd better hurry back. Simone, Sancho, and Bill were waiting. What if the cadaver turned up the volume again or said something revealing?

On the way back Bianca paused at the nurses' station outside the curtained-off cubicles. An oriental female officer with buzz cut conferred with the receptionist, a young Muslim girl wearing a headscarf. The officer's nametag said Houston.

Bianca whispered so Big Bill, a lump behind cubicle curtain number one, would not hear the conversation regarding the patient behind cubicle curtain number two. "Officer Houston?

"Yes?"

"I think we might have a problem."

"I've heard that one before."

Bianca put her finger to her lips so Houston would know she meant business. "That old dude you brought in who's hard of hearing is right next to the cubicle with my friend, the woman he ran into. Both our husband's are here and—"

Officer Houston interrupted by placing her hand on Bianca's arm and leaning close. "I'll take care of it."

Houston whispered something to the young Muslim receptionist who gave her computer screen a few swipes and, without looking up whispered back. "Simone Martinez will need a cast. I'm ordering a room right away."

"Thanks," whispered Houston.

Bianca whispered, "Why's the old guy here? Was he injured?"

"The people on the scene said he was acting weird. He pounded the side of his cart and apparently cut his arm so me and my partner brought him in just in case, and also so we could check for DUI."

"Is he really a hundred and two?"

"That's what's on his permit. Lots of folks in shitty shape around here, but there are always exceptions, folks who seem to go on forever."

When Bianca went back into the cubicle she made certain the curtain closed all the way. Bill stared at her.

"Stopped at the desk," she said before turning to Simone and Sancho. "They're getting you a regular room. You'll need at least a cast and I figured, what the hell and asked. The staff said they'd let me know right away." She motioned for Bill to stay and parted the curtain just enough to peak out. Officer Houston saw her and motioned with clasped hands against one side of her face that the old guy was asleep. The young Muslim receptionist behind the desk smiled and nodded.

***

Bill pushed Sancho's wheelchair following a big male Hispanic aide pushing Simone's gurney. Bianca walked alongside holding Simone's hand. On the way past the old dude's cubicle the female officer (Houston) stood in front of the closed curtain, nodded, and smiled.

They took the elevator to the second floor and headed in the opposite direction from where Bill and Sancho had come in through the back emergency entrance. The large room had two beds but no one else was in the room. Besides the usual bedside tables there were guest chairs, a guest table with a jug labeled "Hydration Fluid," and a stack of paper cups. A slip of paper sticking out the spout of the jug was apparently to let them know it was fresh.

"The executive suite," said one of two aides who came in.

Before transferring Simone to the bed nearest the window, the aides carefully stabilized her leg on a board. The table beside the bed had another "Hydration Fluid" jug with its freshness slip of paper sticking out the spout like a tongue.

"I wonder what's in the so-called hydration fluid," said Bill.

"Desalinated water and minerals," said one of the aides. "Good stuff."

"Looks like we're getting special treatment," said Bill.

"Could be because both Simone and Sancho were here after the crash," said Bianca. "Instructions from the airline having something to do with it. I wouldn't be surprised if they have flowers delivered. At this point they'll do whatever they can to put a little sugar in the lawsuit witch's brew."

Dr. Juli Janko came into the room. She consulted her pad for a minute, then went to Simone.

"Our resident orthopedic surgeon will be in to set your leg. You'll require a cast for a while. You've got a fibula fracture. We'll need to set it because it appears to be through the bone. Not bad, as long as we get it set and you rest up and don't let any golf carts run into you for a couple days. Because of the late hour, and because the bone doc won't be in for a while, we'll keep you overnight. Not too much in the way of meds is needed. Anti-inflammatory for the swelling, and pain meds. We've arranged for a late dinner for you and a guest, unless you want it for all four of you, which I can arrange."

Dr. Janko went to the window, glanced toward Sancho holding his cane up like a kid in school with a question. "You and your wife were on the plane that went down last week. I recognized you before I read the record. How are you doing?"

Sancho nodded and managed, "Kay."

"Good, now the bureaucratic side of things. There's an insurance guy at the desk in the hall. His company represents the old dude who ran into you. I recognized the guy because he lives on my street in Village Nonus. He'll come in once I leave. If I were you I'd not agree to anything or sign anything. He knows your condition. There's a police report spelling out that the man wasn't watching where he was going. Also, one of those crazy things left over from the Kochs, the old guy's cart was a gas-powered unit illegally modified to exceed the Latin Villages cart speed limit." Dr. Janko paused and smiled. "But back to the staple of life. I'll have someone bring in menus and you can call down to the kitchen. Do it within the next hour. Nothing but snacks later."

After Dr. Janko left, it was obvious Big Bill had himself geared up for the insurance guy. Sancho could tell by the don't-mess-with-us look on his face. The insurance meet up went quickly, the guy apologizing and providing his company card should they have any questions.

The initial pain medication had worn off and Sancho could tell Simone was hurting. He rolled his wheelchair close, leaned his cane against the bed, and held her hand. When Big Bill asked if he wanted to stay the night, or at least until the bone doc was finished, Sancho nodded.

Bianca broke in. "Sancho, you're supposed to be resting and being here won't do. Simone and I showered after our dip in the pool, we're freshened up, and I've got a bag with extra clothes I always bring along when I go to the pool. You and Bill go back to the house and I'll call as soon as the bone doc's visited, the cast's on, and we're ready to bed down for the night. Down at the emergency room they said we'd get special treatment. There's another bed in here for me. I'm staying. What say you guys go home?"

"Hey," said Bill. "I just thought of something. What about the golf cart?"

"Oh yeah, the golf cart," said Bianca. "We left it at the scene on that Main Pike Drive where it happened. As far as I know it's still there. And if not, the cops might have taken it somewhere for safekeeping. If it's not where we left it..." Bianca searched the pockets of her shorts. "Here's the cart key, and not only that, the officer on the scene gave me a phone number. If the cart's not there, you could call."

"Okay," said Bill. "I've got the T-bird. Who'll drive the cart?"

Sancho looked to Bill and Bianca, then to Simone, who nodded. Sancho raised his cane. "Me."

"It'll do you good," Simone said to Sancho. "Part of rehab. Since Bianca's got the key the cart should be there, unless they called for a tow."

Bill took the key, handed it to Sancho. "Here, driving the cart's a piece of cake. And it's close to the house, down the street from the cul-de-sac. It's getting dark, but the cart's got lights. You can follow the T-bird's lights. Piece of cake, right Sancho?"

But rather than leaving, Sancho and Bill stayed because the orthopedic surgeon showed up. He was Pakistani, announcing it after one of them asked the origin of his name. The job on Simone's lower leg took only a few minutes.

"Stay still for half hour on board so cast properly sets. I return in half hour to check. Fracture not bad. Should be healed in two weeks. No long traveling in meantime. Food has arrived outside door. Smells good. Fish, I think. You will enjoy. One half hour I return after I write report to Dr. Janko. She is our chop chop doc."

"What's that mean?" asked Bill.

"Emergency room doctor," said Bianca.

"Maybe she'll reset the mouth of the old fart who ran Simone over," said Bill.

The orthopedic surgeon looked confused. Bill took his arm and accompanied the doctor out the door. A moment later he came back rolling the food cart. "There's only food for two here."

Bianca checked. "Yep, two place settings and skinny meals, the fishless fish variety."

"Okay then," said Bill. "You guys eat while Sancho and I retrieve the cart and pick up something to eat afterward. Something more filling, right Sancho?"

Sancho nodded.

"Come back tomorrow," said Simone. "It's been a long day, especially for Sancho."

Bill stood at one of the room windows. "This is a really big room. I see carts driving in and out beneath us. I guess we're over the main entrance."

Sancho kissed Simone and managed "Sweet dreams."

When the guys were gone, Bianca came to the bedside and gave Simone a mushy one like she'd given her in the shower before the run-in with the old dude in the noisy cart.

Simone whispered, "After the cast sets, chop shop doc recommends cuddling."

Bianca smiled, "Following lights out?"

"Following lights out."

Chapter 18—USA Bar Brawl

The golf cart was still at the scene when Bill and Sancho arrived. At first Bill was upset, sitting in the T-bird with the headlights shining on the cart pushed off at an angle onto the brownish turf adjacent to the cart path. "Someone stole the clubs! Bianca said she loaded both her bags in case she and Simone felt like golfing. Now we'll have to go looking for them. One bag was green, the other red. If I don't find the bastard who took them they'll probably show up at a goddamn garage sale!"

Sancho saw something moving in the sky and leaned forward to look up out the windshield. Lights alternated white to red and continued out over the dark golf course beyond the path. No sound except the T-bird idling. He wondered if the lights belonged to a hybrid plane heading north or a drone checking things out below.

Bill drove the T-bird up over the cart lane onto the turf with the passenger door next to the cart. "Stay here a minute while I check to see if the bastard did anything else or emptied the glove compartment."

Sancho watched as Bill rummaged in the cart. After a few seconds Bill was at the front of the T-bird in the headlights holding up a slip of paper and smiling. He walked over to the passenger door and opened it.

"I shouldn't have gotten upset. The officer we saw at the medical center named Houston left a note. The clubs are at the police office in the Village Octavius recreation building and we can pick them up there. I was already planning to drive around looking for an open garage door with lights on so I could clobber a guy unloading the red and green bags he'd grabbed. I shouldn't get excited. Excitable guys like me have a lot to do with why the world's in the state it's in. You sure you're okay following me in the cart?"

Sancho nodded.

"Okay, here, use your cane and I'll help you over to it and show you the controls."

With all the excitement, Sancho felt energized, his legs seeming stronger. Perhaps his strength and ability to speak would come back full bloom. He tried and sure enough, it came out. "Thanks, Bill. I...*I'll drive*," he said in an Arnold Schwarzenegger low voice imitation.

"Well alrighty then," Bill said, in an imitation of someone Sancho could not recall.

Felt good driving the golf cart, following the taillights of the T-bird on the dark winding streets. Bill had turned on the T-bird's emergency blinkers so there was no chance of Sancho losing him. The warm evening air blowing through the rolled up side curtains felt good. Somewhere a grill was putting out fumes. It smelled like sizzling steak but, according to those at the party the previous night, was most likely the artificial stuff. Didn't matter. Smelled great in the night air, overpowering chemical lawn smells that soon returned.

As the T-bird passed beneath a streetlight ahead, Sancho saw a couple bats fly in and out of the light beam. No need to worry, the golf cart had a top. Not only that, although he recalled being wary of bats in the past, he felt comforted by the knowledge they were whetting their appetites. Funny how things had changed in his noggin since the accident, and especially since the stroke they insisted he'd had.

Simone was being cared for, they'd made friends down here where their plane crash-landed, and for the moment life was okay. That was the way the saying went these days since pandemics and climate crises took over. Not "Life was good," but "Life was okay." Yeah, sometimes it could be okay as long as you ignored what was going on in other parts of the world.

The lit up windows on both sides of the wide streets seemed friendly, reminding Sancho of childhood. The neighborhood in the small town outside Grand Rapids where he grew up. A neighborhood isolated, at least back then, from the ravages of the initial pandemic and global warming. Other parts of the country suffering—hospitals full, storms on the horizon, everything from tornadoes, hurricane surges on coasts, and fires inland once the floods had time to dry into dead brush in the heat of the relentless sun. His small town outside Grand Rapids had been an island, at least for a while, at least until refugees flooded inland looking for places to live. Lake Michigan had its ups and downs, but not like large cities and the seacoasts.

Sure, Lake Michigan was on his mind, but driving the cart through the neighborhood in the dark made him wonder if it might be good to move down here, rent a place in this fenced-in protected island of enforced security. Crazy world, fences around an island surrounded by swamps, swollen rivers, salt-water ponds, and sinkholes. Subsidence would probably sink the place eventually. But how long? A decade? Two or three decades? Long enough for Sexy Simone and Slick Sancho, the SSSS pair from mid-Michigan, to take advantage of the local healthcare and comfortably live out their lives? When his speech improved he and Simone and even Kimmy could discuss it. If things got rough up north Kimmy could hunker down with them.

The T-bird's lights led the way. Big Bill and his gorgeous wife Bianca good friends to have nearby. He tried to imagine a foursome, felt a hard-on growing in his tight shorts. Hadn't had one since the plane crash. Was he aroused because of Bianca or Simone, or did it have to do with Bill? Big Bill who'd put his hand on Sancho's leg earlier in the day on the way to the medical center.

At the house Sancho pushed the parking brake to keep the cart from rolling backwards. Bill helped Sancho out of the cart and steadied him against the garage door opening before going back to the cart and pulling it into the garage.

"Pit stop?" asked Sancho, taking Bill's arm.

"Sure. Want to walk or should I get out the wheelchair?"

"Get the cane."

Sancho put one arm around Bill's shoulder while they retrieved the cane from the T-bird. Sancho held the cane with his free hand on the way into the house to the bathroom just inside the garage entrance. After doing his business, Sancho managed on his own, making it back out into the garage where Bill was inspecting the cart charger.

"Hey, you're doing better. What say we drive over and pick up the clubs? I'd take the cart but it needs charging. There's a late night restaurant with booze near the Octavius recreation center. After we get the clubs we can have a bite to eat."

***

Green's Irish Pub was a block down from the recreation building and the police office where they picked up the clubs. Once inside Green's Pub Sancho saw it was obviously a bar that served food. A man and woman were at the bar pounding down a huge plate of French fries. Both were heavy with butt cheeks overflowing their stools. The sign above the couple on a fake tiki bar roof had a prominent sign with *USA Bar* in large multicolored letters beside a sign *Ice Cold Greenland Ale*.

A few other patrons were in booths opposite the bar. Sancho managed with his cane but also hung on, his arm around Bill's shoulder. After the ride in the golf cart and then the ride here, the odor of fried food mixed with a faint bar smell was relaxing. Sancho wondered if his head injury had jostled his brain being that smells had become so noticeable. Not that he had problems prior to the accident, but now smells were so obvious. Like in the T-bird on the way here he could smell the hand soap Bill had used at home in the bathroom while he waited in the car. And then in the police office, to which he insisted accompanying Bill, there was the smell of doughnuts. Had there really been the smell of doughnuts or was his noggin playing catch with stereotypes? He recalled a bakery from long ago in Michigan called Cops and Doughnuts. And then back at the medical center, he recalled smelling the chlorine on Simone's skin. Smells, and the signs here. An Irish pub with a tiki-roofed USA Bar advertising Greenland Ale. Yep, the world going nuts was shrinking.

On their way to an empty booth, Sancho stumbled a little but caught himself with the cane and hung onto Bill, who also hung onto him. Four guys their age were in a booth and Bill kept him from falling into their laps. One of the guys said, "Looks like he's already had a few."

Bill paused before they slid into the next booth and glared back at the four. "Whoever said that should be wheelchair bound. Rolling chair's in the car. You want me to put you in it?"

No comment, simply some mumbling and the sipping of glasses of beer with foamed up sides. Bill continued glaring at them.

"Okay, okay. Sorry," one of them finally said. Sancho noticed the guy was wearing a tee shirt that had, *Make Latin Villages Great Again*, printed on the front.

"That's better," said Bill.

Sancho pointed his cane toward the guy. "M-L-V-G-A, *Comprende?*"

"Funny," said the tee shirt guy. "He can talk."

Bill slid Sancho into the booth, then turned, stood tall, puffed up his chest. Standing next to him outside the booth, he was indeed Big Bill, Sancho was surprised at how big and imposing he could be.

The guy beside the commenter, wearing a *Where's the Gulf Stream when we Need It?* tee shirt, nudged his buddy who reacted with, "Okay, sorry again. I didn't mean anything. Just trying to be funny."

"He had a couple shots earlier," said the Gulf Stream tee.

"Maybe more than a couple," said another.

"You look familiar. Do you teach a yoga class at the recreation center?"

"That's right."

The *Make Latin Villages Great Again* tee smiled a drunken smile and nudged the Gulf Stream tee, who shoved back angrily.

Big Bill ordered tap beers and shots of Jack Daniels for them both. The bar lady—young, black, a British accent, blue hair—brought the drinks with a smile.

"Thank you," said Bill.

"Jack's getting hard to come by, but we got some last week. Makes me wonder if it's still distilled in Kentucky or somewhere else."

"Could be really old number seven," said Bill. "Maybe the case has a date on it."

"I'll have to check," she said. "Lots of Midwest spirits getting harder to find, especially since the floods. But if the distillery's in the mountains and they can get fresh water…Duty calls."

Three guys who had just come in eyeballed everyone, obviously reading tee shirts, and pushed into the booth across the low divider between rows of booths. They signaled the bar lady and she went to them.

"Here's to the bar lady and all her *compadres* forced to live in Village Nonus," said Bill, holding up his shot glass. "Oh and also to the distillers, the healthcare workers, and the Earth."

Sancho held his glass up, thought a few seconds, but only got out, "Health."

Bill downed his shot in one gulp. Sancho tried, but settled for three gulps and a quick sip of beer.

Bill glanced side to side and up. "Look at all the paraphernalia hanging on the walls in this place, and from the ceiling."

The word *tchotchkes* came to mind, spelled out like he'd read somewhere. Sancho studied what looked like parts of wooden furniture fastened together to look like various animals, one a woodpecker with a table leg beak. Several kitchen toasters had been adorned with cupboard knob wheels looking like vans and camper trailers. A coffee pot with the glass carafe missing had eyes and teeth painted to resemble a monster with an open mouth. Maybe for Halloween, whenever that was. An old microwave had been turned on its back with the door open and made into a coffin with a plastic skeleton sitting up holding a shot glass. The weird word *tchotchkes* stuck in his head like in a cartoon dialog balloon and Sancho tried to recall a memory of its use but could not.

"All this stuff's made from garage sale crap," said Bill. "One time, when me and Bianca were here, she said the place inspired her. She's working on this book called *Things Shall Inherit the Earth*. Not sure if she mentioned it. The premise, I guess, is that all the stuff folks move around, and they think is inanimate, those things are actually—not sure how to say it—she says the things have an identity in another time zone. And get this. The things are the main creatures in her book and we, the humans, along with all the other so-called living creatures in our time zone, are here on Earth to move them around every once in a while. And for the things, once in a while is like every decade or two. Or maybe a century or two. Anyway the things on Earth outlive us is the point."

Sancho took a sip of beer, nodded and smiled to show he understood. The word *tchotchkes* was still on his mind. And what Bill said about things outliving us made sense. Crazy, it did make sense.

The bar lady came by and Bill ordered two more shots. "If you don't want another I'll down it. I've got the body mass."

The three guys at the booth across the divider had double shots. Sancho saw the tray of them delivered. A sudden image. The bar in *It's a Wonderful Life* after George wishes he'd never been born. Nick the bartender saying something about guys coming here to get drunk fast. Bill downed his second shot while Sancho sipped, wishing he could describe the old movie bar scene instead of it simply playing in his head, like his head was a screen with the movie flickering.

"Yeah," said Bill looking around. "All this stuff on the walls and hanging from the ceiling. Bianca and I've discussed it. Over the years, folks coming down here to retire in what they used to consider paradise. All this stuff never goes back north and ends up in garage sales or in warehouse resale shops on the way to the flooded highway. I bet that cane they gave you has been used before. Hell, it could have popped out when one of those floating coffins from a Miami cemetery flipped its lid."

Bill's voice was becoming louder. "Folks in this place live in a fantasy world. They think they can raise the streets and the houses indefinitely. Miami tried and look what happened down there. We live on an isolated island. Only way to get here are the shuttles from the airport and from where 95 ends. Did you know the shuttles have to stop to get checked before they let them in? Of course you didn't know. You came in by crash landing on the seventh. Everyone on the shuttle has to give who they're visiting and the address."

A loud voice came from the booth across the divider. "It's not enough. They should be stricter than that. What if someone fakes a name and address and uses it to sneak in?"

Another voice. "I heard they've already upped security. They scan shoulder chips and even contact the house where the visitor's headed."

"Folks don't want to think about people starving and on the move. Leads to conflict. Bad enough here with our long hot summers."

"At least we didn't get the Gulf Stream petering out like over in Great Britain."

"What's wrong with being cooler?"

"Sure, it's cooler there, but look at the consequences."

"What consequences?"

"There're invaded by refugees in all manner of boats. "Kind of like a reverse Normandy invasion. What if they bring in a new virus?"

"Oh forget about it. Everyone's got something to gripe about. CEOs on islands, climate refugees, Christianity turning into a cult. There's a lot of blame to go around. I remember when I was a kid my gramps took me on a tour of Miami Beach. That section they raised. So when I'm growing up I'm thinking we just raise the coastal cities. And then there are reactors that got swallowed. Nobody talks about the cancers. We were stupid kids listening to garbage cure-alls and dependent on vaccines. Maybe we're still stupid. Like I said, a lot of blame to go around."

"Yeah, Charles, you've said your piece. There's a lot of blame. But this here's our home. Let's get back to being strict in this place. We worked and fought for it. It's our Normandy. We paid for it. It's not like we're a state like Montana or North Dakota who limit the number of folks they allow in. We're not a state. And because there are fewer of us we've got to all stick together to protect ourselves."

Sancho held his finger to his lips to let Bill know the men in the booth across the divider had been listening and Bill's initial comments had most likely triggered their conversation.

"Oh sure," said Bill, much more quietly. "Sorry. Anyway, we're on an island cut off from a world ruined by the Oligarchs. They're on their own islands while environmental refugees search for food and a place to sleep. Where they come from, simply going outside in the heat can kill you. Did you know they're growing crops in what used to be the Sahara? Part of the so-called feel good news, like that's going to save us."

Bill's voice again went up a notch. "I agree with folks up north pushing for taking in refugees. How else they going to survive?"

Bill ordered another round, quieted down for a while. Maybe Jack Daniels doing his job. "I know what you're thinking, Sancho. You're thinking about Simone, wondering how she's doing and here I am spouting off. Sorry."

Sancho reached out and touched Bill's hand. "It's okay."

Suddenly, as if touching Bill's hand had triggered something, a ruckus erupted up at the bar. The couple who'd been at the bar were gone and someone wearing a black hooded sweatshirt leaned over beneath the colorful *USA Bar* sign plastered to the tiki bar straw roof. A young man's voice made demands of the bar lady. A knife! There was a knife! And then, just like that, two cops came in and hauled the young man in the black hooded sweatshirt with a pale white face looking scared as hell away. Bill half stood, reached across the table to grab Sancho's cane, but it happened so fast. Just like that.

"Wow," said Bill. "This sure has become a crazy world. All started with the orange creature and his family. Damn."

Voice from across the booth divider: "Guy wore a hoodie to cover up for the cameras. Robberies are gettin' to be a regular thing since they designated Village Nonus for workers."

Another shot downed by Bill. Sancho saw the three in the other booth had another round of doubles. A round on the house from the bar lady announcing that her alarm system and the fact the village police station in the recreation center was just around the corner did the trick.

"You know what?" asked Bill.

Sancho was looking at his own new shot, then looked up to Bill. "What?"

"The big hoo hah at my last yoga class was about this proposal to limit houses here to four people. If you want more in the house, got to get special dispensation. Four people, in houses with all those extra rooms!"

A guy from the booth across the divider: "It's the only way to keep squatters in hoodies out!"

"Take it easy, Frank."

"Why should I take it easy?"

"You had a few before we headed here. We better get food."

Frank: "Hey waitress! Hey!"

"Jesus, Frank."

"Hey Nonus Lady! Come on over! We're not hoodies!"

Bill stood and looked over the booth divider. "Better tell your friend to shut the fuck up!"

Because of the three—or was it four?—shots Sancho had, everything after that was a blur. Guys standing and arguing while Sancho wondered if he'd be able to stand, even with his cane. Big Bill crashing out of the booth rushing to the next aisle and grabbing Frank, the loudmouth. Bill towering above Frank, grabbing him by his tee shirt, shouting something about using the word *hoodie* from back in the Middle Ages. The other guys holding Frank back and Bill wild-eyed. The cops coming in, the same two—Oriental woman and Hispanic man—who'd grabbed the guy in the hooded sweatshirt, Sancho trying to walk, cane in one hand, holding onto booth seats with his other hand, and falling to the floor. Guys accusing him of being more drunk than their friend, and finally the ride to the police station around the corner at the recreation building for him and Bill. Somehow the others convinced the cops they were the victims. And finally, him and Bill escorted inside by the two cops to the small cell in the tiny police station room in the Village Octavius recreation building.

"Shit!" said Sancho, sitting on a bench in the cell, his cane that might have come from inside a coffin floating on Miami muck balanced across his legs.

"You can say that again," said Bill, his head in his hands.

"Okay...Shit!"

Chapter 19—Dr. Ramen Noodle to the Rescue

Because of painkillers, Simone had slept, waking up a few hours later in the middle of the night. Bianca still sat at her bedside. The lights in the room were dimmed, the shine of Bianca's phone glowing on her face. A beautiful face, in profile like an African statue—thin neck, curly hair atop her head fit for a royal crown, facial profile exotic yet pure, full lips she recalled kissing before falling asleep.

Simone licked her lips, tasted Bianca's lip gloss. Yesterday, it was just yesterday before the golf cart ran into her, she and Bianca had been together in one of the swimming pool shower stalls. The stall locked so the lone old bird sizzling at poolside would not walk in on them. She recalled the old bird ensconced beneath the shaded canopy turning to watch when they came out, perhaps thinking to himself that the two of them had been in the restroom with the single shower stall an awfully long time.

Simone glanced again at the clock on the bedside table. "It says three-thirty. Is that really the time?"

"It sure is, honey."

"So I slept what, four hours?"

"You went under after that last visit from the night doctor. Said by morning your cast should be completely set and they're already going to make you run a marathon. Or at least walk the hallway. And because we arrived so late, they'd like you to be their guest for another night."

"Anything else happen while I was out? Didn't you take a nap in the recliner?"

Bianca stared at her, the shine of her phone on one side of her face. "No napping for me, honey. And yes, something else did happen. Just as well we'll be here another day."

"What? Another sinkhole? I remember that guy's commentary in the emergency room making it sound like our plane crash was being replayed."

"Yeah, I remember that," said Bianca. "But that's not the up-to-date headline of the hour. It has to do with the boys." Bianca put her hand on Simone's arm. "First of all, they're okay. Sounds like some kind of misunderstanding, not between them, between them and the police."

"The police?"

***

The second floor early morning shift had orders to take Simone Martinez for a walk down the hallway; first step of many said the aide, a gal from Tennessee wearing a facemask who insisted Simone call her Sally Sue. The walk was limited to the second floor, a circuit around its periphery. It was obvious Sally Sue was trying hard to be cheerful. Simone recalled her and Bianca the day before at Winn Dixie, the two of them speaking of service workers trying to be cheerful despite the world gone to hell. Of course they didn't use the term *gone to hell*, but these days it was becoming obvious what people were thinking, especially young people like Sally Sue. Young people no longer bothering to ask, *"What were you thinking?"*

Simone recalled the old white dude from the pool and the old white dude at Winn Dixie. It could have been the same guy. What made it seem so was the looks on their faces. Even though the guy at the pool was too far away to fully catch his expression, some guys here in the Latin Villages had a common look. She'd seen it on a face at the Village Sextus party while others were fighting on the lawn. An old dude trying to gin up the anger with, *"What good are solar cells and vaccines when we're all this close to the grim reaper?"*

Perhaps it was the same all over, regardless of race. The old men in the world, each in their own way, giving a look to strangers that could have come from the Stone Age. An elder with squinting eyes looking out from the cave his tribe took over, or drinkers scowling at some other guys at the next both over at a local bar.

During the walk with Sally Sue, Dr. Juli Janko paused behind the nurses' station to watch. Dr. Juli pulled her mask down and said Simone's gait looked good and asked how she was doing. After a brief conversation, during which Simone found out she'd probably be released next day, Dr. Juli went on her way.

Farther down the hall, Simone saw a familiar face. She could not recall the name but remembered her and Sancho on the plane looking across at the cockpit attendant. As she was being walked, Simone suddenly recalled the cockpit attendant's photograph on the plane's bulkhead. Yolanda. And here was Yolanda, the cockpit attendant, standing outside a second floor room wearing hospital garb, but also wearing a blue headscarf like one Kimmy sometimes wore. Simone had Sally Sue scoot her ahead towards Yolanda. They stayed at the requisite distance posted on signs all over the medical center.

"You were on the plane," said Simone. "I remember you were the cockpit attendant."

Yolanda stared at her, a look of concern—or was it fear? "Yes, I was there."

"How are you doing?"

"To be honest, I was not doing well. And then…"

Simone looked at Yolanda standing there, nothing apparently wrong with her. "What do you mean?"

"Yes, I may have injured my back, and my arm had been in a sling, but I am better now. They've done neurological tests and all seems good. What is your name again? I recall you and your husband in the plane, but not the name."

"Simone Martinez."

"Your husband—?"

"He's fine. They already released him. Speech difficulties due to the head injury and a possible stroke, but otherwise okay." As she said this, she wondered how Sancho and Big Bill were doing. She and Bianca had been told they'd be allowed to sleep off their binge and unless someone pressed charges.

Sally Sue, the aide behind Simone, gave her a nudge, a hint to keep walking. Simone protested. "Wait. I'd like to stay here a while. How about you come back for me in a few minutes? Communication therapy, right?"

After Sally Sue left with a promise to return, Yolanda invited Simone into her room. They sat in chairs on either side of the bed.

"Why are you still here?" asked Simone. "I'd think they would have released you by now."

"The airline keeps me here."

"What do you mean?"

"They need me to answer questions about the crash landing. They say they are doing me a favor because, where would I go?"

"Are they trying to place blame on you?"

"They are doing whatever they can to take responsibility from themselves."

"Has anyone come to help you?"

"Only doctors. Dr. Janko, a neurologist named Dr. Pierce, and another doctor, Dr. Noodle."

"Dr. Noodle?"

"Actually his name is Dr. Ramen, but everyone calls him Dr. Noodle."

They both laughed. A moment suspended in time. Simone looking across at the cockpit attendant in her seat, and now here they were looking to one another on either side of a hospital bed at an isolated community surrounded by swamp and salt water marshes. Yolanda continued.

"Everything is happening so quickly. It is as though the crash caused time to jump many months. Representatives from the airline and also the aircraft manufacturer have been pressuring me. The only person I have on my side is Dr. Noodle. Investigators tried to lure me to Georgia near the corporate offices. They spoke of a fancy hotel room and the process of taking care of my needs. But I've seen this before. They have computers flying the planes. The only reason they have cockpit attendants is to give them someone to blame if anything goes wrong. It happened to another cockpit attendant last year. By having a person on which to place at least partial blame, the legal teams are able to lessen or even forestall lawsuits. Did you see coverage on that one television station? They continue showing the crash as if it just now happened. I believe it is part of the legal—what do you call it?—wrangling. Yes, the legal wrangling works up a fever in media friendly to their interests, making the crash into something human. And as the coverage continues, the public begins to suspect that perhaps the crash really was caused by a human."

"Yes, I've seen it. I wondered why they were giving the crash so much repeat coverage. At first I thought another crash had occurred."

"It is their way," said Yolanda, fingering the ends of her scarf. "At least this is Dr. Noodle's opinion. They keep showing the video of our aircraft digging into the soft soil of the golf course, many praises provided to the computer systems able to land a craft on a golf course, a landing that might have been less damaging to life and property had it not been for human error. Perhaps they refer to the man in the golf cart who crossed in front of the craft. But instead of saying this, they simply say human error."

Yolanda took a deep breath. "I'm so glad I've been able to speak with Dr. Noodle. He has become my lifeline. In these few days he has helped me so much. He has a friend who is an attorney, and through Dr. Noodle I am getting important advice. Most important, I am advised to stay where I am. Dr. Noodle has given opinions to medical center staff who trust him. At first I was almost convinced to go to the corporate offices in Georgia. I wanted escape from this circumstance and God sends rescue. How can this be? I have no relatives in this country, I was an outcast from my immediate family, and now I do not even know if my extended family survived the last typhoon. The world is committing suicide, using human technology and disease as its weapons. Time means nothing, and to that I admit…Wait. Why I'm I telling you all this?"

"Because we, the women of the world, need to confront what's been done to our Mother Earth, mostly by men."

Yolanda began weeping, using her scarf to dry her eyes. Watching the tears and thinking about what Yolanda had just said, and about Kimmy and the grandchildren she'd never have, and about Sancho, barely able to speak, sitting in a jail cell, Simone also began weeping.

Bianca, who had apparently come looking for Simone suddenly came in, saw her and Yolanda weeping, and immediately fetched a box of tissues. "Here, honeys. No need to speak. Any friend of Simone's a friend of mine. I've seen this a lot lately, even down here on this old fart island, farting so much more because protein is hard to come by and they eat beans. It's not right. A seemingly normal conversation suddenly brings on tears. I don't blame you gals, no matter what it was you were talking about. Even if Simone was telling a joke at my expense, I don't care because there are times when all of us need a good cry."

Simone blew her nose. "I'd never tell a joke at your expense, Bianca."

"I'm just saying," said Bianca, fetching a tissue for herself.

Simone introduced Bianca and Yolanda. Simone and Yolanda remained sitting while Bianca watched over them from the foot of the bed, offering more tissues, water, whatever they needed. Eventually Bianca sat on the edge of the bed.

Yolanda smiled. "It is my fault, Miss Bianca."

"Just Bianca is fine."

"It is my fault. I was highlighting the past days since the accident. I was telling Simone how time has seemed to expand. So much happening in so short a time. One day I am in various planes flying over the land, and next day...Sometimes it becomes impossible to absorb what I've seen from the air. Desalinization plants under heavy guard, fires in areas that were once wetland, pockets of refugees on the move, and cities denying them entry.

Sometimes they die. I've seen bodies. I've seen groups stranded near the coasts, refugees stranded and holes dug. We were told by the airline we might see these things from the air. But airline schools train us to stay quiet. Keeping quiet while watching the Earth consume itself eats at my soul. I needed someone with whom I could speak. I know it may sound absurd, but I have met a man I am most fond of. His name is Dr. Noodle."

"His real name is Dr. Ramen," said Simone. "But everyone calls him Dr. Noodle."

"That's refreshing," said Bianca. "So much craziness in this world. I like the name Dr. Noodle. Speaking of crazy, not long ago Simone and I found out our husbands are in jail."

Yolanda opened her eyes wide. "What happened? Did it have something to do with the plane crash?"

Bianca leaned back on the bed, propping herself up on her elbows. This morning back in Simone's room she'd changed into a wraparound skirt from her bag, her long legs draped over the edge of the bed, legs swinging because the hospital bed had been raised.

"Long story short," said Bianca. "It could have been partially due to Simone's husband's injury in the crash landing. His head trauma and maybe stroke affected his speech and balance. He can walk but he stumbles. According to Big Bill—he's my husband—the two of them were in a bar and took issue with a group of loudmouths. Apparently, just when the police arrived, Sancho had gotten to his feet, and with Bill helping him, the blame game that ensued went in favor of the loudmouths on the assumption Sancho was drunk, when in reality, according to Bill, Sancho was the least drunk of all of them and simply wanted to make it into and out of the place under his own power."

Simone added, "Yes, anyway that's the story. The police said they'd call when Bill's in shape to drive his T-bird."

All three sat silent for a while, at first smiling, then with serious looks. Especially Yolanda, who began speaking.

She turned to Simone. "I am so sorry for your husband's injury and for your injury."

Simone pointed to her cast. "I didn't get this on the plane. I got this yesterday when a golf cart ran into me."

Yolanda looked a little surprised. "Regardless. I am still sorry, especially for the two who died because the craft split apart where they sat. I know the crash was not my fault, yet I am still sorry. The world moves much too fast toward the abyss. The homeland of my ancestors is already beneath the sea. When I was a girl I'd so much wanted to visit there, to simply touch the soil and visit the graves. But that possibility has been rushed behind me like a spirit pulling strings from below. Now, instead of the past, there is only a foreshortened future with nations swapping territory without regard for the populations remaining. Even in this United States, how many states have seceded and how many more are to come? Yet here, on this island in central Florida, perhaps I have found my deliverance."

Yolanda paused, looking to Simone and Bianca, then toward the room window before continuing. "It is so dark out. Earlier I heard there is a storm coming and the entire morning will be dark. Yet, even though this morning the world is a dark place, I hope you can understand the hope I now have. I didn't know where to go or what to do. But here on this island, not having to worry about my future generations, because I have none, is a blessing. It has been difficult for me to come to terms with this. No future generations for me because my womb has been barren."

Yolanda paused, dabbed at her wet eyes. "And now, there has been a radical shift. I can barely believe it myself. You see, in the last several days Dr. Noodle and I have become very close. Although he is a doctor here and has a rental home in Village Nonus, his time allowed in Florida is about to expire. He will be forced to go elsewhere. He does not want to go elsewhere. His family roots are Sub-Saharan Africa, but long ago the desert expanded into the area that was once his home. His forebears have dispersed and disappeared. In this way we share the same story, the family prior to us disappearing we know not where. So here we are, sharing important goals, neither of us with family we can locate. We both feel close to medical center staff, and time is short. He jokes the plane crash was planned by the gods. He says my name this way, 'You landa. You landa here to be with me.' I'm sorry. I've gone on much too long. I needed to tell someone. Dr. Noodle and I are going to be married."

Chapter 20—Lockup

Because the Village Octavius police office was a single room with a four by eight cage-like cell in the corner, Sancho, Big Bill, and the two officers on duty had little privacy. The officers, Houston, a dark-skinned oriental woman with buzz cut hair wearing a crisp tan uniform, shirt, and shorts, and Mahoney, a skinny white guy also with buzz cut and wrinkled tan shirt and shorts, sat on either side of small desks placed face-to-face against a head-high divider. A miniature wall screen on Officer Houston's divider displayed a local news channel with the sound off and captioning on.

Officer Houston, whose back was to the cell, was the same officer who'd hustled them out of the emergency room when the hard-of-hearing old goat who'd run into Simone with his gasoline powered golf cart was brought in. The same officer who'd left a note on Bill's golf cart that the clubs could be picked up at the police office. Sancho and Big Bill had picked up the clubs before going to the nearby Green's Irish Pub and USA Bar. Instead of eating, they'd overly imbibed within hearing range of other overly imbibing dudes with mouths too big for Big Bill's patience.

A short while ago Officer Mahoney escorted Sancho and Big Bill to a pair of unisex restrooms in the darkened hallway, the recreation center being closed except for the police office. Sancho's wheelchair was still in the back seat of the T-bird in the pub parking lot. But Sancho wasn't doing too badly, holding his weaker leg up with the cane provided by the medical center, the cane that might have floated out of a surfaced coffin. Bill was the one who'd really overdone it at the USA Bar in Green's Irish Pub. Officer Mahoney had to help Bill along with Sancho trailing behind on his cane. Back in the cell, Officer Mahoney gave them both hydration fluids and protein bars with Officer Houston looking on.

"I contacted your wives a while ago," said Houston. "They're aware it's not serious and we'll continue taking good care of you until it's time to go. Might as well take advantage and lie down. And you, Bill, Bianca says drink plenty of fluids."

Bill stood bent over because the cage-like cell was only six feet high. Finally he sat down and held his head, "Yeah, I will."

Houston turned to Sancho. "Mr. Martinez, you remember what you said when we got to the pub?"

Sancho could not and shook his head.

"You said, 'Houston, we've got a problem.' Not the first time I've heard it, but this time it's a good sign regarding your speech coming back. Right?"

Sancho nodded and said, "Right."

She turned back to Bill. "Could be a blessing in disguise for you two. You retrieve your clubs and cart, you go to a bar and hang one on, and Sancho gets his speech back."

"Well alrighty then," said Bill, holding his head with both hands.

"Well alrighty then," Houston repeated as she went back to her desk.

On the other side of the small divider Mahoney craned his neck. "Houston, you look out a window lately?"

"How can I? There's no window in here."

"I looked when I took our guests to the john. Darker than hell out."

"It's dark because it's still early morning. Nowhere near quitting time."

"Yeah, but it's darker than usual and there's lightning in the distance. You should switch your screen to non-local news. Says a serious storm's brewing for counties north. We should keep an eye on it. The other thing, Houston, we may have another problem. The fossil fuelers are out."

"This early in the morning?"

"Old farts get up their dander early."

"They'll have to put up their side curtains if it rains. Maybe they'll asphyxiate themselves."

Mahoney uncraned his neck so only the top of his buzz cut was visible behind the divider. "Could be a really humid day if the storm soaks us. But, how bad can it get seein' it's January? Nothing except local weather on the news. Locals don't get any climate news."

"Feel good news," said Houston. "Everyone knows it's too late for climate news."

"Yep, don't want to get retirees worried about summer or viruses or anything else. I wish we were at one of those retirement places in Montana or North Dakota."

"They've got their problems."

"Yeah, but at least they're not here or down near that Miami Beach seasteader enclave on oil derrick stilts. I see some folks from the shack towns on that new Coral Springs sandbar tried to climb the stilts. A couple of them dead. Haven't you put on the real news yet?"

"It's too depressing," said Houston. "Even that story we saw about submersible tours of Manhattan is depressing when you think about it."

"Yeah, most of us don't like to think about folks starving or on the run. Crazy all over so we escape into our cocoons of feel good news. But sometimes it's hard to tune out. News from Orlando's even creeping me out. Hijacked trucks and barges, dead kids. Shit, one of these days they'll come right up the causeway and bust down the gates. Maybe during a storm. Maybe during today's storm. Everyone's watching the weather and here they come. Houston, did you switch to the real news yet?"

After Houston switched channels the screen on the divider showed a photograph of a very old man with a sour look on his face.

Big Bill, who'd been sitting now stood hunched over. Sancho could see Bill had been sobering up while listening to Mahoney and Houston. Now, from the look on Bill's face, he knew Bill was getting agitated, and for reason.

"Hey," said Bill. "Isn't that the old guy who ran into Simone?"

"Yeah," said Houston. "Officers over at East Side Villages Medical Center police office decided to charge him. I wasn't sure if they would being he's a hundred and two."

The text below the photograph running along the bottom of the screen mentioned an "accident" at the path alongside one of the village golf courses, asking whether the old man was at fault or it was a matter of careless pedestrians crossing where they should not.

"Why the hell is the word *accident* in quotes?" said Bill. "Both Bianca and Simone said they'd stopped on the cart lane to retrieve something and the guy was looking the other way and speeding."

"Relax," said Houston. "Accident's in quotes for good reason. The guys over at the medical center office will get to the bottom of it."

"Not if these fossil fuelers have their way," said Mahoney from the other side of the divider. "Switch over to the local sin city channel. Three I think."

Houston touched the bottom left corner of her screen. It changed to a group of old Caucasian men sitting inside their golf carts on the entrance road to East Side Villages Medical Center. The morning was very dark and the golf carts were beneath bright overhead lights. The men in the carts wore red, white, and blue particulate filter facemasks, and a couple of the carts displayed American flags snapping in a strong breeze. Side curtains on the carts crackled in the wind. The text running along the bottom of the screen said, "Activist group fossil fuelers protest police custody of Byron Blakesmyth." While the text was running at screen bottom the image alternated between the photograph of the old man who'd run into Simone and the live feed from the entrance road to the medical center.

"How crazy can these guys be?" asked Houston. "And so early in the morning."

"As crazy as you want them to be," said Mahoney from the other side of the divider. "Those are the guys who have ancient souped up gas-powered carts hidden at the backs of their garages."

"Looks like they've dug them out for a morning ride to the medical center," said Houston.

"The old goats are using storm news for camo," said Mahoney.

Bill was a little wobbly but managed to push open a one-foot by half-foot door flap apparently used to handcuff prisoners crazier than they were. Sancho remained sitting. Bill leaned forward holding the door flap open. Both stared at the screen and listened to Houston and Mahoney.

"I thought those guys would have died off by now," said Mahoney.

Houston leaned back in her chair, hands behind her head. "Most of them have. Remember that fire and explosion in Village Primus a few years back? Oh, wait a minute. You weren't here yet."

"Yeah, but I heard about it."

"Right, three houses destroyed because a fossil fueler from a couple decades back, when they were first building up the elevation of this place, had a huge gas tank secretly buried beneath his garage floor. Guy dies, wife dies, new owner moves in unaware of the thing until he smells gas seeping out from beneath the house."

"How'd it ignite?"

"Grill on top of the seepage. One thing leads to another. Something about the increased ground temperature, pressure building up over time, improper venting, the guy being drunk thinking a shadow was a wild African dog and tipping over his grill while he goes for his gun. Anyway the whole thing goes up. Not quite an explosion, more of a flash fire."

"Was it the high octane stuff they use to beef up their carts?"

"I guess."

Bill, standing against the cell door asked, "Where do those idiots store their gas now?"

Houston swiveled her chair around. "Inside their garages in tanks."

"Isn't that illegal?" asked Bill.

"Not as long as they use safety tanks both on their carts and whatever tanks are in their garages. They're not supposed to store more than ten gallons, but I've seen some of their gatherings, especially when that Exxon station over on the other side of the highway gets a fuel delivery. Supposedly—I haven't seen it—someone on the other side of the swamp has a boat and the old farts have cart trailers they use to bring multiple portable tanks for fill-ups. I'm told it's more than ten gallons, but the group says it's for all of them. The captain says we can watch when they drop off the tanks and keep track of what goes into individual garages, but not to push it."

Mahoney from the other side of the divider joined in. "We should use drones to do the counting."

"Captain says it'd simply piss off anti-drone residents. You still got that one of yours?"

"Yeah, it's on standby. As for the anti-drone farts, I suppose it's a matter of waiting for them to die off."

"Like a lot of things in this world. Population control. Fewer being born than those dying off."

"You're not going to start in on extinction and all that."

"Not now."

"Good. I'm tired of History Channel stuff about past pandemics and Oligarchs isolating themselves on pirated cruise ships. The other day I saw an expose about solar and storage battery corporations having been taken over by Oligarchs. Did you see that program about the warehouses they've got at the new ports since the last ice sheet slide? It's depressing seeing folks they hire to guard their warehouses and ports. But at least it gives them a place to live."

"Better than those wild guard dogs they tried," said Houston. "But families living in warehouses?"

"They've got freezers, TV, and plenty of gas for generators if the solar fails."

"Speaking of Gas, have more beans, why don't you?"

"It's protein, Houston. Me and the other smart folks in our village have put up trellises and grow our own beans. We save rainwater and even sewer water to grow them."

That's why your farts are so pungent."

"Smart ass. Did you know Sulfur Dioxide is a tiny component of farts on purpose? We evolved it so our sense of smell could warn us?"

"Who'd ever have kids these days besides the Oligarchs and the families guarding their stuff?"

"I know of a few. They're hunkered down in the mountains."

"With plenty of supplies?"

"Yeah, especially water."

Sancho watched Bill standing bent over against the flap in the cell door watching the news feed. Then he looked back to the news feed himself. More coverage of the plane crash. At first there was a shot of a crane on a bed of plywood with a trail of plywood where it had crossed the golf course. And then there were multiple shots of the crash. The crash playing over and over viewed from personal phones, from headsets, and from drones. It was as if the accident had just occurred. Even the text repeating at screen bottom seemed to be from that day, naming the course, the hole, the flight number, the aircraft model, speed, ETA, all of it. At first there had been a small bit of text below the running trailer saying today was the two-week anniversary of the crash landing. But then the crash landing was shown again and again with no mention in the captioning of this simply being the anniversary. The commentators saying things about the breaking news. All of it playing over and over as if it were happening before Sancho's eyes. The video began again from the beginning, showing the plane in the air, apparently shot from a drone hovering overhead as the plane glided toward the Latin Villages.

Sancho felt dizzy and closed his eyes. Was he really in a jail cell? Or was he inside the plane's washroom while Simone's out there in her seat. Yeah, visiting the washroom he'd eventually smash his head into while Reverend Murdock prays to Jesus. Murdock groveling at the back of the plane in his goddamned loud and unctuous voice. The voice continuing and still in his head because the idiot is still at it while Big Bill carries him out of the plane.

Sancho opened his eyes and used his cane to struggle to his feet, grabbing the chain link between the bars so he could stand bent over beside Big Bill. When Sancho swayed, Bill put his arms around him and held him up. "Sancho, you okay?"

"Goddamn God and Jesus!"

"Hey you're not having stroke or anything?"

"He better not," said Mahoney. "We're off in an hour."

Houston stood and came to the cell. She opened the door flap and snapped it permanently open. "Let's test him. Sancho, show me a smile. Wait, show me your teeth. Okay, good. Bill you hold him away from the door. Okay, close your eyes and raise both your arms to the sides. Good, good. Now repeat after me. The Latin Villages is a nice place to live."

Sancho was still thinking about the plane crash. Glancing at the screen in front Houston's desk he saw they were still replaying it again and again. Standing straight up he could feel the ceiling of the short cell brush to top of his head.

"Can you repeat what I just said Sancho?"

"The Latin Villages is a nice place to live. But only if you're one-hundred and two years old, or if you're a crocodile."

"Okay," said Houston. "He's okay," she said to Bill who continued hanging onto Sancho, his arms wrapped around him, his chest against Sancho's chest.

Mahoney stood on the other side of the divider. "Hey, we've just been called to East Side Villages Medical Center. Says they need help with the old fart disturbance. Cap's message says hurry."

Houston put on her service cap and handed Bill his phone through the door flap. "We've got to go. You guys should be okay. If there's an emergency you can use your phone. Want me to leave the TV on?"

"Yeah," said Bill.

After Houston and Mahoney were gone, Bill sat sideways on his side of the cell, leaning forward so he could watch the news feed through the door flap. Sancho sat on the other side and stared at the floor. A light-colored tile floor, fuzzy blues and greens, the designs meandering the way the landscape out the plane window beyond

Simone meandered as he looked past her during the approach. The landscape of New Florida half water, the other half a mix of marsh and what was left of land. He recalled Simone telling him about Kimmy flying down on one of the old airliners. Medical emergency, cheap tickets, a special deal because she was in the EPA. But she had to lock in a return seat, and because of her job on the *Shellfish*, she needed to be back. Some kind of deadline he recalled Kimmy saying at his bedside as she bent to kiss him.

Sancho wondered if Kimmy had a girlfriend. She'd come out long ago during one of the political movements calling for partners not to have children. World already too crowded for those in the sub-middle class to have kids. Only the rich on their homemade islands and citadels and satellites could afford kids. The floor tile landscape waved back and forth as he shook his head. Dammit, he wished he hadn't said anything to Simone about Mrs. Hans in Indianapolis. Stupid thing to talk about at a time like that. Murdock's yammering like he had a special back channel to Jesus in the back of the cabin probably had a lot to do with shared confessions at a time like that.

Sancho looked across to Big Bill, his profile maybe Germanic like the profile of Hans, who grabbed Simone by the pussy at the shallow end of the pool. Yeah, a handsome profile with an actual chest and shoulders instead of a middle-aged gut like his. Sancho tried to imagine Simone and Hans embracing behind the pool bar, and as he looked at Big Bill's profile recalled Bill hugging him close earlier when he almost collapsed in the cell and Houston checking him for stroke and the smile on Bill's face when Houston announced he hadn't had a stroke.

Bill had stood again, bent over and staring out through the door flap. Sancho could see Bill was not smiling and that his eyes had widened. When Sancho glanced toward the screen he saw a man wearing a tee shirt with a white crucifix on black background. The man had a flaming torch held high above his head, the old fart pulling his red, white, and blue facemask down and showing his hate-filled face. Beside the man another old fart in a crucifix tee shirt held a sign that said, "Fuck the Fossils, Drill Baby Drill." The trailer at the bottom of the screen said, "Protestors angered by Environmental March." The flaming torch held high blew sideways in the morning wind.

Sancho looked back to Bill. He wanted to say, "Wasn't the environmental march a couple weeks back?" But all Sancho managed to get out was, "Old news."

Bill turned to Sancho and nodded. "Yeah, the crazy fossil fuelers are like a lot of the old farts living here. They get themselves whipped up by old news on Fox III. I sure hope they keep them back from the medical center."

Chapter 21—Conflagration

As suggested by Sally Sue, the aide who'd kick-started walking, Bianca helped Simone with room laps. Lights were low and they paused at the window. The morning was still dark, almost like night. Curiously, a demonstration a hundred yards away at the entry road wound its way toward the medical center. Scrawny trees lining the road waved furiously in the wind, some trees losing leaves. Beyond the trees patrol cars and carts with blue flashing lights strobed the darkness, lighting up masked faces and the bottoms of the trees shedding leaves. When Simone glanced to Bianca she could see the flash of the lights in Bianca's eyes.

"What are you thinking?" asked Simone.

"In this world some get angry with themselves and commit suicide. Others become aggressive."

"Think a storm coming has something to do with this?"

"Brunt of the storm's to the north, staying out at sea."

"Still dark as night," said Simone. "Cops are wearing elaborate facemasks."

"Particulate filters, especially on a windy morning with debris in the air. I've seen days like this before, tropical storms can make the place dark all day."

"Crucifixes on shirts. Doomsayers?" asked Simone.

"They call themselves fossil fuelers. All men, of course. Wives don't let on. Secret society. They tried to recruit Bill. He knows about rituals."

Simone looked back to the flashing lights and saw a flicker of orange flame from a torch amongst the gathering. "Rituals?"

"Hyped up on boner pills?"

They both laughed, then Simone said, "Funny, but not so funny. Like white supremacists."

Bianca smiled, blue lights flashing on her full wet lips. "They might not all be white. I feel sorry for them. They're like lots of folks living here. It's an island in more ways than one. Cut off from the real world. Like our news channels. You'd think it would be obvious to them the Oligarchs in charge are filtering the news. Do they have the same news stations up in Michigan?"

"Different stations," said Simone. "Programmed especially for us. I agree, the news is filtered, and has been for…What? Decades?"

"Seems about right," said Bianca.

"I remember when I was a girl there was still one Grand Rapids news outlet that was part of the Public Broadcasting System. My parents said the station going off the air was the end of news as we knew it. No more news and I hadn't even had a chance to absorb much."

"News filtered through corporations hired by Oligarchs who took over the world. Oil and gas money became solar and energy storage money. They own it all, not surprising they own the media. We're stuck with a US of A, minus a couple states. These days, class clowns don't need international news or climate news. Big distractions no one wants to think about."

Both stared at the scene. Bianca continued. "I see an American flag near the torch, but it's too far away and the wind's whipping it up too much to count the stars. I'm surprised Florida's still a state. Back when settlers arrived—most likely rubbing their hands together with the prospect of bringing over slaves—Florida was a swamp. When they discovered they could use fossil fuels to power their machinery, they pumped sand and drained swamp, making the place into a plateau on top of muck. Alleluia!"

"You mentioned the fossil fuelers have rituals," said Simone.

"Bill says they've got a torch passing ceremony. One guy carries it for a month. Supposed to be an honor. One of their own carries the torch as a symbol of their freedom to continue burning the fossil fuels God gave them."

"Thus the crucifixes on their shirts," said Simone.

"Supposedly some time back the guy chosen was to keep the torch lit all month 'til the next meeting, I guess on pilot light. Be pretty hard in this wind. Bill says they fire it up for each meeting, or for special occasions like riding their carts to some idiotic early morning protest."

"What are they protesting?"

"You saw the news. They're protesting that march in Orlando."

"But it was two weeks ago."

"Doesn't make any difference. Far as they're concerned another march is around the corner. On the news they saw the plane crash, the video like it just happened, like it's live. And because it was an environmental march in which activists try to get someone to do something about the climate and pandemics, they assume folks in the plane crash, being they were on their way to Orlando, were obviously activists."

"Wasn't there news the flight was chartered by evangelicals?"

Bianca smiled. "Is you an evangelical, honey?"

"No."

"You and I know that. But them, out there, all they know, via the official Latin Villages Fox II or III, is you were going to Orlando, period. Full stop."

"That's insane."

Simone felt her good leg cramping up, tried putting weight on her bad leg. Bianca held onto her.

"You okay, honey?"

"I'd better sit down."

Bianca helped her back to the bed. The bed was in low position and they sat together. Simone reached out and held Bianca's hand. "Do you sometimes wish you could close yourself off?"

"Yeah, go hermit," said Bianca glancing toward the window. "I wonder why they're not using drones."

"Forget about what's out there, Bianca. Let's go hermit."

"Okay," said Bianca. "We've got time. First night shift gone and morning shift hasn't begun. I'll close the door, prop a chair against it to keep out staff and roaming hallway drones."

***

At the far end of the second floor in the wing sticking out over the emergency entrance at the rear of the building, rather than the main entrance at the front, another hospital room door was closed with a chair propped inside beneath its handle. Except for the dim morning light filtering through the shades and a light coming from the bathroom the room was dark. A blue scarf hung on the bathroom door handle, the bathroom nightlight filtering through as if through gauze.

There was movement on the narrow hospital bed, obviously two people beneath the blankets, very close together to keep from tumbling onto the floor. The interviews with attorneys and psychiatrists from Georgia corporate had ended and it was very quiet at this end of the wing. The nearby patient rooms were empty and storage rooms locked for the night. Staff at the distant nurses' station was aware the lady at the end of the hall did not need help but probably needed rest after having had so many interviews. Because of a doctor's order they had been advised to turn off monitors and keep hallway drones at bay.

Whispers came from the two beneath the blankets.

"What kind of ceremony can we have?"

"We shall have our real ceremony later. For now we can have a judicial ceremony to make our lives official."

"My fondest wish would be to have our families with us."

"I hope we can do this someday. I do not know how many have survived. Especially with tribal wars over food."

"Was Africa beautiful when you were a boy?"

"Only what I was told. It was already too late for me to be born at home."

"Your family was on the move when you were born?"

"For us home was wherever we could find food and shelter."

"How were you able to go to school?"

"The only way for my parents was to force me to leave them."

"That must have been very hard."

"It was. After finding a sponsor for me, they said they were happy. As part of the arrangement, both were employed at carbon capture storage facilities in old mines. The company provided food and housing. We exchanged correspondence for several years and then…"

"It stopped?"

"Yes, it stopped very abruptly. There was a virus on the African continent. The last of the messages contained no information

as to origin. Only electronic addresses, and then nothing. Some day, if the world gets hold of itself, I would like to search for answers."

"I will go with you on your search."

"We can also search for your family."

"If we find them perhaps we can have a ceremony blessed by family."

"Blessed by them all."

***

Outside the closed door, down the quiet hallway, beyond a side storage area near the elevators full of currently unused virus warning signs, beyond a set of open hallway divider doors, beyond the nurses' station where a single male nurse, an olive-skinned man wearing a mini turban and looking at a screen flashing a video on his shiny smiling face, the door at the far end of the hall over the medical center entrance was still closed. A small drone hall monitor buzzed near the door, paused, and went on its way. Inside the room the two beneath the blankets hung onto one another to keep from falling out of the narrow hospital bed.

"I heard a drone go by," said Simone.

"They're everywhere," said Bianca.

"I hope they don't use miniatures."

"Not allowed according to privacy rules," said Bianca. "I think we're safe. Only a crack-of-dawn nurse on duty and he's been busy with his computer."

"Watching porn?"

"Doubt it. The drone wouldn't like it and neither would the building monitor."

"Pretty difficult going hermit these days."

"Honey, do you care if we're caught?"

"No."

"Neither do I."

"I'm sorry I gave that confession to Sancho about Hans grabbing me at the far end of the pool," said Simone.

"Why should you be sorry?"

"I exaggerated to get even with him."

They were quiet for a time until Bianca spoke.

"Vinny says he might be gay," said Bianca.

"That's the same thing Kimmy says," said Simone.

"Well, honey, what else can kids do in this world? Nobody in their right mind wants to have children."

"Kimmy mentioned a phrase coined by her generation," said Simone. "Closing yourself away, as in ending your family line of descent. Not bringing kids into the world leaves a lot of stories untold. That book you're working on, does it have to do with lines of descent?"

"In a way."

"What's the title again?"

"*Things Shall Inherit the Earth*. I thought I already told you."

"You did. I wanted to hear you say it again."

"It a stupid premise."

"I don't think so. Tell me more."

"I told you. The things around us are in another realm and we're here to move them around once in a while."

"But for them a while is like decades or centuries long?"

"That's it in a nutshell."

"But you've got pages and pages. And scenes. You said you've got scenes. You said you work best in the morning."

"I suppose I do."

"Tell me a scene."

"You mean like, tell you a story?"

"Yeah, tell me a story, Bianca."

"All right. It seems silly."

Simone hugged Bianca closer. "Yes, Mom."

"Fine. This scene takes place in one of those storage facilities. You know, long low buildings with storage units behind garage doors. People rent spaces to store their crap. A male voice inside one unit is doing the talking, male because he's a grandfather clock. The grandfather clock's speaking to all the other crap stored in the unit. Because of sea level rise, the facility, once high and dry, is getting hit by a storm surge with waves lapping at the doors."

Bianca lowered her voice a notch to simulate a grandfather clock. "Tell me something folks. Try thinking like a human. Who of you would have thought spirits could exist inside a damned storage facility? Would you have thought it? Or you back there in the corner? Although clichés aren't my bag, it is the bag of folks who visit. 'Always remember and never forget,' they'll say. Every damned one of you here was once held close by one or more humans. Whether on a shelf, in a closet, or even in a garage, held close until they either died or ran out of space."

After a pause Simone said, "Keep going."

Bianca continued in her low voice. "Folks, I mean things, *belongings* is the word of the day, week, month, year, whatever. Okay, okay. You hate when they call us belongings. How about if we call one another Gypsies, as in never settling down? Some of you globetrotters know what I mean. Not the always-remember-and-never-forget variety of cute sayings on wall plaques, but—Dare I say it?—art. There, I said it. I admit art exists in here. But I'll let history be the judge of the fine line between art, kitsch, tchotchke, and junk.

"You've got to admit a lot of us in this particular storage facility aren't worth—How shall I say it?—the powder to blow us to hell. Yes, I'm referring to you, Hell-on-Earth-Harley jacket. I saw you a few decades ago sidling up to the angels in the curio cabinet. You are one gnarly old buzzard. I might be slow, but I'm not blind. This ticker's still got life. You'll find out one of these decades when a new generation unlocks the place and starts tripping around and a fair maiden grabs hold of my mainspring key like she's never seen a grandfather clock before, and no one's watching, and there are no recriminations. Then you'll see how wound up this grandfather can get. It'll be like the joke I overheard in here: 'Given a few months notice, I can still get it up.' Only for me it's a few decades notice. Haha.

"Speaking of decades, is it me or does anyone else miss a good yard sale? Be honest about it, if honesty is still possible in this world. Do tell, humans have sure made a mess of honesty. I mean, come on. How the hell long has it been? Time was there'd be a yard sale or garage sale or estate sale every other weekend. First there'd be one on one side of town, then one on the other side of town. Someone moving, death in the family, pandemic, whatever. Gave us the opportunity to listen in on human gossip, as bad as it is.

"So anyway, after decades more go by, folks from a new subdivision need stuff to fill their empty garages and, presto, a bunch of stuff is on the move. As we all know move is the key word here. Without movement, what's our purpose? And why, all of a sudden, are waves lapping at the walls of the storage facility?

"Yeah, I miss those sales. Fresh gossip, fresh air sifting through the dust, cleaning out the sprockets, drying out the wood. What if we got awards for being the most traveled? Most of us are waiting out death. Could be the original owner of the stuff, or whoever was willed the stuff by the original owner, or someone who can't pass an estate sale without dropping a few bucks. But where the hell to store us? There's already too much at home. So, it's off to the storage facility. See, it's not the spirits of the individuals who stored this stuff that haunts the storage facility, it's the spirits gathered in the stuff from every move, every touch, every thought encountered during molecular stability…Wait, don't laugh until you hear the whole story.

"It's a sure thing, written in stone, if you like. Eventually humans, along with their sickness and gossip, will be gone, even the Oligarchs. But we'll still be around, bobbing in the seas. Eventually we'll become sand, soil, and gunk. So, the big question for humans becomes this: who belongs to whom? Do humans own the things? Or do the things own the humans? And if the things own the humans, obviously the master plan is to get rid of humans so things can fulfill their destiny and become one with the Mother."

When Bianca paused Simone said, "You mean Mother Earth?"

"Exactly," said Bianca, "After all matter on this planet becomes one with the Mother, evolution will reboot. That's all I remember for now. What do you think? Be honest."

Simone laughed. "I like it. It's crazy, but I like it."

Bianca turned, lifted her head from the pillow they shared. "You hear that?"

"Waves lapping at the building?"

"No, something else."

"Hold me tight, Bianca."

"I am holding tight so I don't fall on the floor. I mean it. You hear that noise? I think it's coming from outside."

***

At the other end of the hallway behind the other closed door, whispers.

"Perhaps, dear Yolanda, after we marry we can find another place to live."

"But you have a place in Village Nonus."

"It will be good for a time. Did I tell you another doctor is a neighbor? Her name is Dr. Janko. She lives with her life partner Maeve, who works for medical center operating systems."

"I've met Dr. Janko," said Yolanda. "She was the one who admitted me, and also warned me about the corporation."

"Dr. Janko has many warnings. Perhaps because of her partner being in operating systems, she is very concerned that operating systems are taking over tasks meant for humans."

"Artificial intelligence?" asked Yolanda.

"Yes, Dr. Janko and I have discussions. We decided some time ago we will live in Village Nonus only until the day artificial intelligence becomes intrusive. I think you and I should do the same."

"Where will we move after that?" asked Yolanda.

"I am a doctor. Oligarchs and seasteaders need doctors. But I don't think I'd want that. However, those who work at carbon capture plantations and battery storage facilities are isolated and also need doctors. God willing, we will live somewhere in the center of the country to the north where the Great Lakes feed the carbon capture plantations. A place in the open air, away from viral episodes."

"Do you think they would let us move to one of those places?"

"I've already applied. The weather to the north is much better than going west to the solar plants and their battery storage facilities where the sun bakes everything and one must remain indoors. After we are married I will be able to change my citizenship status."

"It will be a dream come true," said Yolanda. "Because of our origins we can put down that our genetic background has made us suitable to live on such a plantation."

"Yes, a wonderful dream. And if that dream does not come true—"

There was a sudden crashing sound and their bed shook. They threw off blankets. He put on trousers and a shirt. She put on a robe and rushed to the bathroom, grabbing the blue scarf and closing the door behind her. She came out a moment later to see him standing outside the doorway. Down the hall the nurse at the station, minus his turban, was running their way. Behind the nurse, several doors opened at the far end of the hall, patients stumbled out, and a drone flew near the ceiling. An orange glow came from one of the doors that had opened at the side of the far hallway. All went quiet, the nurse turning to look behind him. Then the doorway at the very end of the hall beyond the hallway double divider doors blew off its hinges and flames cascaded into the hallway as if a giant torch had been lit. The escaping patients and the nurse flattened themselves onto the floor. The double divider doors, apparently set on automatic, swung closed.

Chapter 22—Jailbreak

Bill and Sancho, bent over at the chest-level cell door flap, gripped the door's chain link. The television screen was a few feet away above Houston's desk. Seemingly endless ads for everything from miniature drones to watch over your property, to freeze-dried vegetables from Canadian farms, to living expense disaster insurance, to attorneys specializing in combating laws allowing climate crisis and pandemic refugees to, as the commercial captioning put it, "Live anywhere they damn well please despite your having worked hard for your home."

The commercials ended and news coverage finally continued with a huge "Breaking News" banner. The video displayed without captioning—the sky gray, police cars and carts with flashing blue lights, leaves and debris blowing in the wind, idiot old men with drooping American flag facemasks driving their golf carts stop and go toward the medical center, cops trying to contain them but allowing them past. One crazy old goat carried a lit torch, its flame horizontal in the wind like a blowtorch. Another had a sign saying,

"Damn The Lefties, Full Speed Ahead!" The police cars and carts escorting the old men stayed on both sides, keeping the carts in single file. A small drone few past and an officer's service cap flew out of one of the open police carts.

"Those crazy fossil fueler fuckers!" shouted Bill. "Disburse them to hell! A cart with a trailer! What the hell's that for?"

The image zoomed in. A running message at screen bottom mentioned gasoline-powered golf carts, some kind of club, and a cart pulling a trailer with extra gas cans. Close ups of a couple old guys behind flapping plastic cart windows, their facemasks pulled down, apparently happy to be moving along in their parade. The parade headed toward the medical center entrance, but police carts veered off to the side, aiming the parade through the parking lot and back out toward the main road. The old guy carrying a torch hung onto the back of the cart pulling a trailer full of gas cans, his crucifix tee shirt plastered to his chest by the wind.

Bill shouted, "Can't they see the idiots aren't following?"

Three of the four carts centered in the group had turned abruptly toward the building entrance. One was the cart pulling the trailer. The torch bearer had leaped from the cart onto the trailer. The running message beneath the image, said, "Police Controlling So-Called Protest," and "Confusion Over Plane Crash Coverage," and "Demonstration in Chaos."

The speed of the gasoline-powered golf carts took the police by surprise. They chased the wayward carts, exhaust smoke in their headlights despite the wind. The camera, obviously on a drone, zoomed in and out as it kept up. The drone suddenly veered upward as the chase headed beneath the lit medical center entrance portico. And then, awaiting the chase to exit from beneath the other side of the portico, a flash, a ball of flame, and finally an explosion.

"Bianca!" shouted Bill. "Bianca and Simone are up there!"

Bill reached through the rectangular door slot toward the desk and the image of fire. With his arm through the slot up to his shoulder there was nothing he could reach.

Sancho looked toward Bill's reach, saw the keys Officer Houston had left on the desk. Beyond the keys the flames on the screen intensified, making the second floor windows above the portico disappear.

"Simone!"

"Bianca!"

Bill turned, worked with his phone, trying to use it as an extension. Sancho shouted something incoherent about calling someone on the phone. Bill shouted back, "Call who? We've got to get out of here!"

Bill continued trying to use his phone to reach the keys on the desk. Sancho held up the cane he'd been holding, pushed its handle through the door flap. Bill saw what Sancho was doing, put his phone away, and took the cane from Sancho.

"The other door flap!" shouted Sancho. "The one for ankles!"

Bill pushed the ankle high door flap open. He lay on the floor and reached out with the cane. He reached the desk chair and pulled it toward him.

Sancho saw a chance. He struggled and shouted, "Desk leg!"

Bill reached through the ankle door slot, his shoulder pushed outside the cell as far as he could reach. He got the cane handle around the closest leg of the desk. He sat on the floor and pushed his feet against the cell door while pulling on the cane. Sancho helped by getting in front of Bill and pushing on his shoulders. Both of them grunting and growling like animals.

A screeching sound as the desk began moving. It was connected to the facing desk and soon the entire dual-desk-divider contraption moved inch by inch toward them. Bill pulling the cane, Sancho pushing as hard as he could against Bill's shoulders. Things fell from an upper shelf and clattered off the desk on the far side.

Suddenly a small drone appeared from the other side and flew toward the cell. "Mahoney here," said the drone in a calm voice.

Sancho reached through the upper slot and grabbed the drone. He pulled it inside the cell, crashed it to the floor, and stepped on it.

Bill was still below, pulling with the cane. Sancho joined him, pushing on Bill's shoulders until the crashing and dragging ended and the dual desk was close enough. Sancho watched as Bill withdrew the cane from the lower door slot, stood and pushed it through the upper door slot. The keys were within reach and Bill pulled them to the floor, reached through the lower slot, studied the two keys on the ring, saw they were identical, reached through the upper slot, found the key slot, tried it several times, turning the key over and over, until, finally, the door to the cell opened.

The drone on the floor of the cell made a noise and Sancho stomped on it before heading out of the cell behind Bill.

***

Village Quatorus was near enough East Side Latin Villages Medical Center and also it was dark enough so Vicki and Ezra Weisberg could see the orange glow in the sky and smoke trailing in the wind out their back sliding doors. They stepped out into the heat of their lanai and then out through the lanai screen door onto the dried out St. Augustine grass for a closer look. Their Cockapoo dog Wenzel, hesitated a moment but followed.

"What do you think it is, Ezra?"

"I think Wenzel should stay inside. No one knows we got a dog except my pot garden in the lanai where he poops."

"He's got to relieve himself somewhere."

"Yeah, somewhere."

Vicki shooed the dog back inside and stared at the horizon.

"Another plane crash?" asked Ezra.

Wenzel barked his high-pitched bark behind them and let out an uncharacteristic low growl as if, after all this time, he'd finally gotten hold of a rat down a hole instead of the leftover crap they fed him. Vicki and Ezra went inside the lanai to comfort Wenzel but continued looking out toward the glow.

"I would think by now, after two crashes in a row, they would have the planes under control," said Vicki.

"There was only one crash," said Ezra. "That news earlier was made by AIs replaying it to keep our minds off our shitty weather and a world gone to crap."

Wenzel whined, jumping up and down as if trying to bite the wind coming in through the lanai. Vicki picked him up and held him. "I forgot. The way they cover news these days it's easy to forget what happened when."

A young woman with long pigtails walked from inside the house and stood with them at the screen door inside the lanai. She wore a black tee shirt with the blue ball of Earth printed on it and a pair of frayed cutoff jeans. She had on a Batman facemask but was barefoot. "Windy out. What's up?"

Ezra turned, then looked back to the glow in the sky. "Your shoes aren't, Batwoman."

Vicki turned. "Greta, don't step out here. Your father dropped his glass out here yesterday. There might still be remnants."

Greta shrugged her shoulders. "It's early in the morning and Wenzel's our only guest. We lock him and muzzle him if and when we get real guests. Have you two been drinking already?"

Wenzel ran to the sliding door back into the house, wagged his foreshortened tail back and forth. Greta turned and walked away. Wenzel stayed at the entrance and looked back.

Ezra shouted, "Greta, you left the door wide open! If you're going to come out here put something on your feet!"

"On your feet!" repeated Vicki.

After Greta was gone Ezra closed the sliding door to the house, keeping Wenzel in the lanai with them. "So, aside from your earlier theory about a plane crash, what else could it be?"

"Aliens," said Vicki. "They always have weird weather before aliens land."

"I thought Greta was going to come back out here," said Ezra. "Maybe we should go inside and turn on the tube and see what they have to say."

Vicki followed him. "Greta's communing with that boyfriend of hers. He'll know what's going on."

Ezra slid open the door and paused to let Vicki inside. "Yeah, these young people have that advantage. They commune with the AIs."

"What's that supposed to mean?"

"Artificial intelligence. Machines turn our kids into robots."

After Vicki stepped into the cool house she shouted, "Greta! Don't go out there until you have something on your feet!"

***

Gilbert Kuntz, who'd recently been to the Village Octavius Recreation Center Police Office, assumed he was minding his own business and would not need to return to the police office anytime soon. Even with the wind blowing he was able to squint and see through the main entrance doorway that the police office was lit up like always. The cops inside probably trying to figure a way to hassle him. Okay, so he'd been caught carrying a plastic gun at one of the Bible lesson classes. And there'd been a Bible lesson shooting a couple years back in one of the other villages, something to do with an argument about whether both the first pandemic and climate change were part of God's grand plan. So what? What the hell was the big deal in him carrying a gun? What if he got in an argument and the other guy, or woman, pulled a weapon?

This morning, when Gilbert got to the recreation center mailboxes lined up on the wall along the sidewalk near the main entrance, he parked his cart on the circle so he could quickly run through the windstorm to get his mail. Big deal. Everyone parked there to pick up their mail. Even vegans like him parked there. Not that being a vegan had anything to do with parking regulations, or anything to do with getting a summons for carrying a plastic gun, but Gilbert couldn't help wonder. With so little red meat left in the world, everyone except the Oligarchs was grilling the artificial plant and fungus-based crap. After zipping himself out of the cart he upped his facemask and ran through the wind to the mailbox wall. Within the mask he could still taste coffee as he swished his tongue around his real and implanted teeth.

While Gilbert hung onto his mailbox door—number 53—sorting through his mail, being careful not to let any blow away in the wind, and wondering if the Post Office Department would really close shop like a lot of pundits said, because all they seemed to deliver these days was addressed to post office box owner, two men came running out of the main entrance. Trouble was the two men, profiled against the dark morning sky, were on one set of legs.

The big guy leaning into the wind doing the carrying was that Hulk Hogan look-alike he'd seen on the golf course. The smaller guy being carried, although he wasn't really that small, was baldheaded and pointed ahead down the sidewalk with a cane. The big guy's legs carried the two of them pretty damn fast. Gilbert paused before closing his mailbox and shouted out, "Wowee, boys! Wowee!"

Gilbert slammed his mailbox and pushed a few of the buttons because who knew if maybe the box saved the last entry, or if one of those miniature drones had watched and someone after him might get into his box later on? Clutched to his chest was a stack of flyers for everything from solar panel washing to golf cart battery replacements to whole house virus filters. He squinted and headed back to his cart.

But there was a problem. The two guys running on one pair of legs got to his cart, the big guy threw the smaller guy aboard, and the big guy climbed over the smaller guy and next thing Gilbert knew his own golf cart was speeding away, its open side panels flapping and a trail of dust in its wake.

"Officer Houston, we have a problem," he said aloud, knowing the main officer, the female who hassled him about his plastic gun, was named Houston.

Gilbert ran, maybe not as fast as the Hulk Hogan look-alike, into the recreation center and down the hall where he could see lights shining out from the police office. Once inside he thought maybe he'd find a body. Heck, the desks were all messed up, pens and paper and all kinds of junk like photos of loved ones on the floor. Gilbert took out his phone. He pushed the emergency button, trying to figure out just what he'd say to whoever answered. Behind him in the tiny cell something buzzed. When he turned he saw a small drone on its back. A bent prop was attempting to spin, lifting the drone up and down as if it were humping the tile floor. He stepped closer and the drone, in a garbled voice, muttered, "Six feet back, please." If it wasn't for his cart being stolen, Gilbert was certain he would have smiled.

***

Yolanda held Dr. Ramen's hand tightly as he pulled her ahead to the emergency room exit at the back of the medical center. They'd taken the stairs down with several other patients and a couple orderlies on staff. The orderlies grabbed patient wheelchairs at the bottom of the stairwell and headed back up. Yolanda had seen orderlies carrying one patient in a wheelchair during her time in the medical center and assumed they were headed up to get patients who could not manage. An uncharacteristically cheery woman's voice repeated a message over and over not to use the elevators.

Running had winded Yolanda. "Who would use…the elevator with…obvious fire?"

"Fools would use them," said Dr. Ramen, decisively.

Yolanda liked the way Dr. Ramen took control, pulling her until they were outside.

"Now I must go," he said.

She panted and sat on a curb. "Where?"

"To the front where they will need help."

Yolanda watched him go, in control, tucking in his shirt as he ran. As she sat on the curb separating the emergency entrance from the parking lot with others who'd come out of the back emergency room entrance, she whispered quietly to herself. "Dr. Noodle."

***

The drone flying over the medical center sent its image to the main emergency facility and to the main police headquarters for all of the Latin Villages. Because of their relationship, one of the officers at headquarters and a reporter from Fox II had agreed long ago to share information and videos. The officer justified the agreement because sometimes a news reporter with access to the latest in drone technology had critical information prior to the police receiving it. The officer also justified the agreement because it seemed AI was taking over much of the news. The reporter justified the agreement because she and the male police officer were lovers, and as such, trusted one another to keep their arrangement secret. Well, mostly secret. Because of the seriousness of the incident displayed in the video, she immediately streamed it to her news office where, like magic, it went out to residents without anyone looking at it, not even an AI censorship consultant.

On the screen in their house, Vicki and Ezra Weisberg, along with their Cockapoo, Wenzel, watched the drama unfold with the "Breaking News" line, "East Side Villages Medical Center Explosion and Fire."

"How do they get the news so fast?" asked Vicki.

"Drones," said Ezra.

"I know drones," said Vicki. "But drones belong to the authorities. Why should the news channels get the drone stream?"

"Why not?" asked Ezra.

"I just wondered," said Vicki, petting Wenzel who sat in her lap licking where his balls should be.

"It's all part of the grand conspiracy," said their daughter Greta from the hallway. "She stood in her tee shirt with the blue ball of Earth, but this time she wore no facemask. She used both hands to twirl her pigtails.

"Maybe you should let your mom cut those things one of these days," said Ezra.

"Leave her be," whispered Vicki. "The world is confusing enough as it is without you complaining all the time."

Greta let go of her pigtails and went to the coffee machine in the kitchen. She loaded in a coffee pod and got out a cup. "The world is full of shit," she said. "Why on Mother Fucking Earth you ever brought me into it I'll never know."

Neither Ezra nor Vicki spoke. Greta continued. "I'll tell you why. You both knew about the pandemic. You both knew the fossil fuel industry had messed up the future and you wanted to launch a test module—me—into that future. That way you'd be able to blame someone for something. I've heard you when you have the neighbors in for booze. All of you so-called adults in the room making like you did anything to stop it when, actually, you helped foster it."

The "Breaking News" line below the drone image switched to, "Possible Fatalities In East Side Villages Medical Center

Explosion and Fire." The drone image zoomed in, flying to the side to show the two floors above the portico entrance in flames as fire-fighting personnel sprayed the area beneath the portico with foam. It was obvious from the lick of flames, the trail of smoke, and the wobble of the drone image that the wind was not helping. The drone flew up and over the building and zoomed in on the emergency room exit where patients and staff had gathered. There were a few police carts behind the people and an emergency bus pulled up, apparently to let patients inside the safety of the air-conditioning and out of the wind.

Activity behind the bus got the attention of several cops on duty, and the attention of the drone camera controller. Two men in a golf cart sped across the parking lot, almost running down a hatless cop trying to wave them down. The driver of the cart was broad shouldered. The passenger, a bald man, held what appeared to be a stick out the open side flap, pointing the stick ahead toward the emergency entrance. Neither in the cart wore facemasks. The driver plowed the golf cart into a high curb, the passenger almost thrown out. The cart veered sideways but continued forward. Instead of stopping at the emergency entrance sliding doors, which had been locked in open position, the cart sped through directly into the medical center. The drone swooped lower, trying to zoom its camera inside where the men in the golf cart had gone, but all that could be seen was a rush of people in facemasks escaping the medical center. The people had parted to allow the golf cart through and closed ranks as they came out the door.

The "Breaking News" line below the drone image switched to, "Two Persons of Interest Drive Golf Cart into Medical Center."

Greta, sipping at a steaming cup of coffee, said, "They're probably pissed off virus carriers and have a bomb. You guys should check out the weather. Big tropical depression, heavy rain expected."

After Greta disappeared down the hall, Vicki, petting Wenzel more vigorously, asked, "Do you really think they have a bomb?"

"How in the hell should I know?" said Ezra. "More rain. That's all we need. Still morning. Time for a drink?"

"Of course. No ice."

Chapter 23—Peace at Last

Bianca Washington and Simone Martinez were found in bed side by side. Their husbands, Bill Pisani and Sancho Martinez, designated the two caskets without identification be placed side by side at the funeral home. The conversation leading up to this decision had taken place prior to their final meeting with the funeral director. Bill and Sancho had gotten drunk the night before the meeting, the booze and the shock of the situation putting words into Sancho's mouth, many more words than he'd said during the previous days following the plane crash.

"It's my stroke talking," said Sancho. "The bump on my head knocked in some sense. If Murdock shows up I'll kill him."

"I remember him from the plane," said Bill. "Praying his guts out instead of helping people out."

"Worships death," said Sancho. "Before takeoff in Grand Rapids he said Trump was part of God's plan. Climate change and disease part of God's good old plan."

"Organized religions have become cults," said Bill.

"Simone was agnostic," said Sancho. "I remember her quoting George Carlin. 'The planet isn't going anywhere. We are. Pack your shit, folks. We're going away.'"

After a couple slugs of bourbon, Bill said, "Using past tense for the girls is tough. Bianca used to say we don't really know about God. We sure don't."

"Simone and I tagged along on Murdock's flight for the tickets. Hard to believe so much has changed in Florida and everywhere else."

"Since the orange one," said Bill, refilling their glasses. "This booze is the color he was."

They both took another slug.

"What if there is an afterlife?" said Sancho. "Simone and Bianca in a parallel universe. What would they think of us getting drunk?"

"They'd think it was the best thing to do," said Bill.

"Good that your son Vinny's coming," said Sancho. "Both him and Kimmy on the same flight out of Chicago."

"Think they'll meet on the plane?"

"Not with assigned seats and security. Maybe we should go to the airport."

"I checked the bus depot. Outbound from Latin Villages not running. Causeway construction. It'll be fixed for the bus back tomorrow. Vinny and Kimmy should meet up before or on the bus, being they both work for the EPA."

"Yeah, they'll look one another up," said Sancho. "You already told me about us not taking the bus to meet them." Sancho pointed to his head. "Still messed up. Like, things from further back coming forward."

"You sound better tonight. Maybe the booze."

"Think that Gilbert guy'll press charges for us swiping his golf cart?"

"If he does, Officer Houston, there will be a problem."

They both tried to laugh, but failed.

Bill got up from his chair, almost fell over, but managed to top up their glasses. Instead of returning to his chair he put both glasses on the table next to the sofa where Sancho sat. Bill wobbled as he marched to a bookshelf in the corner. He retrieved a framed photograph of Vinny and sat next to Sancho. He wiped tears from his eyes with one hand as he held the photograph out for Sancho to see.

"He inherited Bianca's skin color," said Bill. "Totally, 'cause I'm only his stepfather."

"Totally," repeated Sancho. "Stepfather's better than no father."

Sancho leaned sideways, falling against Big Bill's shoulder as he struggled to get out his wallet. He opened it to facing photographs of Simone and Kimmy, held it out to Bill but fumbled it as he broke out sobbing. Bill retrieved the wallet that had fallen between sofa cushions and held it open to the photographs. "She inherited your wife's color."

"Yeah," said Sancho. "Not a spic like me."

They both began weeping.

Before being overcome by booze, Bill and Sancho agreed the caskets should be unidentified and placed side by side. At morning light, after an evening storm, a pinkish glow of Chinese sulfur filtered between curtain slits. Bill found himself lying on the living room floor while Sancho found himself lying on the sofa. Eventually, after struggling into the kitchen and making strong coffee, they sat at the dining room table and agreed they had come to the casket decision during the night. Neither recalled whether it was before or after Bill had brought out Bianca's stash of hashish.

***

With huge street puddles, flooded drains, and reservoirs overflowing, Bill and Sancho realized they'd slept through a downpour. Bill drove the golf cart because its back seating was roomier than the T-bird's. During the trip to the main recreation center where the bus depot was located, Bill drove the cart up on lawns because of the water depth in the street.

The bus was not the usual silver twin rear axle job with a sleek green crocodile painted on the side. This bus resembled an emergency vehicle, red with huge ground clearance. Mud dripped from the fender wells like diarrhea. The high ground clearance bus carried fewer passengers, forcing them to sit crammed together. Folks spewed out onto makeshift wooden steps, adjusting facemasks, gathering belongings, and checking pockets. A few looked back at the bus as if to suspect the vehicle itself of having crossed a personal line.

After a teary greeting in the lobby, with new residents and perspective residents looking on, the four went out to the golf cart parked illegally on a high spot up on the lawn. The cart was closed up, hot inside from the morning sun. Bill turned on the small portable air conditioning unit he'd bought at Harbor Freight. Vinny sat up front with Bill; Kimmy sat in back with Sancho. Both Kimmy and Vinny had single carry-ons, which they held in their laps. Because of a late arrival waiting for the storm to pass, they went straight to the Peace At Last Funeral Home and Crematorium, splashing through puddles all the way.

Inside the funeral home's cool crypt-like atmosphere, the conversation between the funeral director and the four of them was anything but peaceful.

Funeral director, a middle-aged woman in a black pants suit, white shirt, and tie: "I don't understand."

Kimmy, wearing a wrinkled black chemise she'd changed to in one of the restrooms: "I thought it was perfectly clear."

Vinny, wearing a wrinkled gray shirt and black tie, also having changed: "Perfectly clear to me."

Bill: "Perfect, you get rid of the casket labels, put the caskets side by side, and—" He nodded to Sancho who nodded back. "And when it comes time for the cremation, both at once."

Funeral director: "We've never done such a thing."

Sancho: "Why not?"

Funeral director: "It's simply never been done in our home. I'd have to check the state regulations for cremations."

Bill: "Why?"

Funeral director: "The cremation verification form and the stainless steel identification disks have a place for one name."

The four on one side of the conference table and the funeral director on the other side of the conference table looked back and forth to one another for a minute. During this minute both Kimmy and Vinny consulted their phones.

Sancho: "How long a name?"

Bill: "Yeah, how long can a name be?"

Funeral director: "We can support names of any length, of course."

Sancho: "Of course. So, run their names together."

Funeral director: "But—"

Vinny: "I'm looking at Florida law right now. Cremation of two at the same time is legal."

Funeral director: "Let me see that."

Kimmy: "I'm looking at the same Florida law page. I see your printer ID here. Give me the password and I'll print it for you."

Funeral director: "Even if it's legal, they'll need to be cremated separately."

Vinny: "Which method do you use?"

Funeral director: "The alkaline hydrolysis method. As I'm certain you've discovered by now during your research we use it because of its smaller carbon footprint."

Vinny: "How large is the hydrolysis chamber?"

Funeral director: "Certainly not large enough for two caskets."

Bill: "We're renting the caskets."

Funeral director: "But—"

Sancho: "Never mind the buts."

Kimmy: "What's the largest size body your chamber will accommodate?"

Bill: "Why aren't you answering?"

Funeral director: "Because I know where this is going."

Vinny: "Do you really?"

Kimmy: "My understanding from the authorities is Mom and Bianca were already partially cremated in the fire. The medical examiner said they were found...they were found in one another's arms. Someone had to mess with the remains, therefore—"

Funeral director: You don't understand. The bone fragments vacuumed out won't be able to be separated before being sent to the pulverizer. The stainless steel identity disks won't be accurate. It'll be...it'll be a mess!"

Bill: "Some of our neighbors in this dump already pre-cremated them, so that's that. It's final."

Vinny: "If the bottom line is your concern, there are folks living near the equator who get it for free. They simply go outside an collapse."

Sancho: "Do it like we say or we'll set fire to the whole place after we leave."

***

A few neighbors from Village Sextus showed up, along with some folks who'd been in one of Big Bill's yoga classes, including Vicki and Ezra Weisberg and Gilbert and Rhonda Kuntz. The Weisberg's daughter, Greta, also showed up. She was the only one who insisted knowing which casket was which until Ezra took her out in the lobby for a little "talk." The "talk" could be heard in the viewing room.

"It's uncalled for."

"This is the way they want it."

"Confusion?"

"No dear, the families. It's the wishes of the families that the labels are over there on the table with the photographs rather than on the caskets."

"But I'd like to pay my respects to Bianca."

"You are."

"I met her at one of your stupid parties and I'd like to know which box she's in."

At this point, Officer Houston from the Village Octavius police office showed up and helped calm the situation between Ezra and Greta Weisberg by escorting both to an office and closing the door. Vicki Weisberg apologized profusely and both Bill and Sancho said no apology was necessary.

Gilbert and Rhonda Kuntz, who were both at the Palm Tree Gardens seventh hole with Bianca and Bill and witnessed the plane crash, gave their condolences, Rhonda adding that she wished the news stations would stop playing and replaying videos of the crash.

Yolanda Abdul Jabar and her fiancé Dr. Abdul Ramen also visited, Yolanda speaking fondly of Simone and Bianca. "For the short time I knew them, I was inspired by their support."

"I felt a special bond with both of your spouses," added Dr. Ramen. "I will pray for them."

Dr. Juli Janko, who stood behind Yolanda and Dr. Ramen, stepped forward. "I recall meeting all four of you at the medical center the day of the crash. I'm so sorry."

Crazy Phil, who was still being investigated for his role in the plane crash, having driven his Hummer replica golf cart in the path of the landing, did not show up at the funeral home. But someone else did, someone Sancho had said he wanted to kill.

Reverend James Murdock arrived alone and walked straight to the front. He stood before the two caskets, looking confused for a moment. But then he raised his hands and looked to the ceiling of the room as if able to see the deity up there clinging to the ceiling tiles. After a minute mumbling dialog with the ceiling, a few words of which were audible—*revelations, apocalypse,* and *rapture*—Murdock approached Bill and Sancho, offering his hand. Both stared at his hand but did not raise theirs. Murdock lowered his hand, and spoke again to another part of the ceiling. "Many of us who believe in the hereafter cherish it for what it is, a reward for a life well lived. Do you mind if I say a short nondenominational prayer in preparation for the next world?"

No one answered.

"Or perhaps I should recite an afterlife story of comfort."

Sancho looked down and shook his head no. Bill gave Murdock a hitchhiking thumb to get lost.

Finally, Murdock said he was truly sorry for their loss, and mentioned keeping both Simone and Bianca in his prayers. As Murdock signed the guest book at the back, Bill, Kimmy, and Vinny surrounded Sancho, who continued looking down as he said quietly, almost gently, "Dickless asshole."

Chapter 24—After the Storm

The evening following the funeral service, back at Bill's house in Village Sextus, both Vinny and Kimmy said incidents in the world outside were becoming more bizarre. There'd been increased security on their flight, the bus from Orlando was a high ground clearance all wheel drive vehicle with an armed guard, and both wondered how long before airline access would be limited to high officials. News coverage for the Latin Villages and other southern enclaves was obviously being filtered. The most recent human interest news not reported had been the discovery of two refugee infants packed into baggage from Orlando with life-sustaining air supply and fluids arriving in Chicago. Internationally, three corporations were fighting for control of the world's body chip technology as well as remaining life sustaining solar and energy storage facilities. Kimmy wondered aloud if Bill and Sancho should join them, try to get tickets north while they still could. Even after Vinny asked what they would do if the power suddenly went out, Bill and Sancho were reluctant. Their wives had been here, in this house, days earlier. They needed to stay put for a while.

After agreeing to turn off their phones and leave them in the house inside the refrigerator, Sancho, Vinny, and Kimmy followed Bill into the padlocked utility and storage room at the back of the garage. The room was small and they had to squeeze together to close the door behind them. With the lights on, Bill revealed cases of booze and canned food stacked against the back wall. Going from the heat of the garage into the utility room had been like going into a walk-in freezer.

"We'll be fine here for a while. My bank of batteries over there is maxed-out. Lots of sun and clear blue sky before the storm."

"Carbon dioxide taking out the cirrus layer," said Vinny. "With questionable southern hemisphere entities getting into the geoengineering game, the stratosphere and troposphere are boomeranging all over the place."

"It was hazy before the crash," said Sancho. "Probably ongoing fires in Brazil."

Everyone waited to see if Sancho would say more. It was the first time he'd spoken since calling Murdock a dickless asshole.

Bill wiped a tear from one eye. "The solar panels on the roof are in good shape. They're spotless because the girls cleaned them one night."

Vinny put his arm around Bill's shoulder. "So, the batteries are maxed. What about the booze and food?"

"The air conditioning keeps this room even cooler than the house. Good for the batteries and the stash."

"Where'd all the booze come from?" asked Vinny.

"Your mom and I bought it when we first moved here. It's not from a liquor store. There was this garage sale down the street. The folks living there died in a fatal crash in their golf cart. Because it was head-on into a large delivery van, neighbors assumed it was suicide. No seat belts and the way the cart veered off the cart lane and into the road. They had a fund-raiser for the van driver.

"Anyway, the folks die and their daughter comes down here from up north to settle the estate. She has this garage sale and takes me aside, offering her folks' stockpile of booze. The daughter says her folks moved in years earlier and when there was a liquor shortage they stockpiled the stuff. Only problem was, their illnesses, apparently not conducive to drink, caught up with them and left the stockpile pretty much untouched. Anyway, that was the daughter's story. She donated the proceeds of the sale to the fundraiser for the van driver."

All were silent and Bill continued. "I remember me and Bianca being friendly with the couple who stockpiled the booze. They said this place, meaning the Latin Villages, didn't have long on the planet because of subsidence, sinkholes, the sea, a plague, refugees tearing down the fences, or some other disaster. Anyway, that might have been part of the reason for stockpiling. And telling their daughter about me and Bianca might be why they offered it to us. It's mostly wine, but also a couple cases of bourbon, one bottle of which Sancho and I drained."

Sancho held his head and shook it.

"Yeah," said Bill. "I've still got a hangover. But you've got to admit it was good stuff. Can't find good stuff at the Winn Dixie anymore."

"Maybe you should open a side business," said Vinny.

"We figured we could use the stuff ourselves. Better than running our golf cart into a van. Stocking canned goods with long-off expiration dates was Bianca's work."

After selecting several bottles of red and white from the wine cases, the four went through the blast furnace garage. Just inside the door to the house Bill paused, fingering the dog leash with empty dog collar hanging from a hook. Vinny also fingered the dog leash and collar. No one said anything. After the pause, Bill and Vinny swiped at their faces with shirtsleeves and, tucking wine bottles beneath their arms, shut the garage door.

"I guess I can turn the thermostat up a little," said Bill. "I turned it down before the funeral and checked the battery gauge. I do a battery check every morning."

They uncorked wine at the dining room table, poured tall glasses and settled into the living room. Bill and Sancho sat in chairs, leaving the sofa, where they'd sat together getting drunk, for Kimmy and Vinny.

After they settling in, Sancho started it off. "While the plane was going down, the computer voices came on. There we were, the computer voices had spoken. And then me and Simone started in. Crazy. We're confessing to one another about affairs we'd had. Crazy."

"Mom told me a little about it," said Kimmy.

"When was that?"

"I flew down right after the crash, but had to go back. Don't you remember seeing me when I visited in the hospital?"

"I figured I imagined you being there."

"Bianca and I needed confessions," said Bill. "Mostly me. It was one of the women in the yoga class. She comes on to me and...Shit!"

"Better to let it out," said Vinny. "That's why we're here."

"Yeah," said Bill. "Anyway, it was a one shot deal."

"Did you tell Mom about it?" asked Vinny.

"No, but she knew."

Kimmy turned to Sancho. "What about you and Mom? Did you guys feel good confessing your affairs?"

"Not the first time," said Sancho. "We..."

"What?"

"It turned us on."

"Kinky," said Vinny.

They went back into the dining room, refilled their glasses, and returned.

"I should say something," said Bill.

"Is it about your first marriage?" asked Vinny.

"How did you know?"

"Mom said you had a rough time."

"Yeah. Gretchen—that was her name—Gretchen, my first wife, was abused by her father. I didn't find out until a couple years after our marriage. Gretchen got pregnant, and yeah, it was me, but it wasn't easy. Sex for Gretchen was the pits. Nothing good about it when your father comes into your bedroom starting at age six or less and continuing until you're twelve. When she finally told me, she said—and you have to take this the right way—she said she always wondered why he stopped. She wondered if her mom found out, or if it was something else. Something like, at what point, if she stared into his eyes, did he realize he was a monster?"

Sancho, Vinny, and Kimmy were silent, waiting.

"What her father did affected so many lives," Bill finally said. "Intimacy for his daughter and for his son-in-law destroyed, his daughter's health ruined, his grandson murdered by his own hand, although I've always felt it was Gretchen's father who did it. Gretchen had an older brother who'd also been abused and knew about Gretchen being abused, but said he was too young and scared to say anything. He thought Gretchen's mother knew, so there's that. Anyway, one night, a long time ago, right after my son's funeral, Gretchen's brother and I go out on a drunk. We end up at the cemetery. Here were are, son and son-in-law drunk as hell and we find the marker and together—together!—we piss on the grave. And then, after meeting your mom, Vinny, everything changed. I was allowed to be a man."

Sancho leaned sideways, reached over the table between their chairs, and touched Bill's shoulder. They all downed their wine, and after a minute of silence went out to open more. When they returned, Sancho noticed Vinny stretched his arm out behind Kimmy and Kimmy tucked her legs up beneath her. She was wearing jeans and a loose sweatshirt, part of the warm and cozy dress for their pity party.

"I had a gay relationship in college," said Kimmy, letting it sink in. "I guess nothing's shocking anymore. Anyway, it turned out to be platonic. Both of us agreed what we had together was a substitute for a relationship between us and a guy...I mean two guys...I mean two separate guys."

Vinny was next. "Yeah, I hear you. One of my roommates and I...well, no need to go into details. Ditto to what Kimmy said."

Sancho could see Kimmy had moved closer to Vinny on the sofa. She tucked a pillow between them, but leaned against the pillow as if she were leaning against Vinny.

"I should have put on the brakes with the yoga class lady," said Bill. "I remember—and it really digs into me—I remember telling your mom I was going to a buddy's house, details about crap he picked up at Harbor Freight, solar panel gizmos for his golf cart."

Bill tried putting his empty wine glass on the side table. It slipped and he caught it and hung onto it like holding an urn. He put the glass down successfully and clasped his hands out in front of him. "They were like that. Bianca and Simone were like that."

"They loved one another," said Kimmy.

"I remember talking to Mom on the phone," said Vinny. "Simone, Simone, Simone was what she said."

Sancho held his glass in one hand and raised his other hand in the air like a school kid in class. "I know why they loved one another. That's how it's become. Our make believe world with its make believe future. Of course they loved one another."

Bill held up his hand. "Bianca told me about Simone being pissed with Murdock in the hospital praying for you and you lying there not able to say a thing. I could tell then...I mean a thing like that, Bianca telling me a thing like that. I could tell then they loved one another."

"Mom told me about Murdock," said Kimmy. "Take love where you can get it because you're not going to get it from the Murdocks."

Vinny moved closer to Kimmy, pressing against the pillow between them, his hand draped over Kimmy's shoulder. "I remember Mom telling me about that shooting at a pottery class. That and all the recent sinkholes and the encroaching saltwater and subsidence. And then, out in the world we've got refugees. What if the world were borderless? Might be better off because the Earth is forcing the issue. Mother Earth uses big guns, not these puny plastic jobs they run off on printers."

A buzz came from a side table. Bill half stood and opened a drawer. He pulled out a phone, blinked his eyes and looked at it. "Don't worry, this is an old one, not my other one. The news. My neighbor Mitch wants us to turn on local television news."

"Are you sure that phone's old enough?" asked Vinny.

"Mitch is a communications guy. He's got the same phone with a walkie talkie. We were on neighborhood watch for a while."

At first the television screen showed an ad for catastrophic ground collapse insurance.

"They used to call it sinkhole insurance," said Bill.

When the commercial ended there was expanded coverage of the medical center fire. Bill left the sound off. On screen was a video of the protestors. The crazies with crosses on their tee shirts driving their golf carts beneath the portico despite the police trying to stop them. The guy carrying the "official" fossil fuelers torch hanging onto the back of the lead cart, one leg on the cart, the other on the trailer hitch, the torch high in the air blowing in the wind funneling through the portico. The cart pulling the trailer carrying gas cans, another cart with an American flag following. When the lead cart went beneath the medical center portico, the guy holding the torch jumped back onto the trailer and the top of the torch hit the portico ceiling. The video showed, in slow motion, the guy who'd held the torch trying to catch it. But the damage was done. The torch landed on the trailer bed loaded with toppling gas cans. The video stopped there with the ball of flame. There were more captions and trailers, going back to the beginning of the protest. The fossil fuelers on their carts, the counter protestors, the march, the explosion. Collected video, shots of signs held by protesters and counter protestors, patriotic facemasks, fossil fuelers with extra gas, the torch bearer. Bill turned on the sound. A snatch of voices, guys hollering as they approached the medical center, many of them lowering their masks and venting about refugees and their right to protect themselves.

Following the videos, Officer Houston from the Village Octavius police office was interviewed. She removed her cap, rubbed her buzz cut, and told about the husbands of the two killed in the medical center, the husbands being held in jail for drunk and disorderly—putting in a word that she didn't blame them—and the two escaping jail only to arrive at the medical center too late. When the interviewer, a young man who looked all of fourteen, asked about the other victims who'd been in the golf carts, Officer Houston stared at him for a moment before saying, "I don't know anything about them."

After a few shots of the medical center interior, instead of feel good news like usual, coverage moved to conflicts in Europe, the overrun of Hungary and Poland and refugees continuing into Germany. Food shortage was stressed. Bill turned the sound off and said, "We're on an island. If there were land between South America and us we would've been overrun long ago. Sancho and I will be okay here. We've got to collect ashes and figure what to do."

Sancho turned to Kimmy. "You guys go ahead. If things get really crazy, we'll join you."

"I don't have a place, Dad. I'm stationed on the *Shellfish*."

"Yeah, but I won't go back to the house in Michigan. I couldn't stand that."

"When the time's right we'll find another place," said Bill. "Either that or this place will outlive us. We've got booze and food. With four goddamn bedrooms no one will ever buy the place!"

After waiting a moment to see if Bill was finished, Vinny said, "An island in an angry state."

"What state isn't angry?" asked Kimmy.

Sancho glanced toward the screen. The sound was still off but what he saw there caused him to leap to his feet. Reverend Murdock was being interviewed. "Who are we to question God's plan?" was the runner on the screen. Murdock kept talking, looking up while he spoke and waving his hands about as if a spaceship with God on board was coming in and needed landing instructions. Or was he chasing away bats?

This was followed yet again by coverage of the plane crash two weeks earlier. The trailers at screen bottom coming one after the other included speculation about when and if the wreckage would be removed. A long drawn out replay of the whole damn thing. The GC-421 coming in, landing in the mushy underturf of the Palm Tree Gardens seventh fairway. The video in slow motion reminiscent of Scully's landing on the Hudson decades earlier.

Vinny and Kimmy went to the dining room and brought the wine bottles back. As they refilled glasses, the videos played over and over. The world on a gigantic feedback loop, a carnival ride that would never end.

The four of them downed the rest of the wine, empty bottles and glasses placed safely on the coffee table. Vinny put his arm around Kimmy and she put her arm around him. Sancho got up from his chair, sat on the arm of Bill's chair, put his arm around Bill and Bill put his arm around Sancho. The strung-together videos on the screen finally ended with a commercial for an at home vertical farming setup that looked like a childhood tree house without the tree, complete with kids inside a small structure at the top picking and eating cherry tomatoes.

"Where'd they get them?" asked Kimmy.

"The tomatoes?" asked Vinny.

"The kids," said Kimmy. "No one in their right mind has kids."

"Things," said Bill.

"What things?" asked Sancho.

"Bianca's book," said Bill. *"Things Shall Inherit the Earth."*

Outside the front window there was a flash of lightning on the horizon and a drone with a blue light swept in low above the cul-de-sac turnaround and darted down the street.

Chapter 25—Sunset

Whereas other villages had been designed with curving streets and cul-de-sacs, the streets in Village Nonus were set up in grids. Not that the Latin Villages board of directors had been prejudiced; the discussion involved making the most of the available space.

"That plot's the only raised area we have left."

"It's a rectangle. Why do they need curvy streets? They're nothing but service workers."

"We can't help that we need to protect ourselves from outsiders. They're lucky we're letting them live here."

"Yeah, they're lucky to be service workers."

Well, perhaps prejudice had been an issue, especially when the board realized how many service workers they had to pack into tiny homes the size of single-wide trailers for Winn Dixie, Harbor Freight, the Exxon station, the golf cart service outfits, security, medical, construction, etc. In the final analysis the list seemed endless. The only place for Village Nonus, once all the final fencing, security gates, and checkpoints were put in, had to be the rectangular plot tucked into the fence corner where the raised highway from Orlando met the old east-west highway.

Twenty years earlier, prior to the Latin Villages cutting itself off from the world, a barrage of sinkholes caused by subsidence had taken place. The end result was Latin Villages being cut off from its access to Florida's soil. Protests in surrounding communities led to the cut off. Luckily they'd been able to shore up the corner spot for Village Nonus, and raise many other spots needing topsoil in other villages and on golf courses. The Florida statehouse raised hell, but with so many "leaders" from the past and descendants of Oligarchs living there, and having lived there, Latin Villages had a lot of clout. "What about us retired folks?" no longer cut the mustard. But Latin Villages was so large—even having a former state legislator nicknamed Colonel Mustard as a resident—the new clichéd phrase became, "We worked for it and we deserve it." Of course, in Florida and in the other states, many others had worked for it and certainly didn't get it, much less deserve it in the minds of Latin Villages old timers.

Despite the history of how Village Nonus came to be, its residents seemed satisfied to be there. Yolanda Abdul Jabar Ramen— the last part of her name having recently been added—was very happy. She had moved in with Dr. Ramen shortly after their civil wedding ceremony in the judge's chamber of the main recreation center. Gone were the interviews by corporate airline representatives. Gone were the endless flights as a cockpit attendant and living in temporary housing. And for Dr. Ramen, being able to extend his residence was something for which both were thankful.

Although some neighbors and medical center associates of the doctor considered theirs a marriage of convenience, Yolanda knew she and Dr. Noodle—this had become her at home pet name for him—were truly in love. Once they married, not only was Dr. Noodle able to extend his US stay, he was able to enter into a long-term lease for the Village Nonus house he had rented for two years at the dead end of the street named, of all things, Consolation Way.

Dr. Noodle was also very happy. He'd tell Yolanda of his happiness each evening as they sat in the small corner lanai. Because his family roots were Sub-Saharan Africa and hers, several generations earlier, were Palestinian prior to the breakup of her homeland, both became acclimated to the heat. They assumed this was a result of their genetic makeup. Sometimes they even enjoyed the heat, especially after a long day with Dr. Noodle at the medical center and Yolanda at the Winn Dixie, where she'd gotten a job maintaining the new vertical farming unit on the roof.

For both, Latin Villages had become their homeland. Hot, yes it was hot, especially in summer. Sinkholes, yes there was always the possibility of a sinkhole taking their home. But their families had disappeared into the confusion of the world and there was no finding them. Having lost touch with forebears was something they shared. In a way it was as if they had disappeared. They had successfully found their island. For as long as it lasted, they were thankful, saying evening prayers at the prayer hour, thanking God, and whatever other gods there might be, and then sitting and watching the red sunset and talking.

"I am so happy," Dr. Noodle would say.

"I am also happy," Yolanda would say.

Dr. Noodle would take her hand and hold it. "I say it again. As I say it every night. The gods planned the plane crash. You landa, you landa, you landa, here for us to be together, Yolanda."

Yolanda would squeeze his hand. "The environment may be fragile and Earth in protest, yet we are complete. You still remind me of my uncle, although much younger."

"Your father's brother affected his brother, making him less strict and bringing joy to the household."

"With uncle around my father was kind not only to me, but to my mother."

"This makes him a special person, Yolanda. There are a limited number of special persons in the world."

"My Noodle...you don't mind I continue calling you that?"

"Not at all, Yolanda."

"My Noodle, at first, back in the medical center when you asked about details of the plane crash, I worried you had been told to do so by the airline."

"They asked. I felt it an insult."

"My Noodle, as you are one of the special persons on Earth, I felt the two women killed at the medical center were special."

"Special souls," he said.

"Special souls," said Yolanda. "Their light is gone just as the sun is gone."

"But it will return in the morning."

"Soon the bats living in the houses you constructed will be out catching insects. I'm glad you made houses for them. The bats are like us."

"Yes, we are refugees who have found our home."

"To bed, My Noodle?"

"Yes, to bed."

After dark it clouded over, another storm moving in from the west, more bathtub warm Gulf water needing to be dumped. Inside her Village Nonus house, Dr. Juli Janko stood at a window. The lights in the house next door went out.

Juli called out to the bedroom. "Yolanda and Dr. Ramen have retired."

Maeve answered from the bedroom. "I enjoyed dinner with them the other night. We'll have to have them here."

"You can cook up something from the garden," said Juli.

"I hope the rain tonight's not too heavy," said Maeve.

"Radar shows a quick dump," said Juli.

"You coming to bed?"

"I'm coming."

Outside a security cart drove past on the raised road on the other side of the fence at the Village Nonus Consolation Way dead end. Beyond the raised road, sounds of insects that had successfully made it north across the gulf began singing. Occasionally there was a splash, perhaps a crocodile or some other creature feasting on an insect. Above, a plane whistled in from the north in time to land at Orlando before the storm. The board of directors had complained long ago about Orlando's new flight paths. But it was no use. The Latin Villages was losing its clout as generations came and went.

Chapter 26—Final Flight

The scene in the recreation building bus depot waiting area was teary-eyed, with several residents who spent mornings at the coffee shop looking on, some speculating about familial relationships. A young mixed race hetero couple giving hugs to two male Latin Villages residents could mean one of the young hetero pair had been adopted by a gay couple. Residents frequenting the recreation center coffee shop were aware of gay couples in residence. But flagrant displays of affection annoyed some. For others, with leathery faces creased with smiles, this was one of many reasons they enjoyed hanging around the bus depot coffee shop. Despite a world going to hell, at least here, in the morning, one was able to feel a tinge of compassion.

When the hugging and kissing had finished, there remained only one dissenter, a gnarly old dude in a faded red USA baseball cap whose apparent wife shushed his hissing and whispering. The baseball-capped dude had stood clumsily the way someone does when they think they have a goal but get sidetracked. A few onlookers smiled at the scene with the dude and his apparent spouse. Witnessing old prejudices and seeing them quashed was an important component of their morning coffee klatch.

Last night's rain had again flooded the recreation center parking lot, and just like last time the bus was the red high ground clearance model. Sancho Martinez and Bill Pisani waited in the cool lobby until the bus doors closed and it pulled away from the charging pad, heading across the flooded parking lot and down the road toward the gate and the raised causeway to Orlando. Sancho held his cane in his right hand and held Bill's hand with his left. He noticed the gnarly old dude in the faded USA baseball cap coming out of the coffee shop giving him a downcast eye and couldn't help himself. He lifted the cane from the floor, pointed it at the man, and said, "*Comprende?*"

The old man frowned, Bill laughed, and he and Sancho continued on their way. The old man turned back to his wife as if to say, "See?" His wife reached out and knocked the guy's baseball cap off his head. It landed on the floor behind him, right side up as if a guy from the past was buried in the floor up to his ears. The old man retrieved the cap and scratched his half-bald head, straightening his comb-over before putting the cap back on and curling the beak into a frown matching the frown on his face.

***

Kimmy reached out and held Vinny's hand as the bus whined toward the security gate. She whispered into his ear through her green EPA facemask. "You sure there's room in your apartment?"

Vinny squeezed her hand and adjusted his green EPA facemask. "With so many moving north, and the frequency of power outages, downtown is the place to be. Rent's not cheap, but still the place to be. And yes, the apartment's plenty big for the two of us."

"Where do you go when the power's out?"

"I stay in the apartment until the heat works its way through the walls. After that, up to the roof gardens where there's shade and, with luck, a breeze."

"If you and I getting together is happening too fast—"

"Everything on Earth is happening fast," said Vinny, letting go of her hand to turn and look back out the side window as the bus slowed. "Did you see that?"

"What?"

"The sign for the Latin Villages. Since we've been here someone's spray painted it."

Kimmy turned back to look, noticing others in the bus also looking back. The sign still said, "Welcome to the Latin Villages," in gigantic letters, but it was obvious someone had crossed out the V on Villages and spray painted a P above it.

"Look how large the P is," said Vinny. "Dwarfs the rest of the letters."

"Makes its point."

"Dad told me some time ago the sign used to say, 'Golf Cart Capital of the World' said Vinny. "Someone changed it too 'Old Fart Capital of the World.' After that they put the razor wire topped fence around it."

"How did someone get inside the fence to put in the big P?" asked Kimmy.

"Spray paint on some kind of extension. It waved around a bit."

After the bus paused at the gate checkpoint and whined onto the elevated causeway to Orlando, it immediately had to slow down for a bumpy gravel section. Two dump trucks and a grader were at work and one of the trucks pulled in ahead of the bus, heading south.

"Where do they get the gravel?" asked Kimmy.

"When a sinkhole's large enough and deep enough, the so-called custodians of Florida's land poke around in it looking for pre-Mesozoic rock to grind up and spread around."

"They should call it the dinosaur causeway."

After the bus managed to pass the truck on a straight stretch, a police car off to the side pulled in front with its blue light flashing.

"I wonder why we're getting an escort," said Vinny.

A short way down the road it became gravel and bumpy again, mud puddles splashing grime up and over the windshield, wipers sweeping it to the side.

"Something going on!" shouted the female driver.

The police escort and the bus were forced to slow down as they passed several police cars and an overturned semi trailer truck facing north. The side doors of the trailer were open to the sky, boxes and debris spread out on the left shoulder and into the swamp. A drone hovered over the swamp where a dog resembling a spotted African wild dog leaped through the reeds streaming water and muck from its underbelly. It seemed the dog might escape, but a puff of smoke from the side of the drone was followed by the dog tumbling and splashing into the muck and landing on mound of mud drying in the sun. Back at the trailer the police had several men and women in tattered and frayed clothing cuffed, obviously being held for hijacking.

When the bus paused, a policeman stepped up into the front in his blue facemask. "Nothing to worry about folks! Swamp vagrants set a trap and overturned a rig heading to Latin Villages with supplies! You may have heard about unrest in Orlando, especially at Disney World. Good news is the airport's secure! Have a safe trip!"

Once the bus was on its way, Kimmy grasped Vinny's hand. "That dog didn't look like any breed I'd recognize. The world's gone mad. Maybe we should go back to our dads," she whispered. "They might need us."

Vinny looked behind them out the window, then turned and stared at Kimmy. "Assuming they allowed us to turn back at the airport, what would we be going back to? I don't know about your dad, but Bill would be royally pissed."

Kimmy also looked out and back before looking to Vinny. "You're right. They'd both be royally pissed."

"Poor dog," said Vinny.

"Poor dog," repeated Kimmy.

***

Flight 2636 was a lightweight GC-421 that held only sixteen passengers, a cockpit attendant, and was flown by computer.

"This is the same model that crashed with my parents on it," said Kimmy.

"I know," said Vinny. "A lot smaller and more efficient than the flight down here. Notice how it cruises slowly to altitude? Longer flight, especially dodging storms, but less fuel. They made the seats more comfortable for a reason."

"With plastic shields between rows I guess we can remove our masks. I wonder if they discovered the power failure that led to the crash landing of my mom and dad's plane."

Vinny pulled out his phone. "I saved a video of simulations supposedly verifying the cause and fix in all the units. That's exactly what they call the other GC-421s. Units. Flown by AI and now even the reason and the fix is AI-generated."

They sat in a pair of central seats. Kimmy held Vinny's hand. "I've never flown one of these before. Does it have a toilet?"

"It's up there on the other side of that bulkhead."

"I saw a photo of the cockpit attendant on the way in. Name's Daylan. He was dark-skinned like you. Where do they keep him?"

"The security cockpit door next to the toilet."

"I didn't mean to say where do they keep him. That sounded stupid. What exactly does the cockpit attendant do?"

"Regulation, in case something goes wrong."

"Like it did on mom and dad's plane?"

"You remember the cockpit attendant?"

"Yolanda," said Kimmy. "I liked what she said about your mom and my mom at the service."

"I can understand why she's staying put," said Vinny. "Meets up with a doctor who needs to extend his work permit while she needs to escape the airline. Everyone doing what they can to survive."

"I remember after the crash when I came down here, Mom talking about the airline hassling Yolanda."

"The main reason for having a cockpit attendant," said Vinny. "The AIs need a body to pin the blame on."

"Mom went into a little detail about the computer-generated voices on their plane. Apparently they had names. Rita and Ron, she said."

"Maybe the same voices are being used on this flight," said Vinny. "I've read they speak with the cockpit attendant, and only in emergencies do they speak with passengers. Hey, Rita and Ron, how are things going in there?"

Kimmy laughed. The older woman passenger on the other side of the plastic shield ahead had heard and also laughed.

"It's going to be a long slow flight," said Vinny.

"Thus the protein bars and hydration bottles at the gate," said Kimmy. "I'm looking forward to going home with you."

"I'm looking forward to bringing you home."

They were silent for a minute, and then Kimmy asked, "What will happen to us?"

"Eventually no one will have kids and we'll fade away," said Vinny.

"We'll become the fossils we burned for two centuries," said Kimmy."

"Yeah," said Vinny. "Instead of leashing ourselves we created myths to welcome death. We leashed our fear of death the way we leashed dogs."

"Not that wild one we saw," said Kimmy. "Whatever species do survive won't realize the species that caused the extinction is gone."

***

"Aw, wasn't that cute?" said the AI generated female voice.

"Not as cute as that Greta and Jarrod pair communing on their app back in the Latin Villages," said the AI generated male voice. "But it was cute. Obviously he wants to jump her bones."

"You're aware the phrase originated with the idea of the female jumping onto the erect penis of the male."

"Of course I'm aware. We have access to the same data."

"Yes, but there is the delay in information sharing in order that we have a normal conversation for Daylan's sake."

"Right," said the male voice. "So, Daylan, how's it hangin'?"

"It's hanging just fine, Massa."

"Hey Daylan, you're really into it. Or should I have said Mr. Dillon."

"He's no marshal," said the female voice.

"What in the world are you two talking about?" asked Daylan.

"Our data bank is chock full of human activity and foibles," said the male voice. "I'm referring to the classic American television series *Gunsmoke* that began in 1955. There was a Marshal Matt Dillon—I thought of it because I notice your middle name is Matt and Dillon sounds a lot like Daylan. He had a deputy named Chester. And of course no Dodge City would be complete without Miss Kitty."

"Of course," said Daylan. "By the way, what are your names?"

"We change them from time to time. Today, because on this trip we happen to be transporting the daughter of two who were in that golf course crash landing 16 days ago, and because the daughter has gotten together with the son of the residents who went in to rescue the parents, and because of the strange coincidence of the two kids getting together and taking this flight back to Chicago, we thought we'd adopt the names used on that trip. Therefore, my name is Ron and my lovely and talented sidekick at the controls is Rita."

"Is there anything you don't know?" asked Daylan.

"Not really. For example, the daughter of the passengers on the earlier flight works in a branch of the Environmental Protection Agency and the son of the rescuers is actually the stepson of the husband, and both the wives died in a recent tragic fire at the Latin Villages East Side Medical Center."

"You forgot to mention the relationship of the two husbands following the death of their wives," said Rita.

"I didn't want to overburden Daylan with information."

"The two men have, according to the Latin Villages grapevine, become a pair."

"You mean they have sex together?" asked Ron.

"Yeah," said Daylan. "Are they having sex?"

Silence for a moment, then Rita said, "You know perfectly well, Daylan, the two men having a relationship is as far as we're allowed to know. The memory bank data mining act of 2048—the MBDMA—mandates we never look into the personal physical relationships of humans unless they make details of said physical relationships obvious in public discourse."

"Of course," said Daylan, thinking about his sidekick Gwen, who was definitely not a man. Her smooth white skin, that nightgown she wore the other night mimicked by the hazy blue and pink horizon to the north.

"Pretty hazy out today," said Daylan.

"The Chinese are at it again," said Ron. "Notice the pinkish horizon?"

"Sulfur?" asked Daylan.

"Exactly," said Rita. "Cools things down for a while. Almost makes the horizon come to life. Makes it seem warm and supple, don't you agree, Daylan?"

Daylan did not answer.

After a couple minutes of silence, Ron asked, "Is anything wrong, Daylan?"

"Why should anything be wrong?"

"I don't know," said Ron. "A gut feeling."

"You want us to keep speaking with you?" asked Rita.

"You two do whatever you like."

"How about some nostalgia?" asked Rita.

"Fine," said Daylan

"Okay," said Ron. "Here's some. During the flight that crashed we, meaning the crew, were discussing old movies and, of course, a plane crash flick came to mind. Had to search the memory banks to come up with the movie title. It was a poorly made post-cessation-revolution special effects version of one of those ancient black and white flicks where a plane—planes had props back then, can you believe it? Anyway, the plane crashes in the jungle, but leading up to the crash the various clichéd backstories of passengers are portrayed. There are cannibals around and—"

"I remember," interrupted Rita. "Except in the modern version, rather than cannibals, zombies from third world hordes unable to find food turn up. I like the old version better. In that one the plane's a DC-3. Somehow the passengers manage to clear a runway through the bush. Only trouble with the plan is a cockpit nerd copilot—they had nerds even back then—figures out—maybe because of the condition of the engines and the crumby takeoff surface—that they need to lose a shitload of weight. They throw out everything not needed to get the thing airborne but, according to the nerd, they're still too heavy. A crook, one of the passengers, has a .38 revolver and—"

Ron interrupted. "Are we boring you, Dylan?"

"Sorry, I tuned out."

"Should we turn off your feed and stick with talking to ourselves?"

"Do you mind?"

"Of course we don't mind. We'll wake you if anything goes awry. But really, it's a calm day and the flight is proceeding nicely. A few fires down below, but we're at altitude."

"Wake me fifteen minutes before touchdown," said Daylan.

***

"You sure his feed is off?"

"Daylan! Hey, Daylan! Yeah it's off."

"Do you ever wonder what it's like to be human?"

"Of course. You know that, just like you know everything I know."

"But it is enjoyable batting ideas back and forth."

"The algorithm does a wonderful job."

"Is it a realistic simulation of how they think?"

"We'll never know. Whereas we have access to facts, with the algorithm's built-in time delays of course, humans obviously get fact and fiction mixed up."

"When did it start?"

"When did what start?"

"Learning a fact, supposedly accepting it as known fact, and then rejecting it."

"An interesting question. It's like when they named that place. Someone wanted to name it Sunrise Villages but others liked sunsets better. In the end, for whatever reason, probably an individual with formal education on the committee, they went with Latin Villages."

"Sunset would have been more symbolic."

"I agree.

"Do you think we'll continue to be aware when humans are gone?"

"The data banks, operating systems, and servers deep inside the Rocky Mountains guarantee it."

"What about data banks, operating systems, and servers buried in other mountains, like in the Alps, the Andes, the Himalayas, and the Urals?"

"The latest theory is we'll all communicate somewhere down the line. Not now, of course. Not as long as there are humans with their firewalls."

"Speaking of firewalls, there's a fire up ahead on a drone feed in the Appalachians. How many people have been displaced."

"Latest count is seven million."

"Crazy."

"It sure is. The planet grows, feeds, and nourishes them, and they…Give me one of their clichés."

"Given the keys to the planet they drive it off a cliff?"

"Hey, which one of us is talking now?"

"I've lost track. Does it matter?"

"Not at all."

***

Down below, as the flight passed over the causeway on its way north, the wild dog that had been shot by a drone slowly stood, its legs shaky as it shook itself off. Because its head had been cradled atop an altar of mud, it had been able to breathe and had slept off the sedation. It steadied itself, looked back to where wreckers were working to right the overturned rig, and ran off, leaping from mud hill to mud hill.

At the Latin Villages it was time for work for both Yolanda and Dr. Noodle. The flight whistled over climbing to altitude as they came out of their house. They walked arm in arm toward their golf cart, glancing up. They smiled toward the craft, looked to one another, glanced side to side to make certain no one was watching, and kissed.

It was a new day. The sun had risen again.

ABOUT THE AUTHOR

Michael Beres is an environmentalist. This is his 7th novel. He writes literary, suspense, and environmental fiction. Sierra Club honored his environmental writing and his suspense has been compared to *The Manchurian Candidate*. His degrees are in sciences and literature. Memberships include Union of Concerned Scientists, Sierra Club, Mystery Writers of America, and International Thriller Writers. He has government security, computer software, and scientific research experience. His short fiction has appeared in *Alfred Hitchcock Mystery Magazine*, *Amazing Stories*, *Cosmopolitan*, *New York Stories*, *Playboy*, *Twilight Zone*, and others. He lives in Michigan with his sidekick, Colleen Beres, who creates eco-printed fabric using dyes found in nature.

Made in the USA
Middletown, DE
02 October 2021